All Keyed Up

by Mary Stella

SILVER IMPRINT

In loving memory of Joe and Lida Mary Stella.
You gave me strong roots and encouraged big dreams.
Thanks, Mom and Dad. I miss you.

July 2004
Published by Medallion Press, Inc.
225 Seabreeze Ave.
Palm Beach, FL 33480

ISBN 1-932815-08-2

Printed in the United States of America

For more great books visit www.medallionpress.com.

Acknowledgments

Heartfelt thanks to:

Beth Ciotta, Jennifer Wagner, and Lyn Wagner.
Treasured friends, wonderful writers, and the best critique partners in the world. Without your encouragement and insight, this book might never have seen the light of day.

My brother Joe, sister-in-law Perri, and nephews Asa and Jonah, whose loving support means everything.

Christine Bush, Shirley Hailstock, Cyndi Klimback, Rainy Kirkland, Terri Brisbin, Colleen Admirand, Mary Lou Frank, Sue Stevenson, Deb Mullins, Julia Templeton, Karyn Monk, Heather Graham, and all the other extraordinary writers I'm fortunate to call my friends. You are walking, talking, writing inspirations.

Marilyn Staron, Lori Guth, Lisa Berger, Robin and Tracy Thompson, Linda Givens, John Hopkins, Martina and David Rossow – for too many good times to count.

Helen Rosburg, Pam Ficarella, Leslie Burbank and the rest of Medallion Press for believing in my book and working so hard to help me succeed.

The passionate, fun-loving people of RBL Romantica and Sanctuary.

Last, but certainly not least, the rest of my Dolphin Research Center family–people, dolphins, and assorted other amazing beings. Every day you teach, inspire, and bring me joy.

Chapter One

"You did what?" Jack Benton pushed a hank of hair away from his face and glared at his aunt.

Aunt Ruby glared right back and shook a letter in his face. "I accepted an offer from the great Dr. Sheffield to do his research project right here at Dolphin Land." Gnarled hands planted on bony hips, she jutted out her scrawny chest with determination. "Don't go giving me that look, Bubba. This here is a miracle falling right out of the sky."

"Let me see that." Mindful of her older bones, he took the paper gently, but still scowled while he read.

Dear Mrs. Maguire,

It will be my pleasure to conduct my latest research on the social communication of Atlantic bottlenose dolphins at your fine facility.

Jack snorted. Dolphin Land hadn't been a fine facility since before Uncle Gus died. It took every penny Aunt Ruby could scrounge to feed six dolphins and keep their lagoons in good shape. She'd let her own conch house go to crap before the animals suffered. Except for the fish house and freezer, every other building sagged in on itself. The next strong hurricane would blow them all to Cuba.

"I know what you're thinking, Jack. Just keep reading."

I appreciate your honesty that Dolphin Land is small and experiencing rough times. However, I don't consider this detrimental to our mutual goals. The intimate setting and established colony of animals should prove beneficial to my methods for study and data collection. Moreover, as I specified in my original proposal . . ."

"Proposal? When did you first hear from this Sheffield? How come I'm just hearing about this now?"

"I wanted to surprise you. Keep reading. You'll like the next part."

". . . *I have obtained a generous research grant to fund the study, and I am quite satisfied with the terms we discussed. I will, of course, purchase all necessary equipment and pay for the installation. I am happy to compensate you and your staff for your time and efforts in the ongoing data collection.*"

"See, Jack! Compensation for me and my staff—that's you and little Jeanie from down the way."

Glee shone in Ruby's eyes as she two-stepped around the battered office. He hated squelching her enthusiasm, but this wasn't the first time his irrepressible aunt had been boondoggled.

"This offer's too sudden. I can't believe you didn't let me check it out first. What do you know of this . . ." He made a show of checking the letter even though he'd committed the name to memory. ". . . Sheffield? How do we know he's the real deal?"

"Jesus, Mary, and all the saints in heaven. Dr. Sheffield practically wrote the book on dolphin research. Open-water studies on family groups, controlled settings for image matching. You name it. He's won the Delphinid Prize at least three times, not that I expect you to bother knowing that that's as big an honor as it gets in this business. Now, he wants to bring himself, his equipment, *and* his money to Dolphin Land, and you doubt he's the real deal? We oughta bend over to kiss the man's—"

"Aunt Ruby!"

"Assets, Jack, assets."

He sighed and then grimaced, mentally kicking himself when the glee in her eyes turned mulish. Hostage negotiations were easier than talking sense into his obstinate aunt. He sure as hell knew better than to get her back up. She'd stand as solid as a concrete statue out of pure stubbornness. Time for a new tactic.

"Aunt Ruby, I know how badly you want to keep Dolphin Land running, and on the surface this looks great, but we have to be practical. It's gonna take a lot more than a few paychecks to get back on our feet. The buildings need to be restored, the grounds redone. We're talking thousands of dollars before we even consider reopening to the public. I want to help. You know I do. But, we have to explore other options."

"Bubba, you think I should just cave in and sell. Believe it or not, I listened when you explained about the bazillion bucks we could get for the land from a developer. But . . ." She turned to the window and looked out at the front lagoon where six sleek bodies glided through the water. She grasped his arm, pulling him to her side.

The afternoon sun sparkled on the Gulf of Mexico as if someone had tossed down a fistful of diamonds. A gangly, teenaged girl stepped down on the floating dock, grasping shiny stainless steel buckets. Immediately, four gray faces popped up. Their excited whistles and clicks carried across the water.

"Jeanie doesn't even need to put their symbols down. Scarlett, Rhett, Melly, and Ashley are always first in line for treats. Robin and Marian over there are more interested in each other than food right now. I don't know if anything will come of it. Marian's thirty. That's getting up there for a dolphin lady, but it won't be for lack of trying." Ruby cackled, but her face quickly clouded over. "I can't do it, Jack,"

3

she choked out. "Those dolphins are family. I won't give them up, and for the life of me, I don't understand how you could even ask me."

The look in her eyes drove a fist into his gut. He gathered her to his chest. Her thin frame ran at odds to her gritty strength. God knows he'd fought enemies armed to their eyeteeth in conditions that rivaled hell on Earth. But only this diminutive, crotchety, old woman that he loved like a mother could bring him to his knees.

He knew he was beaten . . . this time. "I'm not asking you to give them up, and if this is what you want, I'll do my damnedest to make it work."

Feeling the tension ease from her body solidified his determination. One way or another, he'd ensure his aunt's security and happiness for the rest of her life. He rubbed his chin over her sun-bleached hair.

"All I ask is that you trust me. If this research project isn't the answer, if it isn't enough, you have to give my idea a shot." He leaned back to look down into her eyes. "I'll find a way to do it without losing the gang. I promise."

Her grin was all the answer he needed. He'd find a way, damn straight. In the meantime this Dr. Sheffield better be on the up and up. If he screwed up his end of the bargain and left Aunt Ruby twisting in the Florida Keys' wind, he'd have Jack Benton to answer to and it wouldn't be pretty.

***

Jack tilted back in his chair and swallowed more ice tea. Water trickled down his back from hair still damp from the quick outdoor shower. It was hotter than normal for mid-January, but the Gulf temperature hadn't crept above seventy degrees. If he had to spend a couple of hours waist deep in water, tightening lagoon fence lines and scrubbing them clean of sea lettuce, this was a good day for the work.

Propping his feet on a hunk of coral rock, he rested his glass on his stomach. After putting in hours of solid work, a man earned the right to relax, maybe take a nice nap under the shady palm tree and enjoy the cool breeze.

Sure was different from the dense jungles of Colombia where the afternoons grew so thick and hot with humidity, you cooked like a turkey in an oven. Here, you didn't slog weapons and equipment through near-impenetrable vegetation, tracking wily drug runners. Instead, it was feed the dolphins; keep the water exchange flowing through clean fences; and start repairing the front building. He had plenty to keep himself busy while his leg healed and returned to full strength. And he could do it without risking his life—unless he was overcome by the complete lack of excitement.

Compared to the high-octane energy of agency work, Dolphin Land was a tricycle ride on a cul-de-sac. He missed walking the sharp edge of danger and the sense that his job mattered. But, until he healed a hundred percent, returning to the field was suicidal. In the meantime, his aunt needed him, and he needed something to keep from going nuts.

He was overdue for some downtime anyway, so he might as well spend it at home with Aunt Ruby. A little work, a little fishing, and some of her good home cooking would set him up right and let him recharge. To keep himself sharp, he had also planned to work a deal to secure his aunt's financial future. Then Aunt Ruby sprang her latest outrageous scheme.

The hum of an engine and crunch of tires on pea rock interrupted his musings. He cracked open an eye and scowled. A silver SUV, sporting a thick coat of road grime and a few hundred dead bugs, stopped a few feet away. The fly had arrived in his ointment.

The car door opened, but Jack stayed put. Despite the official-looking Sheffield Institute letters and his aunt's assurances, he wasn't even close to sure that this so-called dolphin genius wasn't fifty percent pure crackpot. Old Victor Sheffield wasn't going to stroll in and take over Aunt Ruby's pride and joy. Not while Jack Benton was on the job. No way in . . .

A pair of long, killer, female legs swung out of the car into his sightline. "Aw hell," he muttered. It wasn't Sheffield after all. Still, no matter how good those legs looked, whoever owned them was bound to be a pain in his ass.

He unfolded himself from the chair as he scanned up a line of smooth skin to where a delicate, green skirt brushed a pair of perfect knees. The path traveled to a tailored jacket molded around what looked to be a spectacular set of—

"Excuse me, sir. I'm looking for Mrs. Ruby Maguire. Can you help me?"

Her voice reminded him of blues music and full-bodied wine. Reluctantly, he interrupted his slow perusal and brought his attention to her face.

Talk about a sucker punch.

All the usual features fell into place and created something out of the ordinary. Not beautiful in a classic way. The nose was too pert and the mouth way, way too generous. Her skin held a hint of tan, and silky brows arced over eyes of rich, deep brown. Her hair, pulled back in a sleek braid, was maple syrup-colored, streaked with honey and taffy strands.

Flat-out male hunger kicked in and, almost as fast, pissed him off.

"Am I in the right place?"

That smoky voice again revved his pulse while his mind ran through a list of possibilities. Friends of his aunt wouldn't call her

Mrs. Maguire. Aunt Ruby would have told him if she was expecting someone on business. Besides, this visitor was too well-dressed for the Keys, where casual attire ruled the day. The answer hit him like a coconut falling from a tree. After caving into his aunt's crazy plans, he'd told the realtors and land developers to back off. This one must not have gotten the message.

"Sorry, lady, but if you're looking to buy, there's nothing here for sale." He slowly stepped forward, upping the intimidation factor with his superior height and body language.

Although she leaned back as he loomed over her, she didn't retreat. "I'm not here to make a purchase. I—"

"We're not interested in anything you're selling either. That pretty much covers the bases on why you'd drive in here, so why don't you just climb on back into that little truck and head out again?"

While he watched, her pleasant smile rapidly morphed to narrow-eyed resolve. She straightened and lifted her chin.

"I don't know who you are, nor do I actually care." The rich, contralto voice dripped vinegar. "I'm here to see Ruby Maguire."

"Why?"

"That would be none of your business. My appointment's with her."

"Ruby doesn't do appointments, and the only person she's expecting is—"

A hint of triumph glinted in the woman's eyes. Jack glanced at the SUV and picked out the blue and white of a Massachusetts' license plate underneath the road grime. He whipped back his head. "Who are you?"

The hint burst into victory, and he got his first taste of a full-blown, poleaxing smile.

"Victoria Sheffield. I believe you said I'm expected?"

* * *

Her first introduction to the denizens of Dolphin Land hadn't gone too well. The gruff he-man with too much chest and damp brown hair hanging to his shoulders must be a maintenance worker. He'd barked, "Wait right here!" before storming into a building she guessed was an office.

Victoria stifled the jitter of nerves in her stomach and looked around. Good Lord, the Florida Keys were beautiful. Miles of brilliant turquoise and emerald water shimmered before her like a promise of good things to come. A few brown pelicans with long, pouched beaks and spunky black cormorants perched on a weather-beaten dock. Overhead, an osprey inscribed lazy circles in the cloudless sky, waiting to plunge like a feathered spear and snatch a plump fish for lunch. Right there in front of her, in the first of a few coral-rimmed lagoons, swam the answers to her prayers.

Excitement bubbled inside her like a jet spa. Here, for the first time in her life, she was truly on her own. No more sticking to some-one else's schedule or agenda. Three days ago, she'd turned the lock on the door of her Nantucket home, fired up her car, and hit the road for her new destination. She grinned. Destination as in destiny, she thought, and for once in her life she was going for it! Her future lay in this small place and that family of marine mammals.

"Dolphin Land or Promised Land?" she whispered, amused at the thought. Almost immediately, she clapped a hand over her mouth and then laughed at her own reaction. The air conditioner in the office window made so much noise, surely nobody inside could hear. If she wanted to make a silly, fun comparison and giggle over it, who was here to stop her? Nobody. Not her father, a man she loved, revered, and resented all at the same time. And certainly not her lying, research-stealing, glory-grabbing slime of an ex-fiancé.

This was her quest, her precious little secret. Here, at a facility so small and seedy no others in the field would ever consider it for a project, she would make her mark. Victoria pumped her fist in the air. She would prove her theories of dolphin social communication, present a brilliant paper, and win the Delphinid Prize for research. Along the way, she would show the world she was not merely her father's daughter and unrecognized assistant, but a talented marine mammal research scientist in her own right.

But you wouldn't have made it this far without him. You still needed his name to get your foot in the door. The thought wiggled into her dream like a worm into a tasty apple.

"Okay, okay, so I fudged it a little," she admitted to the pretend guilt imp lurking in her mind. "What's the big deal? I'm qualified to be principal investigator, and I'm using my own money to fund the project. It isn't like I said I was him!"

You never said you weren't either, VIC Sheffield.

Oh, so what if nobody in her whole life, including herself, ever called her anything but Victoria? Everyone had always referred to her father as Victor, when they weren't addressing him in awestruck tones as *Doc . . . tor . . . Shef . . . field.* He'd lived his whole career hearing his name over-emphasized, as if his greatness were too huge for the syllables to flow together naturally.

Be nice. He isn't the man he used to be. Since her father's stroke, he couldn't speak, uttering only grunts. During her daily visits, their conversations were monologues on her part. His caregiver, Rosa, a wonderful warm Jamaican woman, assured her that his mind was active, but Victoria felt him drifting further away. Without his life's work, his teaching and his lecture series, he'd lost his identity as a

9

man, as a person. Surely being a good father had never been one of the ways he'd measured his success.

After the years she'd worked as his paid assistant, without ever receiving a line of credit in the papers she'd helped write, he owed her the loan of his reputation to use as a springboard. It wasn't as if she'd lied to this Mrs. Maguire. She'd merely presented the truth in a creative, maybe slightly misleading, fashion.

She wrestled the guilt imp to the mat and pinned it.

When she succeeded with this project and won the Delphinid Prize, her triumph would also stand as an extension of her father's legacy. Then surely, for once in her life, she would make him proud.

＊＊＊

"Well, I gotta tell you, miss, you aren't who I expected."

Victoria gave her full attention to the small, frail-looking older woman. Anticipating some degree of suspicion, she'd planned her reply and smiled broadly. "Mrs. Maguire, I don't blame you for being surprised. It's a common enough error when people first see my name to assume I'm my father. Over ten years in the field and still . . ." She shrugged and added a nonchalant chuckle, as if to say, *How silly and what does it matter anyway?*

The he-man stared from his post against the wall. He probably thought she'd crumple under his disapproving glare. Little did he know she'd been disapproved of all her life by her own father, even when she'd have crawled over broken glass to earn his respect.

She deliberately ignored him and focused her attention on the woman. "Mrs. Maguire, if we can get past that for a moment, I assure you that my being here instead of my father has no bearing on the research project."

Muscle-brain snorted. She acted like he didn't exist.

"As his senior researcher, I have collected and evaluated data for a number of years." All true, even though she couldn't prove it. "Now, sadly, he is unable to carry out his field studies because of his medical problems, but the work of The Sheffield Institute must continue."

The woman nodded. The man glared.

Victoria adopted what she hoped was a brave smile and a sorrowful look in her eyes, soliciting understanding. "So you see, this project is vital. After all he's done for me over the years . . ." The pause sounded dramatic, but in reality she was close to choking on the words, which were the only real lie in anything she'd said. ". . . it's up to me to continue his legacy."

"Absolutely!" Mrs. Maguire nodded so hard the hair piled on top of her head threatened to come loose from its pins. "I'm sorry if I gave you the wrong impression when you first came in. I was just surprised. Of course, the project must go on, and if the great Dr. Sheffield can't be here himself, who better than the man's own flesh 'n blood?" She patted Victoria's arm.

"It may help you to know that researchers of my father's level very often leave much of the routine field work to assistants and grad students, Mrs. Maguire."

"Ruby. Just plain Ruby. Only people calling me missus are those danged telemarketers. We're going to be working a long time together, and we don't stand on ceremony down here in the Keys."

"Then please call me . . . Vic."

"Honey, you don't have to make yourself one of the guys. Back when we had a full staff, woman or man, everyone worked together and both sides pulled their weight. Equal work, equal money, equal respect, my husband Gus, God rest his soul, always said, and we raised Jack here the same way."

He was her son? Her eyes widened, but she didn't realize she'd spoken the words out loud, until he pushed himself off the wall and approached.

"Nephew, biologically speaking, but she's been my mother since Dolphin Land became my home when I was eleven years old."

The words were underscored with a warning. He moved alongside a window, and with the light streaming in, his eyes glittered with a clear message. *Don't screw with me and mine.*

Her throat went dry as dust. Even with the underlying threat, she couldn't help notice that his eyes were remarkable, almost the same shade as the perfectly clear turquoise water in the Caribbean. She broke eye contact by glancing at the water cooler against the wall. "May I?" she asked, gesturing at the inverted bottle.

"Of course. That's one thing we always make sure to have plenty of. It sure isn't as hot as it can get in the Keys, but the days will come. You keep yourself hydrated but good, Victoria." Ruby frowned. "I'm sorry, darlin', but I just can't call a woman pretty as you by a man's name."

Victoria gulped down the water, unexpectedly moved by the compliment. It was impossible not to respond to the woman's quick, honest warmth. She silenced her misgivings with a fervent promise to do the right thing. Granted, she got her foot in the door by stretching the truth, but her theories and study were legitimate and she'd prove it to the world.

The first step was easy. She crumpled the paper cup and tossed it in the trash. "Let's get down to business then, shall we?" Reaching into her handbag, she pulled out an envelope and handed it to Ruby. "As we agreed, here are the first two months' installments I promised from the grant monies."

"Well, I won't pretend this isn't going to come in handy. Right,

Jack? As it happens, we've got a fish delivery next week and a ton of work to do on the buildings. Oh, we cleared some storage area for your stuff. In a couple of weeks, when we finish the repairs on the other building, we'll be able to make some office space for you too."

"That won't be necessary. I plan to do much of my evaluation and writing at night at the cottage I rented."

"You're all fixed up at Pirate's Cove, then? I told Hank to give you one of the nicer units, and he promised to cut you a break on price."

"I'm quite pleased with the terms, and the walking distance couldn't be more convenient. Thank you for the suggestion." Victoria looked at her watch. "I think what I would like to do, if you don't mind, is unload my equipment from the car." Enthusiasm broke free in her voice. "Then, since we're going to spend so much time together, I would love to meet your dolphins!"

"Well now, that's a fine idea, and I know they're gonna love meeting you. Especially Rhett and Robin Hood, those charmers. Jack, you unload Victoria's stuff while I show her where she can change out of that suit and into something more comfortable."

The watchdog's gaze never left Victoria's eyes, and her stomach jumped a little under the intensity. She'd underestimated his importance before, but the power vibe he transmitted now told her she'd have to stay on her guard.

"Aunt Ruby, I oughta have her input on how she wants her equipment handled." He raked her with a look that made her knees wobble. "I'm getting more interested by the minute in this research project. Suddenly, I can't wait for her to tell me all."

Chapter Two

She surprised him, taking no more than five minutes to slip out of that business-like suit into shorts and a tank top. Another good look at those killer legs made him wish she'd chosen something less revealing—like a boat tarp. *Get a grip,* he told himself with a mental smack. The lady talked a good game, and he sure couldn't fault the personal presentation.

He smothered a *whoa* when she bent over to pet one of Dolphin Land's adopted cats.

Sweet looks or not, he wasn't ready to buy into the whole package.

Something didn't jive with her story. He might be on leave, but he hadn't lost his instincts. For now, with her check in hand, he'd go along with the plans. Necessity dictated they'd spend a lot of time together. She'd need to explain her project in depth, which opened the door to whatever questions he wanted to ask.

He smirked. He was a pro at getting answers.

Swinging open the back door to her SUV, he scanned the neatly stacked boxes. According to the labels, she'd brought enough equipment to give a tech-junkie a wet dream. Hydrophones, video cams, audio tuner, laptop, CD burner, night-vision goggles.

"What are you doing with NVGs?"

She joined him. "NVGs? Oh, you mean the goggles. How else will I observe your animals after nightfall? Spotlights would disturb the natural atmosphere and the dolphins' nocturnal patterns."

"Dolphins have nocturnal patterns?"

"We don't really know, actually. It's fairly impossible to observe them after dark in the wild without intrusion. Boat engines and helicopters are interruptions that influence the animals' reactions."

"So you plan on being here day *and* night?" For some reason, the idea bothered him, or maybe it was the sudden unwelcome image of the two of them watching dolphins while lying close together on a dock.

Victoria laughed, a rich, husky sound. "Not all the time, since it isn't the focus of my study. Still . . ." She looked around, delight on her face as if the place were research-Nirvana and not a collection of junk buildings and overgrown hibiscus bushes. "This is as close to a natural environment as man can make. I won't be able to resist observing every possible situation."

Her enthusiasm obvious, she reached into the car and loaded her arms with boxes. "If you'll show me where to put these, we can get started. I've been dying to see your dolphins since the moment I arrived!"

* * *

Before long her equipment was stored in the cubicle they'd cleared. Ruby joined them, carrying a bucket of fish, and together they walked out to the front lagoon. Victoria never stopped asking questions and mentally filed away each answer.

"Right now, we're feeding them a combination of three fish.

Good size herring give the gang most of their protein, fat, and calories. These guys here . . ." Ruby pointed out a slender fish about six inches long, ". . . are capelin."

"Those are high-moisture fish, correct?"

"Right. So, you know that dolphins get all their fluid from their food."

She nodded and then gestured to the bucket. "I've never seen those tiny, greenish ones."

"Silversides. They're more of a snack, added for taste and variety."

They stepped out onto the boardwalk. The dried, sun-whitened wood creaked underneath. Victoria kicked off her sandals.

"Watch yourself." Jack's gruff order was the first thing he'd said in ten minutes.

She turned around. "What?"

He jabbed a finger at her feet. "These are old boards. You could pick up a nasty splinter."

"Ohh." She glanced down and wiggled her toes. "Thanks for the warning, but I've gone barefoot most of my life. Something has to be pretty sharp to get under my skin."

Take that, buddy. As she jumped down lightly onto the floating dock alongside Ruby, she turned her back on the way-too-intimidating man. Spending her life observing animal behavior had taught her to read a wide range of species. Right now, despite the surface cooperation, he was one suspicious *Homo sapiens.*

I haven't convinced him. He's protecting his aunt's welfare, she told herself. A commendable goal. He didn't know that she herself had only Ruby's best interests at heart. After all, without Dolphin Land, her own dream didn't have a shot. Regardless of the heat and suspicion in his eyes, she'd win him over. But, in the meantime, she wouldn't let him push her around.

16

Water swirled as torpedo-shaped bodies raced toward them from around the lagoon. Instantly, the dolphins bobbed their heads up and down, slapping pectoral fins on the water. They whistled, twirled, and blew an incredible range of sounds out their blowholes.

"Oh, look!" One leaped high, corkscrewing its powerful body in mid-air before reentering the water with barely a splash. "You didn't signal for that behavior, did you, Ruby?"

"Nope. This is playtime. They pick what they want to do. That spiral dive is Robin Hood's favorite." She tossed him a fish snack when he popped back up at the dock. "He learned it all by himself from copying his momma." She dropped a handful of silversides to a dolphin that sounded like she was giggling. "Melly here is our vocalist. She makes more noises outta that blowhole than a high school band."

"I need to learn to recognize them all by sight. Can you begin by giving me some identifying characteristics, please?"

"Sure thing."

For the next several moments, Ruby introduced her to each member of the pod. Rhett, the oldest male, was also the longest. His rostrum, or snout, was scarred white from years of digging in the rocky bottom of the lagoon. White scarring also marked the front edge of his dorsal fin.

Melly was the largest of the females in girth. A star-shaped pink patch of skin in front of her pectoral fin distinguished her from the others.

"Scarlett, well she's the biggest flirt. Whenever Jack's in the water, she won't keep away from him–even on the other side of the fence. She's got her eye on you, for sure, Bubba."

A glance at Jack showed him grinning as he stepped down on the dock, his balance sure, even when the platform wobbled. He squatted to stroke underneath the dolphin's jaw, while the dolphin gazed at him with lovely, dark eyes. "No male can resist you, girl, man or cetacean." He slid his palm down the animal's back, giving her a good rubdown. No sooner had he finished than she turned around and swam under his hand again. He complied with another backrub, and the dolphin continued swimming, first one way then the other, coaxing still more contact.

Victoria laughed. "I'd say she has your number."

"Who am I to disappoint a willing female?"

He'd certainly mastered the art of innuendo. She averted her gaze, ignoring his soft laugh when she didn't respond. Turning to ask Ruby another question, she saw the older woman hoisting herself back onto the boardwalk.

"Willie's truck just pulled up. I gotta talk to him again about that drain in the fish house."

"But I was hoping we could discuss the hydrophone placement in the lagoons."

"Oh, I don't know a thing about that electronic stuff. That's for sure," Ruby called over her shoulder. Her sandals slapped against the weathered wood as she hurried away. "Jack's the man you need."

Terrific. Being alone with him was exactly what she *didn't* need. Although he'd said very little, she'd felt his gaze on her most of the time. That could be trouble. She'd finessed her way this far, but knew she was still on footing as unsteady as this floating dock. Even with all her field experience, this was her first solo effort. She expected to fumble a little getting started and had counted on the fact that Dolphin Land had never before hosted a research project. It stood to reason they might not notice hesitation or minor errors in the beginning.

Unfortunately, Jack watched her as carefully as that osprey overhead scanned for fish. She could sense his skepticism as clearly as if he'd written it on his chest.

His very broad, tan, naked chest.

She gave herself a mental shake. From Belize to the San Juan Islands, she'd worked practically skin to skin with men all her life. Whether stripped down to bathing suits or encased in wetsuits that showed every curve and bulge, comfort and respect ruled when spending weeks together on research boats. She'd grown so used to being around half-naked men, she'd hardly noticed.

Except, of course, for Kel. She'd noticed him all right, and look what happened. The rat. She shook her head, sending the wretched thought back into the past where it belonged. That was one mistake she'd never repeat: falling for a handsome face and charming smile, not realizing until too late that they masked a shark's intent.

She gathered up her resourcefulness. If Mr. Naked Chest Benton wanted to be suspicious, then let him. She'd be that much more careful not to bungle. Instead, she'd present the picture of experienced authority and confidence. Starting now.

Straightening her shoulders, she adopted the firm voice of command she'd heard her father use with his crew. "Very well then, Jack, about those hydrophones. I trust you can recommend a competent electronics company for the installation?"

"I reckon I can handle it myself, Vic. No need to call in somebody else." His deep drawl stretched out the words while he continued lazily stroking the dolphin named Scarlett.

Those components had cost her a ton. Although she didn't know exactly what he did around the facility, given his rough-around-the-edges look, she was darned sure it didn't include handling sensitive audio-video equipment. "I appreciate you trying to save spending

19

money on an outside contractor, but this is a justifiable expense. These hydrophones are top of the line with very acute capabilities. Even though they're durable . . ." She paused, warming her words with a smile. "I'm sure you understand why I can't trust their installation to just anyone."

He stood and flashed a mega-watt grin.

"I ain't just anyone, sugar. Not by a long shot."

Surely it was a sudden rocking of the dock that made her sway, not the power of his smile and those tropical blue eyes. Her arms waved as she struggled for balance.

He caught her upper arm in a gentle grasp. "Easy there."

Mortified, she tried to pull away, but he waited until her footing was steady before releasing her.

"Anyway, Vic, nobody but me puts anything in these lagoons or anywhere else at Dolphin Land. I doubt there's anything you need that I can't figure out how to do." He winked. "But if there is, I'll find the right person for the job. Until then, get used to having me around."

Despite his cheeky wink and easygoing manner, she knew she'd run into an unshakeable force. Silently, she digested his words. Like it or not, she was stuck with him and would simply have to find a way to make it work, without giving up her authority on the project.

"I'm sure we'll get along famously. No doubt you'll enjoy learning how to be a competent research assistant."

"Oh, no doubt." His throaty laugh indicated that he knew exactly what she'd tried to do, darn him.

She sharpened her tone. "All right. Now about those hydrophones. I originally planned six for this lagoon, but now that I see the size, I think nine would be more in order."

"Six, nine, we'll deal with it tomorrow. You've had a long drive down, and it's too late in the day for serious work. Remember what Ruby said? It's playtime. Come here." He grabbed her hand and pulled her down to kneel beside him on the dock. "From what my aunt tells me, you've done most of your research in open water, right?"

"That's correct, so we don't develop personal relationships with the dolphins as subjects."

"Will it mess up your study if you get to know these guys?"

"Actually, since I'm researching social communication in a number of situations, it will help if they learn to accept me as part of their natural surroundings."

"Okay then. Lay your palm flat on the water, like this."

He pressed his hand, warm and solid, over hers. Almost immediately, one of the animals swam up under her hand.

"This is Ashley. Start behind his blowhole and rub all the way up to the top of his dorsal. Perfect. Now try it on your own." In a single fluid movement, he stood and stepped back, boosting himself up on the boardwalk.

Victoria waited for the dolphin's return, and then slid her hand all over the smooth, almost rubber-like skin. The animal came back for more. "Oh, Ashley. You like this, don't you?" The big mammal blew a soft breath out his blowhole in answer.

"Again? Okay, sweetie. Here you go." The water felt cool on her skin, and the graceful creature certainly behaved as if he enjoyed Victoria's touch. Gliding her hand across the smooth back made her smile too. Contact, pure and simple, but a mingling of two separate species and two very different worlds. As a scientist, she could explain conditioned response to stimuli or positive reinforcement training, while rattling off a variety of ways to approximate intelligence in marine mammals. As a human being, learning and appreciating the personality and willing interaction of these magnificent animals was nothing short of magic.

Eventually, Ashley swam off, joining his friends elsewhere in the lagoon. Victoria sat back on her heels and looked out at the Gulf of Mexico, where the sun sank like a deep red, liquid ball toward the horizon. Quiet settled around them, broken only by the soothing lap of water on the dock and the soft, rhythmic exhalation of dolphins surfacing to breathe.

Tranquility filled her heart, taking up residence next to an overwhelming feeling of rightness. She was exactly where she was meant to be.

* * *

From his seat on the boardwalk he watched her, cataloguing every reaction and expression. The lively delight and quick connection to the animals were sincere. So was the simple smile that shaped her lush mouth right now while she watched the sunset.

Her words rang true when she spoke about her research. Her questions were on target, and that mother lode of technology they'd unpacked wasn't stuff for amateurs. She worked up the right attitude, too, and looked mighty cute in the process, puffing herself up a little when she tried to establish authority over the equipment discussion. He squelched a grin. It suited his purposes fine for her to ID him as some sort of handyman. It wouldn't be the first time he'd created a wrong impression to his own advantage.

So, she seemed to have the chops for the project she'd brought to their door, but something didn't sit completely right. He didn't think it was a case of female nerves that put her off-kilter when he'd stood and faced her on the dock. Although, if being close to him kept her off balance, he could use that too.

If there were holes in her story, he could debunk them, using his own highly developed, computer skills and calling in a few favors from old pals at the agency. However, he'd put that part of his life to the side and promised Aunt Ruby to try things her way first. Going behind his aunt's back would piss her off to no end. Besides, they had that fish delivery tomorrow and, thanks to Victoria's check, making the payment wouldn't be such a squeeze.

He had the perfect opportunity to keep an eye on her. Since her own eyes were closed and her face turned to the late-afternoon breeze, he allowed himself a long, admiring scan of her body. No hardship there. She sure as hell wasn't what he'd expected in a research scientist—all long legs, soft curves, and that thick tail of hair he'd love gliding his fingers through. Oh, yeah. They were going to spend a lot of time together. Starting now.

He cleared his throat to get her attention. When she turned her pretty brown eyes his way, he asked, "How long do you need to settle into your place?"

"A little while to unpack and shower. Set up my laptop. Why?"

"I'll pick you up at seven."

"Pick me up? What for?"

"You gotta eat, don't you?"

She quickly stood. "Well, yes, but I'd planned to grab something quick and bring it back to my cottage, and then review my notes to prepare for tomorrow."

"Not on your first night in the Keys. Besides, Aunt Ruby's got a date with old Willie tonight, and I hate to eat alone. C'mon." He rose to his feet and reached down a hand. She took it and stretched a foot up to the boardwalk, while he lightly pulled her the rest of the way. He brought her within inches of his body, keeping hold of her hand long enough for the closeness to register, but releasing her before it became threatening.

"Call it a swap. I'll introduce you to the local atmosphere. You bring me up-to-speed on your project."

He turned her gently by the shoulders and started her moving. There were other ways to investigate a subject, some a lot more pleasurable than others. If Dr. Victoria Sheffield was hiding something, he'd enjoy finding out. If she wasn't, well, he'd enjoy finding that out too.

Chapter Three

"How did I get myself into this?" Victoria groused, pulling a simple sky-blue dress over her head. The hem hit at her knees, but the scooped neckline exposed a little too much skin for comfort. She grabbed a cardigan off a hanger and slipped it over her shoulders.

Better, she decided after a glance in the mirror, although truth be known, nothing short of a nun's wool habit and wimple would make her feel completely protected from the all-too-observant gleam in Jack's eyes.

"This is not a date," she told herself while brushing her hair back from her face and securing it with butterfly clips. She would use the evening to find out everything she could about Dolphin Land, while instructing Jack on the specifications to get her project underway. Accomplishing their business tonight would save time in the morning, and as he'd said, they needed to eat. It also gave her an opportunity to establish herself professionally, portray her knowledge, elaborate on her experiences, and hopefully, quell his suspicions.

If he had any other ideas, he'd discover soon enough that she was not to be messed with. Gesturing with a tube of lipstick, she gave her reflection her best Victor Sheffield stare-down and repeated firmly, "This is *not* a date."

Excellent delivery. Very convincing.

She eyed her dive watch. Its black strap and thick, sturdy dial looked out of place with her outfit, but it was her only timepiece. Not expecting to socialize, she'd traveled with the bare necessities. A dressier watch didn't fit the category. No big deal, she decided. Waterproof, it kept excellent time and doubled as a stopwatch. Those were the only characteristics that mattered. Still, for some reason its chunkiness on her wrist bothered her tonight. Swiftly, she undid the strap and dumped the watch into her bag along with her cottage key.

It was already close to seven. All in all, she'd done a fine job settling into her new home-away-from-home. She'd even had time to log on to her computer to check her email and her brokerage accounts. The market continued strong. Hallelujah! The investments in her trust fund kept producing income as planned. That municipal bond payback had covered her equipment purchases, the first payment to Ruby, and her rent here at Pirate's Cove. The quarterly dividend on her banking conglomerate stock would see her through the next few months.

The guilt imp tickled her nerves. Ruby never asked where the grant money originated, so she didn't have to lie. That truly would have been an un-crossable line. No matter how much she wanted this chance to prove herself, she would never fabricate a story about receiving money from the National Science Foundation or some other official organization. *If anybody flat-out asks, I can honestly say the funding comes from private sources.*

Her trust fund was very private. Not even her father had ever controlled it, since it was set up for her by her maternal grandparents when she was a child. Victoria glanced at the dresser where she'd set out a few personal items. She traced the frame of a family picture taken before her mother had passed away. For once, they'd all been in Nantucket for Christmas instead of on a boat in a distant sea, and they'd shared the holidays with her grandparents. If she closed her eyes, she could still remember the strength in her grandfather's hug and the sweetness in Nana's eyes. No amount of money in the world held more value to her than her memories of their too-few times together.

Thank God, she'd never given in to Kel's strong suggestions that she let him manage the fund when they'd become engaged. He'd robbed her of everything else. He'd have found a way to take that too.

Her gaze drifted to another photograph, snapped at her college graduation. The pride beaming from her mother's face lit up the room. Her father's expression was typically aloof, but smug and satisfied, almost as if he could take equal credit for her *summa cum laude* honors.

A sharp rap on the door broke into her reverie. She put on a cool, professional smile and swung open the door.

"Hello, Ja—" The polite greeting stuck in her throat. The straggly laborer she'd met that afternoon had been replaced by a walking ad for casual menswear, loaded with sex appeal. A crisp cotton shirt with the cuffs precisely rolled back on his forearms topped khaki cargo shorts. His coffee-dark hair was combed back and tied neatly at his neck. Under the overhead light, his gem-like eyes glittered.

"Howdy, Vic." A half-smile quirked out of his suntanned face. "You ready?"

Oh yes! If that wasn't a loaded question. Sensuality flowed from him like some dark, enticing potion. Her skin felt hot and tight, as if pulled straight from the clothes dryer. Her insides jittered and a quivering fullness invaded parts south.

She was ready all right. Ready to melt, to beg for mercy. Ready to be committed to an asylum for the hormonally out of control.

Damn it. Activate emergency control measures.

"This is *not* a date!" Even to her ears the words sounded desperate. Please, bring back the scruffy handyman in the loud print shirt.

"Of course not," he agreed, sliding an arm around her shoulders. He pulled the door shut, and then guided her toward a solid-looking pickup truck.

"It's a business meeting taking place in a restaurant solely for expediency."

"Right." He opened the truck door, and before she could stop him, he lifted her into the seat. "Buckle up, sugar."

"Please stop calling me sugar. My name is Victoria."

"Too formal. I like my choice better."

"But it's demeaning. Demoralizing." God, she sounded like a stuck-up spinster. "It's de—"

"Delicious? Delightful?"

"Deeply insulting. You and I are going to be working together for a long time. I insist you treat me with respect and consideration."

"Trust me. I can consider a hundred ways to treat you in a lotta respects."

Indignation hit the red zone. "Listen to me you, you . . . " Neanderthal, you chauvinist, she intended to say, but got sidetracked by that sexy grin. Speechless, she shook her finger.

He erupted into a full-blown laugh. Grabbing her hand, Jack gave it a swift, friendly kiss before placing it back in her lap.

"Have mercy, you're fun to tease. You've got such a serious look on your face, you're gonna give yourself frown lines." He gently rubbed a spot in the middle of her forehead before turning forward and starting the engine. "Like you said, we're going to be working together, so getting to be friends is important. I'm just breaking the ice. Besides, you need to learn to relax if you're going to hang in the Keys."

Too late she realized the twinkle in his eyes was more buddy-like than sexual. Her insides deflated like a popped balloon. Of course he was only kidding. Hopefully he'd keep his eyes on the road and not notice the embarrassing blush on her cheeks.

How silly to get worked up over nothing. If she'd been paying attention to something other than the spike in her hormones, she'd have properly interpreted the situation. If he'd been a dolphin or a whale, she'd have observed his behavior and nailed the intent. However, despite spending much of her life on boats surrounded by men of all ages, she had a lot less experience successfully identifying human male behavior patterns. Scientists treated each other like colleagues. Crew members and other assistants did not flirt—at least not with, or in front of, the boss's daughter. Victor Sheffield never tolerated such behavior.

Until Kel, of course, but his attentions had been "oh so" proper. He didn't color his remarks in double-entendres, slow burning smiles, and outrageous winks. Always respectful and courteous, he courted her, as old-fashioned as that sounded.

She, like a naïve idiot, had been so flattered by his interest, she'd leapt for it like a sailfish starving for a tasty mullet.

Only in hindsight could she analyze the situation and see that he'd designed his behavior to win her father's approval. She served merely as the means to his end. That first sample of love left her with a bitter taste in her mouth and, she hoped, a much wiser head where men were concerned.

The past could stay where it belonged. Resolved to stay in the moment, she forgave herself for overreacting to Jack's harmless teasing and stuck a cork in her hormone container. She could kid around with the best of them, she reminded herself. She decided to enjoy the evening.

They drove the Overseas Highway for a while, passing strips of stores, restaurants, and resorts. Eventually, Jack slowed and turned off the main road into a gravel lot, parking in front of a weather-beaten, open-air roadhouse tucked inside a tangle of mangrove trees. Muscle trucks, SUVs, and the occasional sedan stood side-by-side with motorcycles with chrome that shone in the overhead lights. Twin guitars and a chorus of voices crooned about changes in attitudes and latitudes, while the rich scent of barbecue smoke drifted in the air from a massive, black outdoor grill.

Jack guided her through the entrance, nodding at a waitress who called his name and pointed at an empty picnic table. Victoria soaked up her surroundings as she slid onto the worn wooden bench. A rough-carved sailor statue sprawled on a seat of stacked lobster traps in the corner. Half a kayak was suspended overhead. Styrofoam trap buoys, colors faded and chipped, bobbed in the breeze. *Cuba 150 miles* with an arrow pointed south was painted on a wall. Bumper stickers proclaiming, *Save the Reef* and *It Beats 40° Below* were plastered on a column.

"What do you think?"

She looked around again. The décor was random and crude, but somehow appropriate. "It all works, doesn't it?"

The comment earned her a smile and a nod.

The waitress dropped two sets of silverware bundled in paper napkins on the table. She handed Victoria a small wooden oar with the menu printed on it.

"Specials are on the board. What can I get you for drinks?"

"The usual, Peg, please."

"Make it a pitcher?"

He nodded. "Throw in some fritters for us for starters, will you?"

She nodded and bustled off.

"You'll have a beer, right?" Jack asked.

"I don't dislike it, I guess, but I don't usually drink, except for wine on occasion."

"Well, the wine list here is pretty much limited to inexpensive white and cheap red. Besides, there isn't anything like a cold draft when you're chowing down on the best barbecue in Florida."

"Delicious, is it?"

"George here makes a pulled pork so good it'll bring tears to your eyes and leave you begging for more."

Her mouth began to water and her stomach registered immediate hunger pangs. "I'm suddenly starving. Bring it on!"

He did just that, giving matching orders to the waitress when she returned with their foaming pitcher of beer and fried conch fritters.

Victoria had to admit the liquid slid coolly down her throat and fit the surroundings much better than a Cabernet or Chablis. Before she finished half the glass or sampled more than two of the chewy, but tasty fritters, the waitress arrived with a massive platter of food.

Forking a bite of shredded meat into her mouth, she moaned as the flavor of garlic, herbs, and a hint of white vinegar burst over her tongue. "Ohhh, that's so good!" She dug in for more.

"Eat up." He picked up his own fork and got to work. They ate in silent, steady, appreciation for a few minutes. It wasn't until they'd put a dent in the meal that he picked up the pitcher and topped off their glasses.

"So, Vic." He shook his head as if bemoaning the nickname. "Tell me more about your research project. What do you want from us?"

She chewed off a couple of rows of kernels from the corncob in her hands, swallowed, and licked a drop of melted butter off her finger. Not sure how technical she could get in her explanation before losing him, she weighed her words. "The basis of my study is cooperative communication. In everyday terms, we believe that dolphins communicate with each other, and there are convincing studies in some areas such as signature whistles, for example. You're familiar with those?"

At his nod, she continued. "So we think all dolphins have their own signature whistles that identify them to the other members of their pod. Researchers have collected data and analyzed circumstances when dolphins use each other's whistles. Fascinating material, really.

"For my study, I intend to isolate an area of communication. It's a given that dolphins are intelligent. They exhibit cognitive awareness and can problem solve to a good degree. And, as Rhett so beautifully demonstrated this afternoon, they learn by copying other dolphins. They can teach themselves, but what I want to see is how they teach each other." The possibilities were endless, and the thought that she would start investigating them tomorrow almost overwhelmed her. Excitement and something like a very unscientific glee bubbled up inside. She tamped it down with a hefty swallow of beer, waiting for his reaction.

He gave nothing away in his expression, merely finished a forkful of baked beans. "You're assuming they actually teach each other stuff."

"Absolutely. I've seen group interactions and teamwork in wild dolphins that make me think more complex instruction, other than imitation, takes place."

"You think, but you don't know."

"True, but I'm making an educated guess."

A dark eyebrow shot toward his hairline. "In other words, you're committing money, time, and energy on a hunch?"

She should have been insulted at the utter incredulity in his voice. Maybe it was the second beer, but she burst out laughing. "I prefer to call it a theory, but if hunch works for you, so be it." Playfully, she waved her fork at him. "It was a hunch, based on some initial observations, that took Ben Franklin into a storm with a key and a kite. Or led Pasteur to wonder if coming into contact with cow-pox protected milkmaids from getting small pox. If he hadn't had a wondering mind, he might not have developed the process of vaccination.

"Come to think of it, Pasteur's theories helped him figure out how to protect beer from getting soured by free-flying yeast microbes. Where would you be if he hadn't? Think about that, Jack."

The furrowed brow told her he was indeed thinking, and thinking hard. It was entirely possible that he'd never needed to ponder the complexities and marvelous excitement of research exploration. He probably caught his thrills from hauling in a trophy-size fish or watching two teams of bruisers fight for possession of a football. Still, she had to give him credit. He'd stayed with the conversation.

Now, finished with his meal, he topped off their glasses again and leaned forward on crossed arms.

"Why us? If this is such a big deal to you, why, out of all the places in the world, did you pick Dolphin Land?"

Oh, now that cut to the chase. She kept her smile neutral. "Your facility is perfect for my needs."

The guilt imp didn't even twitch since the statement was a hundred percent true.

He snorted. "Perfect? C'mon, Vic. We barely keep ourselves afloat. Most of the time people forget we exist."

Which was a plus in her mind. When she'd first hatched her idea, she'd known no established facility would open their doors to her project. Despite her years of experience, she had no credentials on her own, always working under her father's shadow. Her only chance to prove herself had been stolen by Kel. Once she'd gained Dolphin Land's agreement, she realized its relative anonymity worked to her advantage. Nobody else in the field was exploring collaborative communication, and she certainly didn't want to give anyone the idea to start.

Jack waited for her to elaborate, regarding her steadily over the table.

She returned his gaze over the rim of her glass. "You may have hit a rough patch, that's true, but anyone with two eyes can see the potential. The dolphins are healthy and well cared for. Their habitat is in top shape. The buildings . . ." She shrugged. "Okay, so the buildings need some work and the grounds could use sprucing up, but that's cosmetic.

"Where it matters, you have everything I need, Jack. An established colony of dolphins that have not been overworked in a close-to-natural environment. In return, the money I bring can help upgrade the rest of the facility. And isn't that what you and Ruby need?"

"What my aunt needs is a lot less work and worry."

"Really? She looks pretty happy to me."

He sat up abruptly, drained his glass, then nailed her with a look. "She's got it in her head that you're the cavalry, come to save the day. She thinks that if we fix up the place, all of a sudden the tourists will beat down the doors and put Dolphin Land on the map again. So, yeah, she's happy."

"You don't agree?"

"Dress us up all you want but we're still not ever gonna be Disney World. We're too small, too old, too plain. There's no flash, no excitement."

"But people love dolphins! They are almost universally the most fascinating creatures on the planet."

"And there're at least a dozen other, better places in Florida to see 'em."

"I'm sorry, but I think you're wrong. Other places, maybe, but not necessarily better. Dolphin Land may be small, but that doesn't mean it can't be a viable tourist attraction. Surely, there are enough visitors annually to the Florida Keys to sustain the facility. In that case, the size may work in your favor by reducing your operating costs."

"God almighty, here I thought researchers made their observations on facts. Now I see you're as much of a pie-in-the-sky dreamer as Ruby."

"And that's wrong, because . . . Where are you heading with this, Jack? You don't think your aunt's plan can succeed, so you're trying to scare me off? Just because you may not share the dream, doesn't mean it won't work."

Disbelief was evident in his expression, but she refused to stop. "I've got news for you, buddy. Interfering with my work, sabotaging my efforts, would ruin everything."

An ugly thought struck her heart. "Maybe you don't want to support my project because you're hoping for bigger bucks from the land developers. Is that it? Are you ready to sell out your aunt's dreams?"

The habitual lazy look fled his eyes, and he pinned her hand to the table in a less-than-gentle grip.

"Nobody's going to hurt her dreams." Slowly, carefully, he

ground out the words. "Not me, not you, not anyone. I'll see this ride right through to the end. The most important thing to my aunt is keeping her dolphins, and by God, that's what is going to happen. When this plan doesn't work, I'll find another way to save them."

Despite the fury in his eyes, she refused to let him win his intimidation game. "We both want the same thing. I can't complete my research if Dolphin Land goes belly up. For now and a long time in the future, you're stuck with me."

Even though her stomach churned from the confrontation, she met him stare for stare. Gradually while she watched, the laser-intensity in his eyes melted back into his typical good old boy humor. To her complete surprise, he laughed, a deep, full sound that vibrated the air. Releasing her hand with a gentle pat, he leaned back in his chair.

"Jesus, Vic, there you go getting all serious again. The look on your face just kills me." He reached for the pitcher, but she shook her head and put her hand over the glass. He shrugged and put down the beer.

She didn't find the situation at all funny and stayed silent.

"C'mon, sugar, give a guy a break. I had to test you to look out for my aunt's best interests." He gave her a winning, almost boyish grin. "Isn't it the job of the male of the species to protect the female?"

Sugar this, buddy. Loading her smile with syrup, she regarded him as if he were several watts short of bright. "The most developed dolphin social structure is the maternity pod, involving experienced mothers with calves and adolescents, as well as other sexually mature females. They live, feed, and travel together. Females assist each other during the birthing process and act as alloparents—babysitters— for each other's calves. The males live off in their own pairs or small bachelor groups.

"In short, the females don't need the males for anything other than procreation."

He grinned even wider as he tossed down enough bills to cover their meal. Gently grasping her arm, he brought her upright from the bench when he stood. The warmth of his solid body seeped into her skin.

"In your righteous argument on the self-sufficiency of dolphin females, don't discount the importance of those procreation activities. I do remember learning that dolphins are the only mammals besides us humans that have sex just for the fun of it. Lord knows, we see it often enough in our gang." He tickled the sensitive skin at the crook of her elbow.

She tugged her arm free, doing her best to ignore the delicate shiver that rippled up her spine. "I hate to burst your male expectations, but dolphins are also bisexual."

He slid his arm around her waist, setting off another shiver. "Think what you like about our dolphin friends. But when it comes to *our* species, there ain't no substitute for the way a man can make a woman feel, and vice versa."

Victoria stopped talking and kept walking, not sure at all of her next move. She wasn't used to a man whose conversational style ran to innuendo, while his hand spread large and warm on her hip. Jack was trouble in big, fat capital letters. With all that brawn, brown hair, and blue eyes, he was quite the package.

And knew it.

So, maybe he turned on the charm with every woman until she dropped at his feet like a willing supplicant. In which case, she was definitely insulted. She was a scientist, for God's sake, not a bar pick-up. Miffed, she sidestepped, separating their bodies. With a smooth motion, he settled her in again against his hip, keeping her close when she tried to move away.

On the other hand, those eyes of his weren't guileless. He flirted like a champ and appeared the picture of a kicked-back guy, but she sensed he was looking for something behind her reactions, something else lying underneath her words.

Whatever the case, she refused to believe he had any real interest in her beyond the money she brought to Dolphin Land. She represented a windfall, and that alone was reason enough for him to stick close. But there was close, and then there was crowding.

"Don't you ever give your brain a rest?"

They'd reached his truck, and he turned her so her back rested against the door.

She blinked up at him. "I don't know what you mean."

"When you get quiet, I can almost hear your mind humming with hypotheses."

"I'm a scientist. Hypotheses are my life."

"Sooner or later, you have to shut it off for the day."

Nerves sparked a response. "No, not me. When I'm on a project, I'll eat, sleep, and live it for the duration."

The *tsk* sound came from deep in his throat. He stroked the back of his hand down her cheek, and she almost forgot to breathe. "Now, Vic, even the most dedicated researcher deserves a little free time. When you're done eating, sleeping, and living your study, you've gotta take some time for fun."

His gaze dropped to her mouth and she knew, whatever his motivations, he wanted to kiss her. A sensation zipped through her that should have been panic, but it thrilled her instead. The man was too damned sexy for her own good!

She wanted that kiss.

Anticipation shimmered in the night air. His broad chest rose and fell with steady breaths while he waited, his gaze steady.

Oh yes, she wanted the kiss and she knew that he knew it. Still he waited, telling her without words that it was her move to make.

She shut her eyes and he leaned in, bringing his firm, mouth so close she could feel his warm breath teasing her skin in the instant before he—

Common sense returned in a rush. Her eyes snapped open and she slapped her hand against his chest. "No, Jack. Don't." She'd meant her voice to come out steady and strong, but it wavered. She cleared her throat and brought her gaze up to meet his. "Kissing is a very bad idea."

"Not from my point of view."

His body felt solid and strong beneath her hand when she pushed against him, hoping to create much-needed space. She'd have better luck moving the truck.

"Something tells me you haven't had enough fun in your life," he commented. "Now might be a real good time to change that fact."

"Now would be the worst time!" she blurted out, realizing too late that she'd confirmed his observation. "Besides, there's a huge difference between fun and fraternization."

"Frater—" His tongue appeared caught on the unfamiliar word, and she felt small for waging war with a superior vocabulary.

"Fraternization. Having relations with—"

"I know what it means! Vic, I'm not the enemy and I'm not feeling brotherly. That pretty much takes care of both definitions. It's a damn shame that you don't know the difference between causing a problem and having a little fun. Geezus, woman. Do you always have a stick up your . . ."

Stepping back, he unlocked the truck door, grabbed her by the waist, and hoisted her into the seat. Neither of them talked on the entire ride back up the highway. Victoria stared out the window, unable to ignore the deep tide of embarrassment slapping at her insides like waves against a dock. First, she'd wanted his kiss, and then she slammed on the brakes. To top it all off, she insulted his intelligence.

She regretted the wanting as much as she did the insulting. But whether it made good sense or not, the action she regretted most of all was stopping him.

If she told herself from now until the next full moon that she was protecting the professionalism of their working relationship, it wouldn't change the truth.

She was protecting herself as well. The opportunity she'd created for herself at Dolphin Land meant the world to her, and she couldn't afford to make a mistake. Jack was an unexpected distraction. That almost-kiss offered proof positive that his presence drastically complicated the situation.

God only knew how she'd handle the next several months working by his side.

Chapter Four

Victoria's unsuccessful attempts at uninterrupted sleep ended at daybreak. She wished she could claim unfamiliar surroundings and a strange bed as reasons, but she'd given up self-delusion when she returned her engagement ring to Kel. Punching perfectly fluffy pillows and shifting from one side to the other on the comfortable mattress couldn't stop a bad case of jitters.

When the darkness outside her windows lightened to pearly gray, she gave up and grumbled her way to the kitchenette for a hot cup of tea and a toasted muffin. Accustomed to conserving water on research vessels whenever possible, she couldn't even allow herself the luxury of a long, steamy shower to clear out the fuzziness in her brain. After quickly toweling off and pulling on a swimsuit underneath shorts and a T-shirt, she glared at herself in the mirror while braiding her hair.

This is no way to start the first day of the project. Her reflection in the mirror returned a glum look. She'd expected to jump right in with baseline observations of the pod and familiarize herself with the normal routine of the facility. All this could be done at the same time that a competent electronics company installed those hydrophones.

That plan had been jettisoned once Jack declared himself the installer. To think she'd felt a small spate of nerves when he first informed her of that yesterday afternoon. After last night's fiasco outside the restaurant, those nerves were like a soft breeze compared to the current, full-blown apprehension.

Get over it, she told herself. So the incident the night before had been a little . . . uncomfortable. No way could she afford to let it mess things up for her right at the outset. As far as that little . . . okay, significant, sizzle, well, it would surely die out when neither of them fed the flame.

Looking back at the event objectively, Jack's behavior was pretty much textbook. She'd arrived at Dolphin Land eager to carve out some of the territory for herself as head of the research project. As resident male, he'd acted to retain dominance on his own turf. He'd controlled the initial challenge by maneuvering her into the dinner. When she prevented him from gaining the upper hand in their discussion, he had employed subtle, physical intimidation, touching, stroking, and keeping her smaller frame close to his much stronger one. She cast a rueful look at her reflection. If she'd been more observant and less reactive, she would have anticipated his next step—the attempted kiss—before he had even thought to try it.

Textbook and typical. She shook her head. In one way, it was almost comforting to have it all figured out. With a little more concentration, she could have avoided the mess altogether. Jack was no different than any other man, despite going out of his way to prove otherwise. So, she couldn't blame him for normal male behavior. Instead, she'd claim responsibility for the situation getting out of hand. The most direct way to smooth his ruffled feathers and satisfy his male ego was with an apology.

There were two behavioral patterns she could expect this morning.

He'd either be passive-aggressive by barely speaking to her and dragging out the work, or confrontational—signaling his displeasure by arguing every point. No matter how obnoxious he chose to act— and given his larger-than-life attitude she guessed he could act very obnoxiously—she'd respond with calm, matter-of-fact professionalism. She'd keep the apology short and sincere with the understanding that they'd found the line in their working relationship that they were both bett er off not crossing. He'd save face and they'd both forge ahead. Simple as that.

She and her reflection acknowledged each other with a firm nod. Analyzing a problem through to a solution always made her feel better. Bolstered by the process, she strapped on her watch, slipped on her backpack, and marched out the door like a soldier heading into battle.

* * *

Jack leaned against a pillar at the front lagoon, steam from his coffee warming his face. One by one, each of the dolphins swam up and greeted him with various clicks and sounds. His brain was engaged in full debriefing-mode, and he acknowledged the animals with only a nod or half-salute with the mug in his hand. Then Scarlett planted herself in front of him, blowing shrieks from her blowhole, almost as if she was demanding greater recognition.

Geezus, that high-pitched, piercing scream could shatter an ear drum. "All right already, girl. Good morning. I see you. Yeah, you're gorgeous." How glad he was that none of his buddies were around to hear him anthropomorphizing a dolphin and then responding.

The after-effects of a bad night and the unexpected snafu in his mission were the reasons, he told himself. Now, he only had a few more minutes to recap the situation, analyze the results, and counter the damage. He waved to Scarlett when she swam away and tried to figure out where he'd stepped wrong.

He swallowed more of the hot brew. It wasn't really comfortable to admit that Victoria had sneaked in under his radar. He was supposed to be in control and subtly interrogate her over dinner. How could he anticipate that her pretty face would glow with sensual enjoyment with every forkful of her meal, while her enthusiasm for her research project shone like moonbeams in her brown eyes? With the prim scientist replaced by a quick-witted, good-humored woman, he'd forgotten his objective and gotten sucked right into the moment. Over the dinner table, it was damned hard to remember she was an opponent when all he could think was that she'd morphed into a total babe.

Out by his truck, when she turned her face up to him and her eyes drifted shut, his command of the situation went south. It rushed back when she slapped her hand against his chest.

Later that night, half of him kicked himself for making the move in the first place, while the other half regretted it hadn't gone further. He'd awakened before dawn with one thought on his mind: damage control. It wouldn't work to pretend it never happened. He couldn't let her think the rejection stung. Since she probably expected him to be a jerk this morning, that tactic was out too. So, that left him only one option.

* * *

As early as she arrived, he'd still gotten there ahead of her. There he was by the lagoon, still as a statue. So much for the passive-aggressive pattern of not showing up. That left confrontation. He probably set his alarm just to get a head start on giving her a hard time. Suppressing a flare of trepidation, she fixed a pleasant smile on her face.

"Good morning, Jack."

He sipped from the mug in his hand. "Mornin', Vic."

Since he didn't turn around at the greeting, she walked up beside him. "Looks like it's going to be a beautiful day. I'm eager to get started." Say something positive about him, reinforce his cooperative behavior, she reminded herself. "It's good of you to arrive early."

"We always start around this time." The rich scent of coffee wafted from the mug as he took another swallow.

"Well, sure, but still . . . I'm glad to see you here."

"You expecting someone else?" He snickered, the sound vibrating low in his chest.

"No, but . . ." Expecting some degree of antagonism, the nonchalant amusement threw her. "Well, I guess I thought it possible you might at least be a little late." Oh good, Victoria, that came out just short of stumbling.

"Why's that?" The man took matter-of-fact to a new level.

Because! She shouted in her mind. You're supposed to be ticked off, not acting like nothing's wrong.

Obviously, she took too long to answer, because he goaded her again.

"Something bothering you, Vic?" Now, finally, he looked at her, those clear blue-green eyes piercing through her skin straight to her confusion.

Time to regroup. She took a deep breath and plunged in. "Jack, after last night, I realize you have every reason to be . . . annoyed. I overreacted. I insulted you and I'm sorry."

There. She got it all out, less gracefully than she'd hoped, but the apology was complete. Now he could do his part, accept it in the spirit she intended and . . .

He lifted an eyebrow, looking anything but hostile. "Last night wasn't any big deal, Vic. Not anything to freak out over."

"I'm not freaked-out!"

His shrug said "whatever." "Well, if that's been preying on your mind, forget about it." He smiled. "I figured it was better we got that out of the way in the beginning."

"Got what out of the way?" Somewhere lurked a clue to where he was going with this, but she needed a ten magnification microscope to see it.

"The whole guy-girl thing, sugar. With us working real close together, we didn't need you constantly tied up in knots wondering when I was gonna make a move on you. So, the move's been made."

He drained the last of the coffee. "I won't push. When you change your mind, let me know. Until then," he shrugged, "you can quit worrying about it."

His body language, tone of voice, and the smile lurking in his eyes indicated a relaxed, casual, attitude. So *not* what she expected. Her eyes squinted, and her forehead creased while her brain whirled, trying to figure him out.

Using his thumb, he gently rubbed the wrinkle in her brow. "Relax, Vic," he said as he walked away. "C'mon now, we have work to do. Those hydrophones won't install themselves."

When she changed her mind? She snapped out of her shock and strode after him. Oh, that was a whomping assumption. That smug son-of-a . . . whatever. Victoria fumed. If he thought it was only a matter of time until she . . . well, she would prove him way far wrong.

Quickly, she processed her options. Confront him now and tell him off, or . . . no, better not to react at all. If he could act like the previous night was no big deal, so could she. Starting right now, she was so totally not affected by a single thing he did or said.

While he unpacked the underwater microphones from their protective casing, she stifled her anger and opened her backpack. She pulled out the installation manual and a sketch she'd drawn of the lagoon. Jack's confidence aside, if the equipment wasn't placed correctly, the data collection would be useless.

"On this sketch, the red Xs indicate where I need the hydrophones placed for the most effective triangulation of sound."

He studied the drawing for a few seconds. "Got it." Opening another box, he took out a large coil of black, rubber-coated, co-axial cable and slipped it up over his arm to rest on his shoulder. "I'll lay out the cable from land first. Once that's set, I'll go into the lagoons and secure the microphones." He grabbed a leather tool belt and strapped it around his waist. "This is pretty much a one-person job, Vic, so if you've got something else to do, feel free. I'll call you when I need you."

This was not a "learn-by-doing" endeavor. He hadn't even asked for the installation manual, yet alone read it. Last night in preparation for today, she'd studied it thoroughly and highlighted the most important instructions. "Hang on a minute, Jack."

He stopped in mid-stride and turned toward her. "Yeah?"

She held out the manual and pointed to the first broad stripe of fluorescent pink highlighting. "The hydrophones need to be placed at a certain angle to record sounds properly, and the way the wire is laid affects that placement. Don't you think you should read a little bit about it before plunging right into the work?"

With a look that clearly said he was humoring her, he reached for the book. He glanced at the page, flipped over to the schematics diagram, and then shut the manual in less than ten seconds. "Piece of cake." He tossed the book into an empty box, leaving her stunned and staring as he strolled away.

∗ ∗ ∗

The whole time he measured out cables, running them to a central location where they would connect to the recording equipment, she kept an eye on him from afar. When he finished the north section and walked into the office for a short break, she quickly carried the hydrophones to the lagoon, plopped down beside them and waited. Like it or not, this was her sensitive equipment, and she was going to make darned sure they were correctly secured.

"This part *is* a two-person job, Jack," she said with a sweet smile, when he joined her a few minutes later.

He set down the tool belt and cordless drill on the boardwalk. "Whatever you say, boss lady. You can hand me the tools when I need them." He dropped down on his belly next to her, and the air temp increased by five degrees before he swung his legs over the side and effortlessly lowered himself into the water.

His biceps bulged underneath the snug wetsuit. Distracted, she didn't realize he'd relegated her to landside helper until it was too late to argue. Resigned, but still determined to supervise, she, too, stretched out on the boardwalk.

"According to my measurements and calculations, the first hydrophone should go there." She hung her head over the side, her single braid hanging down while she pointed to a post. "I think if you put the first clamp about six inches from the . . ."

Tilting her head up with his hand, he pressed his thumb against her mouth. "I saw the diagram." He flipped her braid back over her shoulder. "Hand me the drill, will you, please?"

"But—"

"Vic, believe it or not, I'm pretty good at this kind of work. We'll even get the whole job done today if you let me get started."

Pressing her point now would sound like she questioned his competence. Even worse, he might think she was picking on him in retaliation. Without another word, she grabbed the cordless drill off the dock and held it out to him. He reached up and, either by accident or design, stroked the sensitive skin between her fingers when he slid the tool from her grip. She jolted, and he wrapped his strong hand around hers.

"Easy there. Salt water wreaks hell on this equipment," he said.

Heat suffused her face. She wanted to blame it on hanging over the boardwalk's edge and making the blood rush to her head. It had nothing whatsoever to do with Jack. She was unaffected. Completely. Repressing a shiver, she boosted herself to her knees and rummaged for the other things he'd need to secure the first hydrophone.

"Clamp, please," he said, sounding like a surgeon.

She carefully handed it down to him. No skin contact, no jolt, no problem. See, she was right. Totally unaffected.

So why did it feel like his fingers caressed hers even when they didn't touch? Surely it violated some law of physics that a man immersed waist-deep in water still emitted hot energy waves. The waves shimmered over her skin like tangible things when she held out the screwdriver he requested. Breathing in deeply, she caught a whiff of saltwater and the clean, potent scent of Jack. But, oh no, she wasn't affect—

The screwdriver slipped out of her grip.

"Oh no!" Grabbing for it, she lost her balance.

"I got it." Somehow, he caught the tool before it hit the water.

With his free hand, he braced her shoulder. "You okay?"

Peachy. Great. Embarrassed as hell. "Yes. I'm fine. Thank you."

To prove it, she snatched up the first hydrophone. "Here." It shot from her hands as if coated with oil.

"Whoa, sugar." Lightning fast, he snared it in mid-air, and then had the nerve to laugh while she gaped at her clumsiness. "Having one of those days, huh?"

She'd *never* had this kind of "one of those days" in her life. For some reason, her steady hands and smooth coordination had abandoned her. Not good. Instead of answering him, she bit down on the inside of her lip and mentally scolded herself. If she didn't get a grip, on herself as well as the tools, she'd look like an inept idiot. Not at all the impression she meant to project.

"The protective casing is slick," she offered as an excuse.

"Oh yeah. That must be it."

Whistling softly, he fastened clamps around the baton-shaped hydrophone and screwed them tightly into the post. While she watched, he gave it a couple of strong tugs to make sure it was secure. Apparently satisfied, he gripped the edge of the boardwalk and pulled himself out of the water as easily as doing a chin-up.

Smooth grace and undiluted male power. She swallowed hard and clenched her jaw to keep her mouth from dropping open in pure admiration.

Thank God he didn't notice her reaction.

"Ready for the next one?" he asked and picked up the tool belt.

Nodding, she scrambled to her feet and reached for the crate of hydrophones. "Let's go."

"Uh, Vic?" The question in his voice stopped her. "Maybe you oughta let me carry those. Just to be on the safe side." He said it so kindly, she was positive he was holding back laughter, which only made her more determined.

"Don't be ridiculous. I have them." A withering look dared him to disagree, and head high, she turned to lead the way to the next location on her chart.

Her sandal snagged on something and she tripped. With the crate in her hands, she couldn't catch her balance and toppled forward.

Jack grabbed her upper arms before she crash-landed. He steadied her, his hands warm on her skin. Thank God her back was to him so he couldn't see the total mortification splashed in blotchy red all over her face.

Stock still, she waited for her heart to stop pounding and her flushed face to cool. When she felt under control, she turned. "Thank you for the save, Jack," she said as calmly as she could manage. "I can certainly see that you really don't need my help with the installation." Or her hindrance, as was obviously the case. "No sense both of us working on a project that one can accomplish. I think my time is better spent going over my video equipment."

Without waiting for agreement, she thrust the crate into his hands, banishing the memory of how good they'd felt on her bare arms. Gathering her beautifully designed diagrams and the tattered remains of her dignity, she smiled brightly and hurried off the boardwalk.

Chapter Five

That had gone even better than he'd planned. Back in charge, Jack whistled cheerfully while he installed one hydrophone after another. Yeah, things were back on an even keel. A far cry from the night before, that's for sure.

The surprised look on her face earlier had told him she bought the story that her stopping the kiss was no big deal. Score one point to him.

Following it up with the assurance that it was only a matter of time before it happened again was the tactic he needed to reestablish command. Her clumsiness around him was an added bonus. She couldn't broadcast her awareness of the heat between them any louder than if she used a 50,000 watt radio transmitter. And damned if she didn't look a hundred percent adorable at the same time.

He got the message loud and clear, which went a long way toward smoothing the ragged edge of his ego. He couldn't afford to get smug, but he was entitled to that much satisfaction. Particularly when, for the time being, she'd made it clear it was the only satisfaction he was likely to get.

He looked at her across the lagoon. The location for the next hydrophone to be installed was closer to where she, surrounded by video components, sat at the edge of the boardwalk. On her lap was a remote camera. As he strolled over, he saw her pick up the lens, glancing between it and the manual.

"Making progress?"

"Uh-huh." Her forehead crinkled, while she apparently absorbed every word of the directions.

"So am I. Six mikes installed, three to go."

"Great, Jack. Thanks."

He almost bought the indifference act, but he caught her glance at him from underneath her lashes and noticed the light pink that tinted her cheeks when she realized he'd spotted her peeking.

She put down the lens and stood, turning her back on him and picking up long pieces of pipe that she quickly screwed together.

The hydrophones could wait while he deviled her for a few minutes with his company. He leaned against a nearby post, but it gave a little. The fence wasn't much steadier, he realized when he propped his hand on it. More chores to add to his "Jack to-do" list.

"How does this set-up work again?" he asked.

She bolted a platform to a swivel on the end of the pole. "The camera goes on the platform. Extra height provides wider visual coverage of the lagoon, and I can change the direction of the camera with the remote control."

"An eye in the sky."

"Right. The video feed travels back to the recorder. By matching the video of the dolphins and the timing to the sound recordings during the test sessions, I can look for a pattern of communication between the pod members."

He focused his attention on the equipment. Knowing what she thought of his intelligence-level, she'd expect him to show more interest in the electronic "toys." "Sweet. You using VHS?"

"No. DVD."

He whistled long and low and winked. "Pretty hot stuff."

She countered with a baleful stare, obviously using her expression and posture to indicate that she'd picked up on his double-entendre, and it didn't faze her. Yeah, right. That's why she held the pole in a death grip.

His wide grin triggered her narrow-eyed glare. "Jack, I can go over all this with you again later on, but I'd like to finish my work. Today."

He grinned again. "You're the boss." Sauntering off to the next location, he called back over his shoulder, "Call me if you need . . . anything."

Oh yeah. The day was going better than planned. Although, he had to give her credit. She'd regained her composure and looked to be handling her video equipment with ease. Clearly, she had the electronics covered. He slid into the water to clamp in the next hydrophone. She might not, however, have taken into account that the wind was flat today, unlike most days in the Keys. Out here on the causeway, without protection, that extension pole alone most likely wouldn't hold steady when the wind came up again.

When he next glanced over, she was standing with the pole in her hand, looking up at the sky. Something told him that, with her high-powered brain, she'd come to the same conclusion and was quickly trying to figure out a solution. They didn't have the supplies on hand, or the permits, to build a stronger structure. He considered the problem while tightening another screw. Once he finished his installations, he'd go over to lend her a hand and suggest building some braces for the pole.

Gathering up his gear to go to the final location, he looked at her again. Holy crap! With the pole in one hand, she was climbing onto that worn-out fence and eyeing the post that had shifted when he'd leaned his weight against it.

She's thinking of attaching her extension pole to that weak pillar. He dropped the equipment and ran, hoping he wasn't too far away. "Victoria, get off that thing!"

"What? Why?"

"Get down. It's not safe."

At the same second that she looked down at her feet, a sharp crack echoed through the air. Shit! The fence was falling.

Ignoring the stiffness in his bum leg, he accelerated. Victoria dropped the pole and wrapped her arms around the post to save her balance. It wobbled in her grasp, and he prayed for it to hold just a few seconds more.

Suddenly, the fence board she was standing on broke in half. Lunging forward, he grabbed her around her legs, jamming his bad knee in the process. Biting back a curse, he did his best to ignore the throbbing pain while he steadied her against the post with a hand on her excellent butt.

Sucking in air, he rasped out, "I've got you."

"Okay," she answered, equally breathless.

The stiff tension in her legs was a marked contrast to the soft curve of her butt in his hand. "Let go of the post nice and easy while I lower you down."

While she complied, he held her securely, sliding her slowly down his body. Once her feet touched the ground, he turned her around and gripped her shoulders as he gave her a thorough once over. Little scratches scored the inner skin of her forearms, but they weren't deep, thank God, and he didn't spot any other injuries. Sharp relief was swept away in a knee-jerk rush of anger.

"What the hell were you thinking, going up there without me to spot you?"

"I—"

"You could have been hurt, damn it. Everything around here is falling apart, so smart money sure as shit oughta tell you that the last thing you do is climb fences like they're jungle gyms!"

"Jack, I—"

"No buts, Victoria. If I'm not with you, don't climb as much as a stepstool." Thoughts of her falling and breaking a bone or, even worse, hitting her head, knocking herself out, and tumbling into the water, rushed through his brain like doomsday scenarios. Suddenly, her earlier clumsiness wasn't nearly as cute. "I swear, if you try, I'll bolt you to—"

She pressed three fingers gently to his mouth, stopping the lecture. Well, if she thought she was going to argue this point and win, she had another—

"Jack, you're right. I should have waited. I'm sorry." Her hand dropped from his mouth to her side, and she barely met his eyes while offering a tiny smile. "I'm not used to asking for help. Or receiving it. Thank you." Her gaze slid away, but not before he caught the wistfulness in those pretty, dark eyes.

Aw hell. What happened to the spitfire? Faint shivers rippled through her body, prompting his anger to evaporate like rain on a desert tarmac. Right now, she looked so vulnerable that, instead of driving home his point, he wanted to tease away the sadness clouding her eyes and kiss away the quiver in her bottom lip. Before he realized what he was doing, he slid his hands from her shoulders down her back.

Hold it, Benton. He quit in mid-slide. Those shivers signaled the aftermath of her near-miss, not attraction. If he traveled any further down this path, he'd end up right back where they'd been the night before, but this time he'd be taking an unfair advantage.

He released her instantly. "Fine. You're welcome and we understand each other. No more risk-taking." He spun away, and the jolt of heat in his leg unbalanced him. Choking back another nasty word, he grabbed the fence, covering the action by yanking on the broken board. A single rusty nail held it fast. Of course. "If you can hold off until this afternoon, I've got scrap two-by-fours handy. I'll brace that post and attach your video platform to it. In the meantime, let me get rid of this mess of splinters."

Thank God he was facing away from her, or she'd have seen him flinch when he took the first step. Taking a deep breath and clenching his jaw, he forced himself to walk slowly and steadily to retrieve his tool belt.

Didn't that just cap the day? So much for the Superman routine. He'd aggravated his injury in the process. Sweeping up the tools, he returned just as carefully to the fence. Not bad. He'd made it look like a casual stroll, a . . .

"Jack, what's wrong with your leg?"

Freakin' A. "Nothing."

"You're limping. That's not nothing!"

Great. Now she stared at his knee like it was a test subject. Denying he was hurt would make her more suspicious. "I have a ba— a back history with an old football injury." Geez. He'd almost called it a bad leg. "Nothing major. It acts up every once in a while."

"Did you hurt it again when you saved me?"

"It's nothing, I'm telling you."

"You might need ice, or to elevate it or something. Let me see."

The kicked-puppy expression was gone from her face, replaced by that narrow-eyed determination he'd already seen numerous times.

With the knee already swelling inside the tight leg of his wetsuit, the last thing he needed was her pushing the issue. Diversionary tactics were needed pronto.

Instead of pulling away, he stepped forward, backing her against the pillar. He met her dogged stare with his best, disarming "good ol' boy" grin. "You know, if you're that eager to check me out from the inside of my wetsuit, all you have to do is ask."

"Your leg, Jack. I want to check your leg."

Deliberately misunderstanding, he pressed another step closer. "We're a little out in the open, darling, but if you want me to unzip . . ." He rubbed the back of his hand down the smooth skin of her cheek and watched it flush under his caress.

"That is not what I said."

"But you don't deny it's what you're thinking. In fact," he mused as he toyed with her braid, "this whole day you've been itching to stay close. Maybe we should study this in depth." He lifted a brow. "Seems to me it's your way of expressing a subconscious desire to get your eyes and your hands on more of my body."

The outrageous suggestion worked. She gaped at him like a very surprised fish.

"I . . . You! I do not have a desire, subconscious or otherwise," she sputtered.

"So you say, but Vic, an observational genius like yourself should be able to spot when her actions contradict her words." He winked, guessing the look would rile her even more.

He guessed right.

Indignation wiped out the last trace of vulnerability in her eyes, making them snap with fire. "My main observation right now is that you're insane!"

"Nothing insane about what we're feeling, sugar, try as you want to deny it." The damn leg throbbed for attention, so he took his weight off it by cocking a hip. With that and a tilt of his head, he pretended to carefully consider the situation. "You know, if we don't do something, it's only gonna keep growing. Pretty soon, you won't be able to concentrate at all on your study." He slipped his hand from her cheek, threading his fingers in her hair and cradling the back of her head. "In the interest of, ah, experimentation, let's you and me act on it. We'll get it out of our systems as easy as that."

He moved his gaze from her eyes to her mouth and then back again, smiling his best, I'm-going-to-kiss-you-now smile as he lowered his head and . . .

Right on cue, she slapped her hands against his chest. With a quick side step, she ducked under his arm and practically charged over to her gear.

"You're preposterous, Jack," she huffed, keeping her back to him while shoving cables into their boxes. "If I wanted to put my hands on your body, which, trust me, I did not, it had everything to do with concern and nothing at all to do with desire."

Now that her focus was directed elsewhere, he tested his leg with some tentative stretches. With any luck, it was only strained with no serious damage done. As soon as Victoria finished stowing her gear and left, he'd get his ass over to the fish house ice machine. He had a hot date with a cold ice pack. If that didn't take care of the problem, a visit to Doctor Wagner for a quick check and a cortisone shot would fix him up right. In the meantime . . .

"Gotta tell you, sugar, I'm a little concerned that a researcher who deals in facts won't acknowledge the evidence right in front of her face."

He practically saw her hackles rise and had to bite the inside of his cheek to keep from laughing. Any minute now, she'd take off like a bat out of hell and—

Instead, she dropped the pile of equipment and spun around.

"The only evidence I see right now is that you have far too high an opinion of your appeal and way too little an idea of what I'm really all about. The only males around here that interest me at all are swimming in that lagoon, and that attraction is purely academic." She stalked over, jabbing him in the chest with her finger. "And another thing. . ."

Catching him off guard, she slapped her hands on either side of his head, pulled him toward her, and nailed him with a world-class kiss.

Releasing him just as quickly, she stepped back. Fury mingled with hurt in the darkness of her eyes. "For the record, I don't 'experiment' with people's feelings—ever—and here's a news flash for you, hot shot. Nobody, least of all me, likes being considered someone you think you can get out of your system 'as easy as that'!"

Good thing she didn't wait around or she would've seen him struggling to regain his breath. *I'll be damned.* He whistled softly as she hoisted the equipment into her arms and marched back toward the office. Stiff indignation didn't erase the sexy swing of her walk. Now, underneath his wetsuit, more than his knee was swollen and hot.

When her back was against the wall, the woman didn't pull any punches. As kisses went, that little number carried quite the jolt. So much for him staying in control and deciding how this game played out. If that kiss was just a sample of the feast in store, he might not be able to wait for her to make the next move.

Chapter Six

Over-sexed redneck. Impossible cretin. Walking, talking libido with legs. If she tried for a week, she couldn't come up with enough disparaging terms to aptly describe him. Of all the outrageous claims—that she harbored such a hot, latent desire for him that it influenced her every move. Pardon her for caring that he might have hurt himself, while saving her from possible injury.

Ungrateful ass—

Victoria bounced her knee so hard the desk shook. If Jack's behavior drove her to name-calling after only two days, their working relationship—the only relationship of any kind that she could afford—was sadly in jeopardy.

Get a hold of yourself. She could not afford to let him affect her this way. He was no more than an over-stimulated Y chromosome, and if she couldn't handle him, then she knew nothing about the complexities of adult behavior.

She looked out the window and watched him make his way toward the fish house. Even though he didn't limp, the careful way he held his body and placed each foot down confirmed her suspicions. Ha! That pretty much refuted his outrageous claim that she just wanted a peep inside the wetsuit that hugged his body like a second skin. As if! She'd known darn well he was hurt. With the evidence right in front of her eyes, she'd feel downright smug if not for the lingering guilt imp reminding her that she was mostly responsible for the problem.

Subconscious desires? Double Ha! She no more wanted her hands all over his body than she . . . than she . . .

Oh, for goodness sake! What was the point of self-congratulation for her superior hormonal control, when she couldn't even finish her thought without a whopping lie?

He was at least half right, maybe more. She was attracted to him physically, but there was nothing subconscious about it. She didn't need his intolerable declarations to prove the case. If her own clumsiness didn't serve as evidence, the heat still churning in her belly certainly did. As much as she wished she could blame it on anger, the reverse was true.

She didn't want to feel anything at all for him. Not desire. And, not a treacherous soft glow that had spread through her when he'd rushed to her aid. Even though he elevated obnoxiousness to new levels, she couldn't discount that, first, he'd been gentle and concerned. Almost tenderly lowering her to the ground and assuring himself that she wasn't hurt.

Even him yelling at her immediately afterward didn't faze her a bit. It was, she suspected, a reaction to the adrenalin rush. The bottom line was that, for at least a moment, he'd cared that she was okay. That attention was even more dangerous to her than the attraction. A physical pull she could fight more easily than a far more treacherous tug on her emotions.

Whether he realized it or not, he'd done her a favor when he switched on the Don Juan routine. Teetering on footing less steady than that broken fence, her anger froze her soft melting and gave her the power to break away.

Once free, she should just have kept moving, but that "get it out of our systems" comment hit harder than she would ever let him know. Between her lifetime of struggling for recognition from her father and the Kel-catastrophe, she was darn tired of men discounting and discarding her as if who she was and what she wanted meant nothing. Even knowing deep inside that Jack was aggravating her on purpose, something snapped. Before she could stop herself, she'd stalked back to give him a taste of his own medicine.

Unfortunately, with her lips pressed tightly to his, she'd gotten a taste of him too. Like crème brûlée, French pastries, and sweet milk chocolate, one taste left her craving more.

But she couldn't afford to do anything about it, not without consequences.

Consequences she'd already learned from Kel.

No question about it. She needed to go on a no-Jack diet.

Eyes skyward, she studied the stained ceiling tiles as if they were cave paintings illustrating the secret of the world according to Jack. Surely there had been other women who, with little trouble, successfully resisted his potent male package.

There were also women in the world who never ate sweets, but she wasn't one of them.

You've got a brain. Use it and find a solution.

During her college years, her roommate quit smoking by developing aversion techniques. Every time she got the urge, she told herself that smoking was a filthy-tasting, yucky-smelling, lung-clogging habit. She ended up loathing the cigarettes she used to crave and hadn't lit another one since.

Aha! So that was the answer. Focus on all of Jack's bad qualities—arrogance, ego, innuendo overload, et cetera—and his good points would quickly be overshadowed and then fade from her consciousness.

Shouldn't be difficult at all. She looked out the window again and spotted him with Ruby, in the midst of what appeared to be a heated discussion. Arms akimbo, the older woman planted herself in his path and talked a blue streak. He raked his hand through his hair and narrowed his eyes while responding. She didn't need to read lips to figure out that neither one of them was happy with the other, even though she didn't know why.

Look at the lug arguing with a woman thirty years older and a hundred pounds lighter. He couldn't possibly look handsome with his mouth twisted into a scowl. How dare he give his aunt a difficult time?

There! She'd launched her own aversion therapy technique. Satisfied, she picked up her notes on identifying and cataloging underwater dolphin sounds. Later on, she'd run out and hook the hydrophone cables up to the recorder for a test-run. As long as Jack behaved like a jerk, she'd have no problem fighting the attraction. For today though, just to be on the safe side, she'd wait until the coast was clear.

∗ ∗ ∗

"What in the name of Jesus, Mary, and all the saints do you think you're doing, Bubba?"

"I—"

"Don't even try giving me some lousy excuse. I saw you putting a move on Victoria."

Nobody could rag on him like his aunt. She shook her finger at him, reminding him of every time he'd gotten into trouble as a kid. Twenty-five years later, and that stern look and jabbing gesture still made him feel like he was eleven.

"Aunt Ruby, I—"

"This woman is our partner, not a plaything for you!"

A plaything? "Now just a minute, I'm telling you—"

"You aren't telling me a thing I didn't see with my own two eyes."

Geezus. He couldn't get a word in edgewise. Gagging her might work, but even if he considered trying it, she'd like as not bite his fingers off first.

"Bubba, back off. If you've got an itch, you know plenty of women in town who'd be happy to scratch it. You might not agree, but Victoria's doing serious scientific work and, in case your memory sprang a leak, she's paying us to do it here. You scare her off, and Dolphin Land is as sunk as a Spanish galleon in a killer 'cane."

Now that was just too rich.

He snorted. "Aunt Ruby, I'm more likely to scare off an invading army. In case you didn't notice, that woman doesn't back down an inch."

"Well, it's about damn time somebody stood up to you, but that's not the point. Don't make her uncomfortable about working with you. You hear?"

His head started pounding in perfect syncopation with his knee. Nobody, but nobody won an argument with Aunt Ruby when she was in a serious snit. "I hear. I hear."

"Now, I don't know how you antagonized her into kissing you and then hightailing it off the causeway like you left a bad taste in her mouth, but whatever it was, you see that you make things right. Got it?"

"Yes, Ma'am!" He'd salute but that would only prolong the scolding.

"That's better. Now, get off your feet. I'll fetch you an ice pack."

Crap. The last thing he needed, next to this lecture, was his aunt knowing he'd hurt himself. "Ice pack?" he repeated, blank-faced. "What for?"

She gave him a "puh-leeze" look. "Love ya, Bubba, but if you think I can't tell when my boy's hurting, you're an idiot."

"I'm fine, Aunt Ruby."

The look on her face said she didn't buy it.

"All right, I'll *be* fine. A simple strain. That's all."

His aunt's expressions and moods could change as fast as the Keys' weather. She'd flashed through irritation to compassion in nothing flat.

"Nothing about your injury is simple. What those bastards did to you makes me want to shoot them myself." She scowled, looking like she'd pick up a gun in a heartbeat and take on the whole herd of drug lords single-handedly.

He had to grin. "Aunt Ruby, if they knew you were after them, they'd run for the jungles and hide."

"Too damn bad they didn't stay in the jungles in the first place instead of going after you. I know you hate to hear me say it, but I'm damn glad you're out of that life."

"Only for the time being." And every day he told himself he was one day closer to resuming active duty. "As soon as my leg heals all the way, I'm going back to kick some ass."

Her eyes changed again, now to worry. Always apprehensive about his work, her concern had logically grown when he got hurt in the line of duty. Still, she knew how much the DEA meant to him. "But, Jack . . ."

Nothing he said would change the way she felt about his job, and the longer he stood there, the more his leg throbbed. Changing the subject was his best option. "You know, I think you're right about getting off my feet. If you don't mind bringing me that ice pack you mentioned, I'll sit over there on the sea wall where I can put up my leg."

It worked.

"All right. You want one of those pain pills the doctor prescribed?"

Only if he wanted to be flat out and snoring within minutes. "No thanks. It isn't so bad that I need anything more than a couple of ibuprofen tablets." Because she looked like she wanted to disagree, he gave her a hopeful grin. "Got any of your good iced tea to wash them down?"

"You know darned well I set some out to brew in the sun first thing."

"Before or after you started baking whatever smelled so good when I passed by this morning?"

"Ever since you were a boy, you had a nose for my sweet rolls," she laughed, swatting him lightly on the arm. "Go on with you now. I'll be back in a minute with the ice pack and your snack."

He made his way carefully to the sea wall. Damned if the women in his life hadn't put him through 180s all morning. Keeping up with his aunt was an exercise in mental dexterity. Then, there was the whole morning's match with Victoria.

He sat down, leaning back against the concrete wall. The idea was to keep her off balance, but just when he thought he had the advantage, she surprised him again. She sure as hell never acted like he expected for very long. He thought he'd pissed her off enough to make her leave, so when she advanced on him, it caught him off guard. His life often depended on adjusting to unexpected developments, so he knew he would have been prepared for whatever she tossed at him next. Then he'd looked into her eyes.

Anger he expected, but not the hurt churning in the bottomless brown depths. In an instant, he wanted to take her in his arms and cuddle her instead of driving her away. As a result, he never saw the kiss coming until it was too late. Quick as a sniper shot, it packed real heat, and then just as fast, she'd spun away again and was gone before he could react.

Remembering her words he ought to feel bad for goading her into action, even though the action wasn't what he'd anticipated. But the kiss tasted too damned good to regret.

The vulnerability in her eyes was a different matter all together.

"Where'd that come from, Victoria?" he wondered. He carefully replayed her last words and winced. Someone, somewhere must have made her feel irrelevant, or worse. Who and why, he couldn't figure, but just the thought sparked an innate protectiveness.

He winced again. He'd wanted to distract her, not demoralize her. So as uncomfortable as it made him, he could applaud that she'd delivered her wallop and walked away with her head held high. She was a whole hell of a lot more woman than he'd first believed.

Seeing Aunt Ruby hurrying toward him, first aid and sweet tea in hand, he carefully arranged a neutral mask on his face. He'd take out the situation and study it again later. At the very least, he figured his aunt was right, although not for the reason she figured. He couldn't apologize for sort of making Victoria kiss him—not when he'd enjoyed it so much. But, unless he wanted to be a total jerk, he needed to quit giving her a hard time. This meant an end to strategizing and the beginning of a real working relationship.

The realization didn't make him altogether happy. Calling a truce usually led to peaceful resolution, but the aftermath of that kiss made him doubt that peace was anywhere close on his horizon. In fact, if the fire in his wetsuit was any indication, he could now expect to battle with himself every step of the way.

Chapter Seven

"Hi, Rosa. It's me." Early the next morning, while she walked over to Dolphin Land, Victoria chatted on her cell phone to her father's caregiver.

"Girl-child! So good to hear from you. How you doing?" The woman's softly-accented, lilting voice was as rich as her cheerful nature. "You settled in wid your project?"

"I'm getting there, thanks. The equipment's installed, and I'm testing it out today so I can collect some baseline recordings."

It was nice to have someone in her life interested in what she was doing. She shoved the resentful thought away. What was past, should stay there. "How's everything up home?"

"Good. Very good. Victoria, it is amazing, but in de last two or dree derapy sessions, your fahder, he's made some progress!"

Bless her warm heart. Since his stroke, her father had been an absolute curmudgeon. When he realized his speech was affected, rather than work against the aphasia that scrambled his words, he nearly stopped talking all together. Still, he managed to convey cold dismissal with a turn of his head or a halting wave of his hand. In physical therapy, he let the therapists manipulate his muscles, but didn't push himself. Rosa never let it get to her. She showered tender care on him, drove him to the rehabilitation center three times a week and, every time, encouraged him to try, no matter how much he glared at her.

"What happened?"

"In de speech derapy, for de first time, he paid attention and den forced himself to answer yes and no instead of just moving his head. And in P.T., he pushed his leg against de derapist's hand!"

Little steps, but compared to his uncooperativeness in the last six months, these were major improvements. "That's great news, Rosa. Tell him . . ."

She stopped herself. What could she say that would make any difference to him?

The heck with it. Regardless of the condition of their relationship, she was still his daughter, and as she'd acknowledged the day before, she was darned tired of being disregarded. She'd encourage him in spite of himself.

"Victoria? You still dere, girl-child?"

"Yes, I'm here. Please tell Father I said . . . I'm glad and to keep up the good work."

She reached the front gate of Dolphin Land and spun the numbers on the combination lock. "Rosa, I'm at work, but I'll call again tomorrow and we'll talk more, okay?"

"We'll be home."

"Great. Bye for now."

"Oh, Victoria, wait. I forgot to tell you someding. Dat Kel man. He call here asking about de Doctor Sheffield and den wanting to know about you."

She jolted as if the fence were a live electric wire. "What? When?"

"Yesterday. I was at de store and de new lady dat helps wid cleaning de house answered de phone. She gave him your cell phone number, but I got de phone before she could say anyding else. So he don't know where you are or what you're doing."

Thank God! Victoria exhaled. Okay, that wasn't the worst case scenario. All he knew was that she wasn't at home. With the Massachusetts area code on her cell phone, he had no way to pinpoint her location. She could be anywhere from Alaska to the Texas coast.

The caregiver continued. "I told him de doctor not up for visitors. And after he hung up, I tell Joan not to speak to him again if I'm not here. So, you don't worry, okay?"

"Yes. Okay. Thanks, Rosa. Talk to you later."

What the hell did Kel want? She disconnected the call and walked through the gate, closing it behind her and shutting down her misgivings at the same time. Darned if she'd waste her valuable research time figuring out the mind and motives of Kel Griffin. Whatever he wanted, she wasn't interested. If he called, she'd handle it.

She had enough on her plate handling Jack, but with a plan of action in place, she felt stronger and more confident. After all, she'd gone the rest of the previous day without running into him again, which gave her more than twelve hours of practice with her aversion therapy.

Stopping by the office, she stowed her backpack under the desk. Stacking a clipboard with her equipment schematics and lagoon diagram on top of her coiled recording cables, she picked up the box and headed out.

Seemed pretty quiet around the facility, she realized as she called hello to the dolphins, laughing when they responded with shrieks and squeals from their blowholes. Ruby's pickup was over by her little conch house, but she didn't see any signs that the older woman was around. Jack, she'd been told, lived on that sleek sailboat out in the bay. So the fact that his truck was on the grounds, didn't mean he'd made it over yet either.

Terrific. She'd have time alone to hook up her audio receiver and perhaps begin her preliminary sound checks. There was still that problem of elevating and securing her video camera, she pondered while rounding the lagoon. Still, if Jack fulfilled his promise to build some braces, she'd be—

Holy wow, what was that?

Sometime between their clash yesterday and right now, he'd built a small platform on top of sturdy construction scaffolding. The pole that would hold her video camera was securely attached, and he'd even drilled a hole through the platform to run the cables.

She wrapped her hand around one of the scaffolding pipes and shook hard. It didn't budge. Placing the clipboard on the ground, she clambered up the structure and stood on the platform. The pole was a couple of feet taller than she, and with the height provided by the scaffolding, her camera would sit an ample twelve feet above ground—the perfect height for wide-angle surveillance.

"Like it, Victoria?"

Focused so completely on the surprise, she hadn't heard him approach. Looking down from the platform, she couldn't help but grin. "It's perfect, Jack. Thank you. How and when did you have time to accomplish this?" she asked as she climbed back down to stand on the ground next to him.

"Not that big a deal." He'd toted out the boxes with her recorder and video equipment and now placed them down carefully at the base of the structure. "A buddy of mine owns a construction company in town. He doesn't need the scaffolding right now and dropped it off for us to use until I can build something."

Walking around his creation, he tested one or two clamps and nodded, obviously satisfied with their strength.

She observed closely. It didn't look like his leg troubled him at all, so he must have rested it well. Still—

"You must have worked overtime putting it together."

"Nah. Steve helped, so we had it up in no time." Judging from the easy, relaxed tone, his attitude was as greatly improved as his leg.

"Well, it's terrific. I really appreciate it."

"My pleasure." He smiled at her. Not an angry show of teeth or an "oh yeah, baby" sexy grin, but an honest to goodness friendly smile.

Absence of malice or mischief didn't make the smile any less powerful.

Feel no pleasure. Uh-uh. She was not veering from her plan. Just because he demonstrated that he knew how to be civil didn't mean she had any less of an aversion to him. Absolutely not.

"Okay, well then. I'm anxious to set up some tests, so I'm going to finish connecting the recording equipment." Crouching down, she consulted her schematics and rummaged through the box of cables.

"Um, you know, I had another idea this morning, and I'd like to know what you think about it."

What? No "I think, therefore we'll do" directive? She tried not to look suspicious when she answered. "Sure. What's up?"

"Instead of hauling out all the components separately every day, I thought I'd build some sort of rolling container. So then all you have to do is plug in the wires and get started."

Very carefully, she kept her mouth from dropping open as she stood up. "That would be really helpful. If you're sure you have time."

"I can knock it out in an hour or two."

"Okay. That's a plan. Thanks again."

You're supposed to be like a cigarette, Jack, she thought to herself. Disgusting and bad for her health. Not smooth and sweet like her favorite, fine chocolate. She studied her clipboard, barely unwrinkling her brow while she pondered the huge change in his attitude. *Just give it time.* He'll revert to his unpleasant self any minute now.

"Hey, Victoria? One other thing."

"Yes?"

"I know we won't leave the equipment out here without permanent shelter, but I'm still a little concerned. As fast as a squall can blow in around here, you might not have time to disconnect everything and wheel the gear back to the office. Even contained, it could get wet in a hurry."

"You've got a point." Staring out at the open sea, she pondered a solution.

He beat her to it. "Ruby's got a pile of old boat tarps in the shed. With a little help and some sail stitching, I bet we can rig a rain cover for protection.

Good Lord, somebody'd woken up on the right side of the berth.

"Yes, Jack. You're right. That would be great."

Helpful solutions. No antagonism. Outrageous flirting replaced by friendly smiles.

It shouldn't have any affect on her, but except for the worst case scenarios—like Kel, for example—she'd always had great difficulty holding a grudge.

Could she be that easy? Where was her resolve?

It was all Jack's fault, darn it. How dare he show up here today and act nice?

Think cigarette. Foul, addictive substance.

"So, you want some help with these cables?"

"No!" Darn. Watch it, Victoria. She drew in a steady breath, forcing a smile. "No, thank you. You've done so much already this morning, but I appreciate you offering."

"You're sure?"

"Yes!" *Breathe.* Smile. Her lips felt like shrunken rubber, but she managed. "Again. Thank you."

"Okay then. I'll get started on those tarps and check back with you later." He ambled off, as annoyingly carefree as if he hadn't just thrown her for yet another loop.

Chapter Eight

He was in deep.

Not deep as in the level of water that came up to his waist and the mud sucking at his dive boots, while he picked seaweed out of the fence line on the outside of Lagoon Two. Deep as in the lust level that rose whenever he found himself around Victoria.

Jack scrubbed dried sea grass and tried to figure out where his plan first backfired. Like an agency debriefing for one, he reviewed the steps he'd taken since her arrival at Dolphin Land two weeks ago. He'd begun with a con job. A damn good one, filled with heavy come-ons and sly grins. That she first figured him intellectually inferior suited his purpose. *An opponent underestimating you always works in your favor.* His first agency instructor taught him that, and the knowledge had served him well.

If Victoria considered him over-sexed, under-smart beefcake, she wouldn't notice how carefully he oversaw her work, watching for the first sign of a screwup that could jeopardize the facility. He'd know in advance when it was time to step in and save their ship from sinking.

The developers who wanted Ruby's property weren't going anywhere. Waterfront lots you could build on in the Keys were as scarce as pregnant nuns. Rafe Escovar had called him again the other night to scope out the situation and dangle the bait of big profits. All Jack needed to do was keep his head in the game and his eyes on Victoria.

No hardship there. He quit pulling weeds and looked across the lagoon.

She was sitting in front of the contraption they'd built to house her audio receiver, carefully videotaping the dolphins swimming in the lagoon. Her lips were moving, and he knew she was identifying the dolphins as they swam past, marking the time according to her stopwatch. Later, she would synchronize her tape with the sounds recorded by the hydrophones they'd installed. It was the only way, she told him, to match each dolphin with specific sounds during the test session. From there, she'd progress to the next stage of her research.

Already she had Ruby and their part-time helper Jeanie doing preliminary training with a couple of the dolphins. First, they had to teach the experiment to some of the gang. Then, they'd test if some of the others learned by observation and imitation. Finally, they'd run trials to see if the ones who already knew the procedures actively taught or "told" the remainder of the gang.

Victoria was optimistic. "We're going to prove that *tursiops truncatas* communicate with each other, Jack," she'd explained in that kind, easy way she had, speaking slowly so he could keep up.

What if she proved her theories wrong, he'd asked? Damned if she didn't sound just as enthusiastic telling him she'd write those conclusions and publish anyway.

This whole scientific process was complicated, painstaking, and slow enough to make his skin itch, much the same way he felt when on a surveillance mission.

He was a man of action—and he wasn't getting any.

Not the kind he was used to when working for the government. Certainly not the kind he wanted when in close, near-constant proximity to a good-looking woman, which brought him back to his original dilemma.

Rising lust levels.

In the beginning, all he wanted to do was reinforce her conclusions about him, with some healthy male intimidation thrown in for good measure. He'd known she was smart, but he sensed some sort of insecurity behind the brain. She rallied quickly, he'd give her that, and her verbal sparring ability kept her in the game. Still, the uncertainty was present, although carefully concealed, and he'd exploit it if necessary.

Or so he thought at the time. Now he had to admit that even that plan, along with every other single plan, had failed. Oh, he knew where it all went wrong. He could pin it down to that first full day, installing the hydrophones, when she'd planted that kiss on him and walked away.

So much for him shaking up *her* balance. Somewhere, that idea corkscrewed, and the increasing desire to take a good long taste of that lush mouth had long since knocked logic out of his head. Add on the combination of Ruby's lecture and his own growing respect for Victoria, and he ended up with a drastically altered perception. Now, instead of considering her a possible threat and a pain-in-the-ass intrusion, she'd become a smart, hot woman he was dying to explore.

And he couldn't, because, when he'd changed his strategy, he'd marched himself right into the trap of terminal niceness. The guns of seduction had been effectively spiked by a long-legged woman who treated him like—say it ain't so—a buddy.

Now a whole separate set of rules entered the game. A buddy could joke around and throw out a spicy comment now and then. Just as long as he didn't sound serious, so they could both laugh. A buddy didn't invite a woman to dance the horizontal cha-cha. A buddy didn't stare at her when she wasn't looking, wondering if he had a chance to get her alone and kiss her until her head swam. Would she reciprocate or run?

The fit of his wetsuit tightened below his waist. A man could fantasize about that lithe body with those firm, round breasts pressed against his chest, while those legs wrapped around his hips. A buddy didn't walk around stiff as an axe-handle, with no promise of the situation changing anytime soon.

For a man, known to all his DEA colleagues as the one who never lost sight of his mission, he was fast losing his objectivity. Like an untied boat on an ebb tide, the decision to be helpful, cooperative in a hands-off kind of way, and not give Victoria a difficult time, was swiftly heading out to sea.

As things stood, the only one having a hard time around here was him.

Splat!

A glob of sea lettuce hit him on the cheek.

"What the hell?" He looked down through the fence and saw Rhett backing up to lob another clump. Melly's high-pitched giggle skittered through the air.

"Very funny, you two."

He grabbed a handful of green goop and tossed it back to the dolphins. One of the things that most surprised him when he came to live at Dolphin Land was that, very often, the dolphins themselves initiated contact. Ever since then, as a recently-orphaned kid, he'd gone out to the lagoons and had the dolphins divert him from whatever weighed heavily on his mind.

Granted, he wasn't, like Aunt Ruby, prone to attributing human characteristics to the gang, but some things were obvious.

They liked to play. They'd chase each other around the lagoons, rolling in fits of white water and leaping high, sometimes alone, sometimes as a powerful, matched group. Then there were times, when they went out of their way to engage his attention for goofy seaweed tosses or backrubs.

It was a pretty simple life really, for them and for his aunt. She didn't think he understood, but he knew that she loved her gang and the life she shared with them. It just wasn't the life for him.

It was too far a cry from the battles of deadly intent played out in the steaming jungles and airfields of South America, or the elegant mansions in Miami, Cartagena, and Mexico City, that were no less dangerous. Those days, even when he felt like he was balancing on a high wire over a snake pit, the importance of the battle kept him focused and driven. He'd give his life to keep more cocaine, heroin, and weed from hitting the streets of his country.

He almost had.

The scar tissue between his shoulder blades itched, a permanent reminder of a near-fatal knife wound. First, the perps had shattered his knee with a sledgehammer, trying to make him give up his informants' names. He'd choked out "Up yours" in pain-accented Spanish, so they'd stabbed him and left him with his blood pumping out on the crude airfield's runway. By some miracle, his backup arrived in time to save his life.

Now he told anyone who noticed the scar that a knee replacement had repaired damage from an old football injury. His leg, so far, had recovered well, although it hampered him in the rain. Even with the temporary setback that day on the causeway, he was at least back to ninety percent. The remaining ten percent kept him off active duty for the time being, and he damned sure wasn't ready to serve out his career behind a desk.

So, in the meantime, he rehabbed at Dolphin Land. By the time he had his aunt set for life, he'd be physically ready to return to the work that really mattered.

The job identified him as a man. The work made him feel alive.

Thwap!

More seaweed nailed him in the forehead. With his thoughts focused inward, he never saw it coming. The dolphin pair hovered on the other side of the fence. Physiology made them always look like they were smiling, but there was something about the expression in their eyes right now that looked ticked off. It was almost as if they were saying, "We aren't important enough for you? What's your problem?"

Yeah, right. There might have been studies done on the intuitive capabilities of dolphins, but to his knowledge, their gifts didn't include reading minds. Ruby claimed they knew what she was thinking as soon as she did, but she'd never been logical where her dolphins were concerned. These two couldn't possibly know how he felt.

Melly razzed him—the rude sound spewed mist from her blowhole.

Guilt twinged in his stomach. "C'mon. You know I care what happens to you."

Rhett sank beneath the surface, ignoring him. Melly did one better. She spun a quick 180 and slapped her tail, showering him with water before swimming away.

She'd told him! Yeah, right, Benton. Too much time in the sun for you, man, if you're projecting human emotion onto a dolphin.

For the next several minutes, he scrubbed twice as fast, finishing the fence line in near-record time. Dropping the brush into the floating basket, he waded toward shore. A glance across the lagoon showed that Victoria had rolled over to her stomach and was writing something in her ever-present notebook. From a distance, with her legs bent at the knees and swinging in the air, she looked like a teenager doing homework. But her body didn't belong on any kid. She was all woman for sure, and in all the right places.

He banished his dark mood with a grin and a bright idea. With the work he'd planned for the day completed, he might as well enjoy a break. At the moment, hanging out with his good *buddy* topped his list of ways to have fun.

✳ ✳ ✳

"Break time," he announced, stepping onto the boardwalk with two cans of soda.

"Thanks." In a smooth motion, she rolled and sat up, taking a can after he popped the top. Pressing her lips to the opening, she drank deeply.

Leaning back on one hand, she tilted her head and slid the cold metal against her sun-kissed throat. A tiny drop of condensation slipped down her skin like a liquid gem and disappeared in the V between her breasts.

He itched to follow its path with his tongue.

Have mercy! She looked like a pin-up poster girl. If he wasn't careful, he'd forget the last of his good intentions. If she wasn't careful, he'd have her flat on her back on the boardwalk.

"Is something wrong?"

The question brought his attention away from her chest. She'd obviously caught him staring, but instead of a knowing woman-smirk, she wore a puzzled look. Could she honestly not realize the effect she had on him?

He stood over her with a playful grin and couldn't resist teasing her. "Just checkin' to see that you're okay, Vic. You're looking mighty . . . hot."

She flushed. The instant color charming.

"I'm fine. Really. Thank you." Consternation filled her chocolate-brown eyes. She swung her legs around, dangling them over the boardwalk's edge while she stared across the water. Then, she drank some more soda.

Geezus! What a walking, talking contradiction. Usually, she took his suggestive comments and lobbed them back into his court. Other times, she didn't seem to have a clue. Most women would laugh them off or, if interested, respond with one of their own. Now, she seemed flustered. It was sort of cute, actually, endearing in a backward kind of way. He could only guess what kind of experiences she'd had in her life.

Judging from her smarts, she'd spent a lot of time studying in school and in the field. He figured much of the time she worked around men. You'd think that would be enough to teach her how they acted. Maybe that's where she'd learned to spar effectively. Then, there were odd moments when she looked lost.

Forget acting like her hands-off pal. He wanted to take her in his arms, wipe that lost expression off her face, and find out what put it there in the first place. When in the field, an agent had to be flexible. Sometimes a development you didn't anticipate cropped up, and plans had to change on a moment's notice.

Now was one of those times.

Asking her straight out what was bothering her wouldn't do him any good. The woman had walls, for sure, but he could be a patient man. Depending on the situation, he could break through, climb over, or with great precision, pick the lock that opened the door. With Victoria, he decided, finesse was definitely in order.

Casually, he took a seat on the boardwalk close enough so she'd feel his heat, but not so tight that he invaded her space. He let the silence and the rhythmic sound of the water hitting the dock ease the mood before he spoke.

"So tell me, Vic. What progress did you make today?"

Like someone flicked a switch, excitement filled her eyes and voice. "I finally identified Robin's and Marian's signature whistles! They were the most difficult because they're almost always together.

"Ruby's idea of gating them out to separate lagoons did the trick. Each kept repeating two particular whistles. It's almost like they were calling each other by name and also saying, 'Here I am.' The only problem was assigning the right signature to the right dolphin."

Damned if she wasn't cute with her face all lit up, even if the topic only interested her and maybe a couple dozen other scientists in the world. He was charmed in spite of himself, and suspicious warmth hovered in his chest. "So how did you decide whose was whose?"

"Oh this is good, Jack! We brought them back to the main lagoon separately, and I taped the greetings from the other dolphins. Sure enough, we heard one of the whistles from the gang when Marian returned and the other when they welcomed Robin! This is huge, you don't even know!"

"How come?"

"Well, even with loads of research done before, there are still many who doubt signature whistles even exist. Although this isn't the key part of my project, it's nearly indisputable evidence! I can't wait to—"

Beethoven's *Fifth* interrupted her in mid-sentence.

"Rats, that's my cell phone. Hang on." She scrambled to her feet and grabbed the phone from the backpack she'd brought out to the dock.

"Hello?"

The light in her eyes clicked off.

"Hold on just one minute," she snapped. Lips thin and face tight, she hurried off the boardwalk.

What's going on, he wondered, his instincts alert. Unfortunately, the wind carried her voice away, but he didn't need to hear her exact words to know she was upset. The stiff posture of her body and uneasy way she tugged on her ponytail communicated her tension.

Whoever had called was saying things Victoria didn't like. She stamped her foot and shook her head. Her voice got loud enough for him to make out a few words.

"No way! That will never happen." She slapped the phone shut to disconnect the call. Her shoulders rose and fell while she sucked in deep breaths, and he swore she trembled.

Now this was a new development. She'd been ticked off before, mostly at him, but always kept it together. This was the first time he'd seen her struggle.

She stormed back. Grabbing the pack, she stuck the phone into a side pocket, and then shoved in her notebook.

"My work is done for the day," she announced, while packing away her video camera. "Since you're here, you can help me roll the equipment box back under cover." Clearly, she intended to act like the phone call never happened.

The hell with her intentions. He wanted to know why she was upset. He stood and laid a hand on her arm, stopping her from disconnecting the audio wires.

"What's going on, Victoria?"

"Nothing. I'm fine."

"Well, ma'am, if you don't mind me saying, you look hot and bothered. And not in a good way."

"I said, I'm—"

"I know what you said, and I know what I saw. In this case I'll take my word for it. Who was on the phone?" Tilting her chin up so she'd have to meet his eyes, he asked, "Was it about your father? Is he okay?"

The spirit returned to her gaze, and she bit out her answers. "My father is fine. I'm fine. The caller wasn't anybody important. Certainly not worth discussing."

"Does it have to do with Dolphin Land?"

For a nanosecond she broke eye contact, but when she answered, her voice was almost steady. "No. Not at all." She tried to pull her arm from his grasp, but he squeezed it gently.

"Then why are you so upset?"

"I'm not upset."

He raised an eyebrow.

"All right, Jack. I am, was, a little upset, but it's a minor annoyance, nothing more."

"So who was it?"

"Not to be rude, but it isn't any of your business"

"If it affects Dolphin Land, it's my business."

"It doesn't. Trust me."

He might have if her gaze hadn't slid to the side again. One way or another, he'd find out the whole story. For the time being though, he let it go.

Releasing her hand, he took her backpack. "How about a swim?"

She looked around. "Sure. Off the causeway?"

"Nope. Right here in the lagoon. You, the gang, and me. What do you say?"

As he expected, the suggestion drove the clouds from her eyes. Her whole face lit up again with a brightness that lifted her from pretty to pure knockout.

"You're offering me a swim with the dolphins? Of course, I'll say yes."

"Cool. I'll stow the equipment. You slip into your suit."

"Stow the equipment? No way! We have to hook it up again. I need to record sounds made by the dolphins when humans enter their environment." So excited she practically danced off the boardwalk, she yelled over her shoulder at him as she hurried off to change. "There's a new writable CD in my backpack."

He waited until she was far enough away, then unsnapped the side pocket of her pack and retrieved her cell phone. Pressing a few buttons brought him to the history of incoming phone calls. The last one identified the caller as Kel Griffin with a 508 area code.

Friend? Colleague? His thoughts turned dark. Old boyfriend?

He snapped the phone closed and replaced it in the pocket. "It won't take me much time at all to find out who you are, Kel Griffin, and how you're connected to our Victoria." He smiled and made a bet to himself. Half an hour on the computer, tops. It might not be the fieldwork he craved, but it never hurt to keep his investigative skills sharp.

Chapter Nine

Victoria yanked her bathing suit up over her hips, shoved her arms through the straps and pushed her feet into water shoes. She ought to be more worried about Kel's phone call, but the only emotion that registered was a strong case of disgust. Obviously he thought he was still dealing with the same, naïve fool she'd been months ago. As if she'd buy his old-colleague-checking-in routine and not recognize it for a fishing expedition.

Funny how she'd never noticed his short fuse before. Then again, when they'd worked with her father, she'd bent over backward to be agreeable, helpful. They were a team, Kel had said. Partners in work and, as soon as their careers were more established, marriage partners as well. He'd promised.

Oh, but eventually he'd shown his true colors. Behind her back, he'd stolen their research data and the draft of their paper. She'd slaved over that document, with scant input from him. The day it had appeared in the *Journal of the Society of Cetacean Researchers* credited to Kel's name, she'd felt as sick as if she'd eaten a bucket of bad bait.

Now, six months later, he called pretending to be interested in what she was doing and to propose they rekindle their partnership?

Pinnipeds would fly first! Kel Griffin was about as welcome in her life as a red algae bloom. This was her project and nobody was going to mess it up. Nobody!

Consigning Kel to the backburner where he belonged, she snatched up a towel and a pair of swim goggles and dashed back to the lagoon. The opportunity to encounter the dolphins in their environment fascinated her professionally, while at the same time a most-unscientific delight bubbled up inside.

"I'm ready," she announced to Jack as if it weren't obvious from her return. "What do we do first? Is there a trained procedure for in-water interactions?"

"Whoa, sugar. You'd think a couple weeks in the Keys would've cured you of rushing around like a Yankee."

"I'm not rushing. I'm evidencing scientific zeal." She smiled. "Bubba."

He chuckled at her use of his aunt's nickname for him and gave her shoulder a friendly squeeze. "We'll have to talk more about that zeal of yours. Right now, we've got friends waiting in the lagoon." His gaze skimmed her body and he frowned. "You're wearing that into the water?"

"What's wrong with it?" She'd chosen the one-piece suit specifically for comfort and the fact that its racing-design completely covered her breasts. Even her father had approved the modest style for their work. Surely Jack couldn't consider it inappropriate.

"Nothing if you don't mind freezing. You monitor the water temperature three times a day. You didn't notice it's barely seventy degrees?"

The comment sparked a laugh. "You must be joking. This is practically bath water."

"Bath water, my ass. Put on a wetsuit."

"I don't need one. I'm from Massachusetts. This is almost as warm as it gets in Nantucket Sound." The skepticism on his face prompted another laugh, but she muffled it into a *tsking* sound and returned his studying expression.

Smooth, snug neoprene encased every inch of his big body, from ankles to shoulders and, holy wow, several interesting parts in between. "C'mon, are you telling me you have thin, wimpy, Florida blood?"

"Wimpy? There's nothing wimpy about me." He snorted, and then narrowed his tropical blue eyes. "That wouldn't be a challenge, would it, sugar?"

She'd meant it as a joke, but his slow, confident smile triggered a spurt of recklessness. "Maybe it is, tough guy." *Now what?* hung unspoken in the air.

The grin spread wider, and he reached behind him, grasped the zipper at his neck and pulled it down. With the back of the suit open, he maneuvered his broad shoulders out of the form-fitting material. Never taking his eyes off hers, he slowly pulled the sleeves down his arms, uncovering deeply tanned skin inch by mesmerizing inch. A striptease couldn't have been more fascinating. First, he revealed a wide chest accented by crisp, dark hair. Taut abs, defined from God knew how many sit-ups, a lean waist and . . .

Her mouth dried up like a puddle in the Sahara. She grabbed his hand. "Jack, wait!"

"Problem, sugar?"

She ordered herself not to blush. "No, at least I hope not. I mean, you do have something on underneath there, don't you?"

"What's the matter? Your wimpy, Yankee blood make you scared to find out?"

He snickered, damn him, and with the challenge reversed, she knew she couldn't back down. She shoved the suit past his hips and forced herself to look.

She barely stifled a sigh of relief at the sight of black swim trunks covering whatever remained in her imagination.

He exploded into broad laughter. "You asked for that, Victoria."

Suddenly, the situation struck her just as funny, and she laughed too. "You're right, I did. But I'm calling it a draw. Now, what about our swim?"

"Yes, ma'am. And in answer to your earlier question, we did use a training procedure for structured swims back when we had tourists. When it's just us, we take a more relaxed approach."

"So, what do we do first?"

He undid the zippers at his ankles and pulled the wetsuit off the rest of the way. "Since it's your first time, we'll take it slow. Go off the side of the dock nice and easy and hold on for a minute. The dolphins will come over if they're interested."

Victoria slipped into the lagoon, her body adjusting quickly to the cooler temperature. As long as she grasped the dock with one hand, she didn't need to tread water. The Gulf's salinity kept her buoyant. Small fish, some sort of snapper, darted around her legs, diving underneath the dock when Jack slid behind her into the lagoon.

She turned and faced him. "What should I do if one of the dolphins approaches?"

"Let 'em look, if they want. Put your hand out in front like I showed you and offer a backrub. But, and this is serious, if one of them turns on its side or back, don't rub."

"Why not? Oh. Of course." Realization dawned. Dolphins were highly tactile and very sensual. Comprehension must have shown on her face, because Jack nodded.

"You got it. We don't want to start something with one of them that we're not prepared to finish. They've been taught what's appropriate and what isn't. So, if one of them acts up, bring your hand back smoothly. They'll get the message."

"Anything else I should watch? Do you have any observations on standard responses by dolphins to people in the water? I wonder if they exhibit different behavior for strangers than for people they know. Jack! Did you switch on the hydrophones and recorder?"

"Woman, don't you ever slow down?"

His smile chided her gently, and she was pretty sure she caught a hint of fondness in his expression, so she knew he wasn't criticizing.

"Yes, the recorder's on. No, there's nothing specific you should watch for." Big hands gently squeezed her shoulders as he turned her in the water. He leaned in close, his breath warming her ear when he whispered, "For once, shut off the research part of your brain and enjoy the experience. Look, here they come."

As if on cue, Robin approached, hovering in front and gazing at her with his dark, unblinking eye. Slowly, she offered her hand, palm down on the surface of the water. The big male blew a soft breath through his blowhole, almost like a greeting, before swimming beneath her palm. It was impossible to tell who enjoyed that first contact more.

"That's a girl," Jack said. "Now, come with me."

He took her hand and swam away from the dock toward the center of the lagoon. Robin followed, joined by two of the other pod-members so that all of them swam together. Victoria slid the goggles over her eyes and ducked her head below the surface. The rhythmic up-and-down tail motions under water combined incredible power with incomparable grace in their streamlined bodies.

Scarlett swam alongside, returning her study, although if the animal could think in descriptive terms, Victoria knew she wouldn't consider her human companion either graceful or powerful.

"Victoria, check this out."

Jack waved as two dolphins propelled him through the water with their rostrums pressing against his feet.

"I want to try!"

"Okay, float on your back."

Perhaps the positioning served as a signal. Within seconds, Ashley and Marian came up to her feet. Their rostrums, hard as baseball bats and strong enough to ram a shark, pushed gently on her feet. She brought her arms to her sides, streamlining her body for a smooth trip across the lagoon. At Jack's direction, she lowered her feet before reaching the far fence, and the dolphins stopped. To thank them, she offered backrubs by resting her hands on the water's surface. Instead, one of the animals popped up vertically and bumped her pectoral flippers against Victoria's hands.

"That's a dolphin-style handshake. Just rub the flippers until she backs away."

Thoroughly charmed, she stroked the fins, talking nonsense to the animal until the dolphin dropped below the water's surface.

On an impulse, she took a deep breath and sank down, too, looking around. The dolphin's gaze met hers, and for a long, incredible moment, they simply studied each other.

What is she thinking? Is she inquisitive? Wary? Do they feel real affection for people, or do we merely project that emotion?

Every curious part of her wished she could discover actual answers, but for now the mysteries stayed locked in the cetacean's dark, placid eyes.

When she ran out of air, she resurfaced. "Now what?

"Swim slowly on your stomach."

She complied, and before she'd gone more than a few feet, two dolphins returned, one on either side. She stopped and they appeared to wait.

"Jack?"

"Hold on to the front of their dorsal fins with your thumbs down."

No sooner had she done so, than the dolphins took off across the lagoon, pulling her between them. Water sluiced over their bodies, and their powerful tails pumped, powering them forward. Victoria hung on tightly, grinning ear-to-ear.

"Go!" she yelled, and the dolphins hit turbo speed. Excitement rushed through her and she cheered, an exhilarated sound that echoed across the lagoon. When they neared the dock the dolphins dived in tandem, ending the ride. Sheer momentum propelled her forward.

Jack caught her around the waist before she plowed into the dock.

"That was wonderful!" Breathless with laughter, she tossed her wet hair back from her face. "What a thrill. I've never experienced anything like that." She grabbed his shoulders, popped up, and planted a kiss on his cheek. "Thank you so much."

His grinning expression changed, his eyes glittered, strangely beautiful in his sun-bronzed face. His voice sounded deeper than normal.

"My pleasure."

The look he gave her stole what remained of her breath. No smiling, good old boy camaraderie now, unh uh. This look was steady, incredibly focused.

Oh my God! Victoria pushed against his shoulders, but he tightened his hold and she realized their bodies were plastered against each other. Suddenly, she wished he had worn his wetsuit after all. Then, instead of the thin material of her swimsuit, there'd be inch-thick neoprene between her breasts and his broad, naked chest.

She swallowed hard. "I, um, better go. The recorder . . ." Her voice came out shaky. She pushed again, but he didn't release his hold.

"The recorder's fine." He shoved them away from the dock, treading water to keep them both afloat.

"Jack, I—"

"Hush, sugar," he said, the command a soft, husky whisper. With his free hand he swept the hair back from her face, tangling his fingers in the strands. He studied her without saying a word, looking deeply into her eyes, then at her brow, her chin, and finally lingered on her lips.

There wasn't anything scientific in his leisurely observation, not when the intense gaze felt like the stroke of a hand against her skin. Or when heat began to glow, turning his eyes the same blue as the base of a flame.

She should break away, demand her release, but, Lord help her, she was just as fascinated. So, she let him hold her suspended in the water like a seahorse while he seduced her with no more than the banked power of his steady regard.

You shouldn't allow this, she told herself. *Can't allow it.* She was a researcher, a scientist—

A woman. One whose insides were melting while her pulse kicked into double time.

Desperate, she broke eye contact and squirmed, only to feel his grip tighten. He cupped the back of her head, lifting it so she was forced to meet his gaze.

"You should see yourself, Victoria. Big dark eyes open wide. Bottom lip trembling. I make you nervous."

"I'm not nervous!"

"Sure you are, and that's fine. You're so smart, you could intimidate the hell out of most men. Not me, of course, but I'll take any advantage I can get." He smiled, converting the fairly obnoxious statement into gentle teasing. "If it makes you feel better, consider this—interaction—a scientific experiment."

"You can't be serious." Oh yeah, that pitiful, weak retort did a lot of credit to her advanced degrees. Too bad her graduate studies never covered the phenomenon of seductive eyes. Her experience in this field was woefully inadequate.

"On the contrary, I'm absolutely serious." He traced the contours of her ear with his thumb. "I'm conducting research, learning all about your responses to certain stimuli."

"But, Jack, I—"

He smothered her protest with his mouth, gently pressing against hers until she parted her her lips. When she did, he deepened the kiss, taking full possession, and she felt the rest of her common sense slip away. Who could think about science when firm, warm lips moved over hers and his bold tongue slid inside, caressing, teasing, and stealing the air from her lungs? She started to sink and grasped his shoulders to keep from going under.

His big hands slid down her hips to the backs of her thighs, lifting so that her legs came up around his waist.

"Breathe in, Victoria," he ordered.

When she did, he fit his mouth to hers and took her deeper. Literally. They dropped beneath the surface, locked together in the kiss. Figuratively. Body to body, mouth sealed to mouth, eyes closed and sound cushioned by the water. In the sudden absence of vision and hearing, pure physical sensation took over. Strong arms holding her tightly and the latent power of his big body between her legs. The suede texture of his lips and salty taste of him on her tongue. As her senses melded, passion came to life, stunning her like a jolt from a nine-foot electric eel.

She stiffened and shoved against his chest, her lungs desperate for air. With one powerful kick, he sent them upward. Victoria broke the surface and gasped, sucking in a great gulp of fresh air.

"C'mon." He came up beside her and grabbed her hand, pulling her toward the dock. One boost and she was kneeling on the fiberglass surface, still breathless from the kiss. He levered his body out of the water and reached for her.

She blocked him with a hand to his chest. "No, wait!"

"For what, sugar?"

For her common sense to return from outer orbit. What in God's name had she been thinking?

"For heaven's sake, Jack, we cannot do this."

The shriek on the end of her sentence should have shattered his eardrums. Instead, he looked around and shrugged.

"Not that the dolphins would mind us getting naked, but we don't need to give passing boaters an eyeful. So, lady's choice. Your place or my boat?"

His smile could have incinerated steel. She felt herself melting again, then the memory of Kel, the last man she'd let herself get involved with on a research project, chilled her hormones down out of the red zone. "My choice is neither. We can't do this at all."

"Darlin', last time I checked, all our working parts were in order."

"This isn't a question of whose parts are working."

"You're not going to lay that fraternization stuff on me again, are you? I'm pretty damned sure it only applies to the military and not to two healthy, unattached people knowing they want each other and doing something about it."

He slid closer and she scuttled backward like a crab.

"That's my point. I don't. Want it!"

The arch of his eyebrow was as sexy as his smile. "Yeah, right."

She'd run out of dock and had nowhere to go when he planted his hands on either side of her body and loomed over her, scanning her with a look that should have left scorch marks. She didn't know it was possible for her entire body to blush, but she felt the heat from her soles to her scalp.

If he made love half as good as he kissed . . . *Don't go there.* She stifled the thought. Soul-searing kisses and promises of passion weren't enough. Giving in to desire had made a fool of her before.

She must have been silent too long, because Jack smiled and leaned in, obviously ready to kiss her again. Before she could weaken, she brought her hand up and reinforced it with her knee—not hard enough to do any damage, but enough to act as a barrier.

"I said no. I meant it."

The knee must have given him the message because he sat back. "You're serious! Victoria, what's the matter with you?"

She had just enough space to roll out from under him and jump up onto the boardwalk. "There's nothing the matter with me. I told you before that the only thing I'm interested in at Dolphin Land is my research. Don't blame me if you got the wrong idea."

He rose to his feet, but, thank goodness, remained on the dock, hands on his hips and "you've gotta be kidding me" written all over his face. "The wrong idea? Wasn't that you sucking on to me like a remora?"

"You kissed me first!"

"You kissed me back. And we'd still be kissing if you'd get over this hang-up about your precious project."

"Okay, I'll admit it. I enjoyed the kiss, but I still won't risk my dream for . . . a roll in the lagoon. No thank you. I make it a point never to repeat a mistake."

He started to say something else, but she talked over him.

"I'm sure I'm not the only woman in the Keys who'd be willing, thrilled to . . . oblige. But I am off limits. Totally. Keep your distance."

"You're forgetting something, Vic." His voice turned dangerously soft. "Without my help, how will you do your research?"

Oh God, he's right! The apparatus and blind they'd rigged for the next phase required the extra boost of his muscle to maneuver. She needed him and had just told him to stay away. The realization hit her like a blast of frigid air, and she shivered.

He swore under his breath and tossed her a towel. "Wrap yourself up before you freeze."

Stricken, she could only stand there letting it dangle from her hands. If he walked out on the project, her dream would sink like the Titanic. She was beaten and knew it. Whatever the cost to her pride, she had to keep him involved.

"Jack, I'm sorry. I . . . I shouldn't have said what I did. You're right, I can't do without your help and . . . and, if you agree to stay on, I'll—"

The scowl on his face stopped her cold.

Leaping onto the boardwalk, he grabbed the towel and pulled it around her. "Woman, don't you dare act like I'm blackmailing you into sleeping with me. Trust me, I'm a long way from being that hard up."

"I didn't mean that!"

He had the look of a man holding onto his temper by the skinniest of fraying threads.

"At this point, I don't care what you meant. Get out of here and into some dry clothes. Now." Two not-so-gentle hands spun her in the opposite direction.

She took a couple of steps, and then turned back, needing to know that her work hadn't all gone down the tubes. "Jack, about tomorrow?"

"I'll be here, damn it. Now get your butt moving."

As a commitment, it wasn't much, but she ran off before he could change his mind.

Chapter Ten

He watched her scurry back to the office. She didn't bother changing, just grabbed her gear and hightailed it off the property, heading in the direction of Pirate's Cove.

What the hell had she been thinking, looking at him like he was a mugger about to take her on the dock? Jack Benton had never forced a woman in his life. Of course, he'd never lacked willing partners. He sure as hell didn't need some stick-up-her-butt brainiac so badly that he'd attack her, even if she did have legs up to her neck.

Oh hell. He knew better than to troll in home waters, so what was he thinking grabbing Victoria when they were swimming? News flash, Benton, you weren't thinking. That's the whole problem. *Better face it, Bubba. The woman's gotten under your skin.*

At the moment, the idea was as welcome as sea lice.

When she'd first torpedoed back to the dock with her eyes glowing, laughing like crazy, his common sense shut down. On autopilot, he'd caught her and then pulled her close. When he had her in his arms, he could only stare, fascinated by her big dark eyes, the honey-smooth texture of her skin, the delicate molding of her cheeks, and those ripe lips.

There wasn't a fully functional man alive who could have kept from kissing her at that point. How could he anticipate that she would ignite in his arms? They'd zoomed from zero to hot so fast, the lagoon should've been steaming. Could she blame him for thinking she was more than willing to go farther?

If they'd been anywhere the least bit secluded, he'd have had her naked. He knew it, and he'd bet his last buck, she knew it too. So what had happened? She'd put on the brakes fast enough to leave skid marks. Sure, he'd been ticked off, but that was no reason for her to act like the situation was completely his fault and he should be banished like a criminal.

Then she got that kicked-puppy look when he'd reminded her that she needed him on her project. Inferring that he'd, geezus, extort sex from her—well, that capped it. But the crushed expression got to him, even though he was damned sure he hadn't done anything wrong.

No, kissing her had not been wrong but, instead, too damned right. Given the chance, he'd do it again, as often as possible. But he wouldn't force her cooperation by making her think he'd let her twist in the wind. They'd worked side-by-side for chrissakes. Knowing he needed this for his aunt's welfare should have been enough for her to realize he wouldn't screw up her project.

Damn, but the woman was serious about her work. He had to admire that trait, even though her refusal to mix business with pleasure had left him with a woody that rivaled a two-by-four. What the hell was wrong with the woman that she couldn't put it aside for a little while and enjoy some healthy fun?

Something jigged at his brain. While shivering on the boardwalk, she'd spouted something else at him. That she wouldn't make, no, wouldn't *repeat* a mistake. He blew out a breath, while that bounced around in his brain. Had she thrown away a project once before over a man? Somehow that didn't seem like her style but, then again, she'd surprised him on a regular basis since the day they'd met.

Grabbing his wetsuit and towel, he strode away from the lagoon. After a quick shower, a cold beer, and a snack, in that order, he'd fire up the computer. As long as he was investigating Vic's caller, he'd see what else he could discover on the Internet.

* * *

He'd barely cracked open the second bottle of brew when he found the information he wanted. A quick search on the name Kel Griffin took him to the *Journal of the Society of Cetacean Researchers*. Griffin's credits appeared on a paper pompously titled, *Studies in Familial Recognition among Migrating Tursiops Truncatas Groupings in the Northern Atlantic*. According to the article, Griffin conducted his study over a two-year period. This issue of the journal was about six months old.

"So, what's old Kel been doing since?" Jack sipped his beer while scanning more web pages. This article proved the most recent, so he went back further. Griffin showed up in a story about a talk he gave to his alma mater and in a few alumni newsletters, but no other articles or professional papers. Then a match linked the man to an old issue of a small Massachusetts paper called *The Nantucket Courier*.

Sheffield's Daughter to Wed Colleague read the headline.

"Well, I'll be damned." He put down the bottle and scrolled through the article.

Dr. Victoria Sheffield, Nantucket, has announced her engagement to Mr. Kelvin Griffin, Seattle, Washington. The bride-to-be is the daughter of Dr. Victor Sheffield and his late wife, Gloria. She is a summa cum laude graduate of Boston University, where she majored in biology and behavioral psychology. She later earned both her master's and doctorate degrees.

Leave it to Victoria to define herself in terms of her education. To hold a brain so big, her pretty little skull ought to be the size of a hot-air balloon.

She is employed as a field assistant by The Sheffield Institute, which was founded by her father, a world-renowned, marine research scientist.

Field assistant, huh? Pretty modest title for the boss's daughter. Guess her old man made her work her way up the ladder.

Mr. Griffin graduated with a B.S. in biology from Washington State University, earned a master's degree in marine sciences, and is also a field assistant with the Sheffield Institute. A wedding date has not been announced.

Well, wasn't this cozy as hell? Talk about keeping it all in the family. From the tone of the phone call earlier in the afternoon, she hadn't enjoyed hearing from lover boy. So, what was Victoria doing down here all alone? Why hadn't she mentioned a fiancé? Granted, he'd pretty much limited their conversation to dueling innuendoes, but surely she obviously hadn't talked about it to Ruby either. His darling Aunt Motor Mouth certainly would have passed on the information.

Jack logged offline, tilted back in his chair, and reviewed the facts. Victoria had a fiancé. He frowned as he pondered this revelation. Said fiancé was heretofore unmentioned, unseen, and based on her reaction to his call, unwelcome.

Why didn't she want the man around? More importantly, if she were engaged to someone back home, what was she doing plastered to Jack's body, kissing him for all she was worth?

He rose from the chair, pitched the empty bottle into the recycling bin and grabbed his keys from the hook by the door. He could wait until tomorrow, but he considered himself a man of action. Especially when it came to getting answers.

* * *

The loud knocking exacerbated her stress headache. Victoria choked down a bite of sandwich and went to answer the door. Her neighbors in the RV resort were all so friendly, always inviting her to join a cookout or bringing over some extra fish they'd caught earlier in the day. Tonight, however, the last thing she wanted was company or food. She wouldn't even have slapped together peanut butter and jelly, except she knew hunger would worsen the headache.

Her neighbors didn't deserve the brunt of her bad mood, so she arranged a careful smile on her face and opened the door.

"Hey, sugar, long time no see."

"What are you doing here?

"I missed you. Did you miss me?"

His cockiness grated tender nerves. "No. Goodnight." She tried to shut the door, but he blocked the move with one hand. Shoving against his superior strength would be stupid and childish, so instead she crossed her arms over her chest and glared.

"What do you want that couldn't wait until tomorrow?" Before the sentence was out of her mouth, she wished it back. The last thing she needed to do was hand him an opening line. Before he could answer, she pointed a finger at him in warning. "Don't even go there."

"Relax, Victoria. I didn't figure you were going to rip off my clothes and jump me, but we gotta talk."

Her temples throbbed as if tiny demons tap-danced on them with spiked shoes. All she wanted was a fistful of aspirin and him gone. "There's nothing to talk about. Things got a little, well, out of hand this afternoon. I take full responsibility for my part, but that doesn't change anything. You and I need to maintain a professional working relationship."

A lifted brow signaled he wasn't buying a thing she said. Well, she didn't care if he liked it as long as he at least accepted her logic.

"So, anyway, I apologize," she continued. "I'm sorry if I gave you the wrong idea."

"Bet your fiancé, Kel, would have gotten the wrong idea if he'd seen us in the lagoon."

The PB and J suddenly hardened to iron in her stomach. She'd never thought it possible for the blood to drain from one's face until she felt it actually happen. "Kel?" she croaked. "How do you know about Kel?"

The good old boy grin disappeared and his blue-green eyes turned arctic. "You'd be surprised what I can find out." He brushed past her into the room.

Possibilities spun in her brain like a juiced-up hamster. Then the answer hit. "My cell phone. You went through my backpack! How dare you?"

A big shoulder shrugged with his answer. "When it comes to Dolphin Land, I'll dare anything."

"This has nothing to do with the facility. It's personal business. And how did you know he was my fiancé?"

"You're not the only one with Internet skills."

"You did a web search?" Her shrillness pierced her aching brain like a sliver of glass. This was her worst nightmare come true. God only knew what else he'd uncovered.

Calm down, Victoria. Finding random bits of information didn't mean he'd connected the dots. She took in a deep breath and released it slowly. The only way out was to brazen through.

"Okay, you know Kel and I were engaged. So what? That's past history. Our relationship ended months ago."

He leaned against the dresser. "You were major league upset this afternoon when he called. Bad breakup?"

"How is this any of your business?"

"That answers that question, but I'm puzzled. You don't kiss like a woman who still pines over a man."

"He didn't dump me! I broke off the relationship."

"So he called because he wants you back?"

"Yes, that's it in a nutshell. Absolutely. He wants me back, but since I'm not interested, the topic's closed. Over. Done."

She yanked open the door and made an ushering-out gesture with her hand. "If you don't mind, I have a headache. You got your answer, so I'll see you at work tomorrow."

"Shut the door before the gnats fly in. You're lying, Victoria, or at least only telling part of the truth. I got all night, so you might as well spill the rest."

"Do you realize you're a monumental pain?"

"I've been called worse. Quit stalling."

Hoping she looked casual, she pushed the door closed, then, with an exaggerated sigh, strolled over to the desk and perched on the edge. "I don't know what else you expect."

"I don't either, but you tried too hard to convince me that the only reason Kel-boy called was to make another play. That alone wouldn't have upset you so much this afternoon. There's more to the story."

Don't sweat. Keep your cool. He's only fishing. Purposely, she kept her face bland.

A shake of his head chided her silence. "Okay, let's see what I've learned so far. The two of you worked together for your father's institute. According to stuff I read, Griffin was involved in a project up north about the same time you and he got engaged. Was this separate from his work with the institute?"

Oh God, how should she answer?

"Yes. Kel had his own project planned, apart from the team's work." No lie there.

"I couldn't help noticing that he lags behind you in academic accomplishments. I'd think that could make it rougher on him in your field. Although, I guess it didn't hurt to be involved with the top guy's daughter."

She flinched before she could stop herself.

"Struck a nerve, huh?"

Only stubborn pride allowed her to shrug as if it were no big deal. "No woman enjoys being a stepping stone for someone else's career."

"I don't imagine you would. Bet it made you good and mad."

Mad, mortified. She had a running list of the negative emotions stimulated by memories of Kel. Even now, all she had to do was think about how easily she'd believed his declarations of love to feel the hot sting of humiliation.

Caught up for a moment in her feelings, she didn't realize Jack had left his spot across the room and approached.

"Aww, sugar, it still hurts, doesn't it? I'm sorry, but if you come clean, I won't have to keep pressing."

"You didn't have to start in the first place." His gall was incredible. She seethed with growing resentment.

"Yeah, I did, and something else keeps niggling at me. You said you'd never repeat the same mistake. Is that what happened? Did you mess up a study because of Griffin?"

"The only mistake I made was falling in love with him in the first place."

"So what broke you up? Did he cheat on you? Undermine you? Make you look bad in front of your father?"

The headache demons quit dancing and picked up mallets. Suddenly her aching brain reached its limit. "He did worse than mess up my research, he took—" She clapped her mouth shut, wishing she'd swallowed her tongue.

Of course Jack jumped on the sentence like a snapper on shrimp. "Took what? Tell me."

Furious, her eyes shot darts at him.

He kept coming. "He took . . . advantage of you? Took your virginity?

Flaming hot darts, dipped in tar.

"What would upset you more than anything?"

Suddenly, he stopped the barrage of questions, and an odd light grew in his eyes.

"Son-of-a-bitch. That project of his wasn't so separate, was it, Victoria? I'll be damned. The bastard stole your research. That paper I read wasn't his work, it was yours."

The look he gave her made her feel like a culture growing in a petri dish. She opened her mouth to tell him in scathing terms that he was so wrong, but to her horror she couldn't speak the lie. She focused on his shirt buttons, unwilling to see her own stupidity reflected in his eyes.

"Fine. You guessed correctly. You win the prize. Now please get the hell out of my room and leave me alone." She shoved against his chest, pushing him back far enough to escape the desk and walk away.

So much for maintaining her authority. Now that he knew how thoroughly she'd been made a fool of, she'd lost whatever edge she'd hoped to keep. Any second now, he'd make some sort of belittling comment, give her his superior laugh, or . . .

Strong fingers gently massaged her temples. Pure surprise kept her from jerking away.

"Even smart women sometimes get conned," he said, his voice low and soothing.

"Now that's a whopping load of comfort."

"Would you rather I said that, with all your brains, you should have known better?"

She broke away, but he reeled her back in, continuing his tender ministration. "You're ticking me off, Jack," she said, but the words lacked bite.

"I'd rather you get pissed off than look like a spanked puppy."

"I do not look like a spanked anything!"

"Shhh. Yelling will only make your head hurt worse."

Strong fingers massaging her skull felt incredibly good. Like magic, the throbbing pain eased. She stifled a groan of pure pleasure, and this time he did laugh, but there was nothing snide in the sound.

"Feeling better?"

"Much. Thanks."

"See how much healthier it is when you don't keep things pent up inside? You could have told me sooner, without making me force it out of you."

She couldn't let that pass, although she was too tired to put much *oomph* in her argument. "It still wasn't any of your business. What happened in the past doesn't affect the work I'm doing at Dolphin Land."

He turned her by the shoulders, bringing them face-to-face. "But Griffin wanted something from you, more than getting back together, didn't he? Come on, sweetheart, you've told me the big part, you may as well finish the story."

What's the use? If she didn't, he'd badger it out of her eventually. Sighing, she admitted the truth. "To be a good research scientist, you need more than the ability to observe and collect data. It takes, well, in the most basic terms, real curiosity and the drive and dedication to spend years finding your answers. Kel wants the results without making the effort. He'd rather cut corners. My guess is that he hasn't found someone else to latch on to and figured he'd see what I had going."

"So he thought he'd call, and you'd welcome him back?"

At her nod, Jack snorted.

"Well that proves he's two times the jackass."

"You think so?"

"Sure. The only reason he tricked you before was because you were in love with him. You're the smartest woman I've ever met. Only a fool would believe he'd be able to pull the same stunt again."

"Well, thanks for that."

"Is he gonna keep bugging you? Do we have a potential nuisance on our hands?"

"Kel is my problem. I'll deal with him."

"If he shows up at Dolphin Land, he's my problem and trust me, I'll kick his sorry ass all the way to the Overseas Highway."

Victoria laughed. "Nice visual, but he doesn't know where I am. I'll call home and make sure nobody tells him, if he asks. Honestly, I think he got the message this afternoon. He's arrogant, but he would have to be completely obtuse to think he has a chance. Although, when you peel away the surface smugness, you find he isn't as smart as he believes."

"I'll second that, sugar. Because . . ."

Jack slid a hand up to cup her cheek.

". . . only a complete idiot would double-cross a woman like you."

More tenderness showed in his eyes than she believed him capable. She could float away in that brilliant gaze.

His voice dropped to a husky drawl. "Don't look at me like that."

"Like what?"

"Like you wouldn't mind if I kissed you."

Maybe she didn't. She was so tired, so overwhelmed by the ups and downs of the day, that she could no longer separate what was wise and what wasn't. Maybe, in fact, she wanted to feel his arms around her and lose herself in his warmth.

"I—" She reached for him, but he stepped back.

"Victoria, I'm not going to kiss you. Not that I don't want to, but if I do, I'll be taking advantage. I can't believe I'm hearing myself say this, but you're on overload, so I'm going to do the right thing." He backed away, opened the door, and stepped out into the night.

"Remember this after I'm gone. I left for your sake tonight, but I won't promise to do the same next time."

With one more look, rich with frustration and promise, he shut the door, leaving her alone with a half-eaten sandwich and a swirling, tidal pool of emotion.

As if slogging through wet sand, she walked to the door and turned the deadbolt lock. The engine of his truck roared to life on the other side of the door. She rested her forehead against the painted wood. "Help," she whispered. Handling Jack when he acted bossy or hormone-driven was difficult enough. Dealing with his caring, borderline sweet, side was a lot more dangerous. Somehow, she had to do it all again tomorrow.

Chapter Eleven

Soaking rain hit the Keys the following day. Chilly winds blew in great gusts from the Gulf, and Victoria struggled to keep the tarps from blowing off the electronic equipment. At high tide, with waves cresting over the docks and boardwalks, setting up the apparatus was impossible. Even the dolphins seemed affected, diving deep down in the lagoons, surfacing only to breathe.

There was no sense trying to proceed when neither the weather nor the test subjects cooperated. She gave up. Hanging her foul weather gear on a hook, she decided to spend the day analyzing data and steering clear of Jack as much as possible.

Being around him this morning proved unsettling. All it took was a greeting in his deep, rich voice for her stomach to flutter like wildflowers in the breeze. When he cupped the back of her neck and pressed his mouth to hers, she'd nearly jumped out of her skin. Before he left to build a new thawing rack for the fish house, he slid her a heated look that curled her toes.

He certainly seemed to think their relationship had set sail on a new course.

So did Ruby, who'd watched them the whole time with an

exceedingly pleased smile plastered on her face.

"Well, now, if this isn't a fine day at Dolphin Land," she proclaimed after her nephew left the office.

"Ruby, last time I checked it was blowing gale force winds and pouring down rain." Victoria sipped from a mug of steaming tea, her eyes scanning the sheaf of reports in her hand.

Ruby chortled. "Girl, you don't have to act discreet in front of me. Jack sure isn't."

"Nothing happened."

The older woman *tsk tsked*.

"Okay, all right. Something happened, but it was just a kiss!" A kiss hot enough to turn coral rock into lava.

A smile bright as sunrise beamed across Ruby's face. "I knew it! Just as soon as I saw the two of you this morning, I could tell."

Victoria ducked her head, her cheeks burning.

"Oh now, darlin', don't be embarrassed. I may be getting up in years, but I sure haven't forgotten what it's like to be hot for someone. Hell, old Willie and I don't spend all our time playing pinochle in his double-wide."

The mental image of the two dear sprites getting intimate was definitely not on her need-to-know list. Desperately, she wondered how to stop this conversation.

"Let's not get ahead of ourselves. I mean, Jack and I have to work together, and we need to keep things professional."

"Hell, it's not like he's gonna roll you around naked on the causeway. Besides the fact that pea rock digs into your butt, me and my Gus taught that boy the right way to treat a lady."

"But—"

"Now, it's easy to get the wrong idea 'bout my boy, especially when he's into that rough-around-the-edges look, but he's a gentleman all the way. Which isn't to say he doesn't know how to show you a good time, if you know what I mean."

Victoria was painfully sure she knew exactly what Ruby implied. She couldn't begin to imagine ever having so outrageous a conversation about human sexual attraction with her father. In fact, when she reached puberty, Victor commandeered the "birds and bees" discussion from her mother. He took a rigidly scientific approach, complete with diagrams and flip charts.

The embarrassment she faced at age twelve, didn't come close to the churning in her stomach now. Her face must surely be as flaming a red as the setting sun. She nodded weakly to acknowledge the comments and hoped the woman ran out of steam.

"Well, I'll leave you to your work, darlin'. I gotta find Willie down at the marina and tell him the news so I can collect on our bet."

"Bet? You wagered on us?"

"Sure did! When you first got here, I know you thought Jack wouldn't take to you, but he was all bent out of shape that I'd sealed our deal without consulting him. Men purely hate being out of the loop, you know? He's a suspicious sort anyway because of what he used to do, and he'd been hanging around here brooding for too long. But I knew from the first that you'd be good for him, and I was right.

"Lordy, this makes me a happy woman. My favorite researcher and my favorite nephew getting together." She grabbed her rain slicker off a hook and donned it. "Time to go get my ten spot! See you later."

She scooted out the door, but her energy lingered in the room. Victoria slumped in the chair, shaking her head in disbelief and smiling at the same time. Ruby might be outrageous and outspoken, but she was also incredibly special. In such a short a time, they'd become good friends, and she cared a great deal for the woman, and for her dolphins.

As for Ruby's nephew, well, Victoria realized her feelings for Jack required considerable study. The situation was entirely too complicated. This would all be so much easier if he wasn't such a smart, sexy package with more charm than he should be allowed.

"Why couldn't he at least have been as dim as he let me think?" She thunked her head on her stack of file folders. Maybe then she could have kept her attraction to him at bay, despite his powerhouse body.

Right now, it felt like she was rowing against the tide in a leaky boat. But she couldn't afford to let go of the oars. In spite of the sizzle that danced between them, she had to concentrate on her work. *Focus on the end goal.* Above all else, that took priority. Unfortunately for her resolve, he didn't consider their professional connection a conflict of interest. To him, work was work and sex was . . .

Amazing. Alone in the office, she allowed herself a single, dreamy sigh. No way would it be anything less. The fundamental data might be inconclusive, but preliminary observations—the way his touches sent heat waves through her body, his nitro-packed kisses, left zero doubt.

If Jack had his way, the hypothesis wouldn't go unproven. So, it was up to her to keep the boundaries of their relationship clearly defined. With so much at stake, she couldn't afford to let those lines blur, not when she'd already lost so much with Kel.

What could I gain?

Now that was a question worth asking. The obvious answer shot a tingle from her scalp to her thighs. She sipped some tea, burned her tongue, and fanned her face with the papers.

Oookay! Moving on. What else?

Nothing sprang to mind. It wasn't like they'd discussed the matter.

Stymied, she swiveled from side to side in the chair and studied the scarred paneling on the office walls. Unless some ancient mystic hieroglyphics were hidden in the fake-wood grain, she wouldn't find answers there either.

Hmmm. *All right, smart girl, what would I like to gain?* This was tougher than studying the sound print data from the recorders. She'd been so burned by her previous relationship, that she hadn't given any thought to looking for a new one. Not that she'd gone looking for Jack. He'd been on the premises when she arrived.

What was the use in speculating? She had already mapped out her plans. Digging through a container of paper clips, she laid them side by side on the desk to act as little counters as she listed the phases in her strategy. Complete the project. Publish her paper. Win the Delphinid Prize. After that, she'd never have a problem getting grant money, and facilities would line up to host her studies. Once she'd earned her place among the leaders in the field, she would . . .

What? Victoria stared at the paper clips like they were rune stones. Everything in her plans focused on a successful, rewarding career. Where were the paper clips representing her personal life?

When Kel talked about the two of them as a professional and personal couple, she'd always assumed that one day they'd have children to complete the picture. Now she was on her own. A strange picture materialized in her brain—an image of herself as a single working mother strapping her baby into a miniature life vest and water wings.

Doable? Well, sure, she was woman, hear her roar. Desirable? That was another thing all together.

Snap out of it! It isn't like I have to prove the theorem right this moment.

Giving herself a mental shake, she returned to the original question. Should she put aside her misgivings and say yes to Jack's seduction? If so, then why? Because her cells jumped to attention in his company. Because his kisses made her nerve endings snap, crackle, and pop.

Because she liked him. Scratch the tough, stubborn, my-way-or-no-way attitude, and you found a solid, good man. One who was busting his butt for Dolphin Land, all to solidify his aunt's future happiness.

She was positive he liked her too, and it seemed to go beyond pure physical attraction. Even when bedeviling the heck out of her, he made no secret that he respected her abilities and admired her intelligence. That alone earned him several gold stars. In short, he was everything she'd thought she'd found in her ex-fiancé, minus the backstabbing.

Of course, this whole train of thought could remain in the depot. Strong sexual interest didn't mean he wanted an eventual walk down the aisle, and that might be the easiest solution of all. Enjoy his company and say goodbye once she completed the research. She'd go with the keys to her future in her hands, or at least on her data disks, and when she headed back up the Overseas Highway, she'd do so knowing that Dolphin Land and its family were in better shape than when she first arrived.

For a minute, she indulged in the image of herself as a love-'em-and-leave-'em woman. Yeah, right. That was so not her. On the other hand, like he'd said on the dock yesterday, there wasn't anything wrong with two healthy, unattached people wanting each other and doing something about it.

He wanted her. He'd signaled that message loud and clear.

She wanted him. No matter that she'd tried to deny it, hidden it, and on at least two occasions, run like hell from it, but her actions didn't change the truth. Even out of his orbit, just thinking about him made her heart pump fast and her blood swirl in her veins.

That was more than enough evidence for even her skeptical, scientific mind. Now that she'd admitted it, what next? The choice was clearly hers to make. Jack's final words the previous evening left no doubt that another bone-melting embrace was in her future. His kiss this morning served as a reminder. When the time arrived, would she lose her nerve and run away again, or put away her fears and run toward him?

Rain splattering the roof marked time for the debate. Would she or wouldn't she? Should she or shouldn't she? Only her libido knew for sure. Yes, no, maybe . . .

Stop mooning over the problem, already, and get back to work. She wasn't going to make up her mind staring at rows of paper clips. Annoyed that she'd veered off track, she swept them back into their container and spread out her data sheets. At least this area of her life wasn't one whale-sized question mark. In fact, the test results thus far were so completely in line with her theories, she wanted to run most of them again. The scientific community would scrutinize her findings down to the minutest detail looking for flaws. Conducting twice the number of tests in every phase of the study would prove her results weren't a fluke. She would need to tack on additional time, of course, but the extra months and money were more than justified.

Speaking of which . . . Victoria faced the computer, hit a few keys, and logged online. The next installment from the "grant" was due to Ruby. Better make sure the bank dividend she expected had been wired into her account before she wrote the payment. She had no idea how long the others would be gone, so now was the perfect time to check.

Within minutes, the screen displayed her brokerage account

records. She winced. The market had suffered some rough weeks with a sudden, strong correction, and a number of investments had lost significant points. Still, her broker had assured her the fund's overall portfolio was balanced enough to weather a slower economy.

She highlighted the line for recent deposits, but before she could click the mouse to download the information, the door to the office opened and Jack stepped inside.

Quickly, she hit the stop button and signed off the web site. Swiveling in the chair, she mustered a smile. "Look what the wind blew in."

After pulling the door shut behind him, he shrugged out of his jacket. "It's getting nastier by the minute. I finished the new thaw rack, but there's no chance I'm gonna get to any of the outdoor work."

Rain trickled down his face. Walking over to the counter, he grabbed a fistful of paper towels to dry himself off. When he reached up to slick back the damp tangle of dark hair, his biceps bunched and flexed.

Watching him perform even that simple act did strange things to her insides. Another swallow of tea eased the cotton texture in her mouth. "There's no hope of running tests today."

"Nah, this isn't weather you want to be out in. Aunt Ruby'll stay put at Willie's marina until it clears." He leaned his hips against the counter. "That leaves only you and me to keep each other company." A slow grin spread across his face as he straightened and approached her chair, much like a panther closing in on its prey.

Uh oh. Victoria jumped up, heading for the file cabinets, slipping out of his reach. "I have data to analyze."

"Even genius researchers need break time." He caught her on the second pass and gathered her close. "Baby, it's cold outside," he said with an exaggerated shiver. "How about warming me up?"

Wrapped in his hug, she fought the temptation to rest her head on his big strong shoulder. She'd never had anybody to lean on, and it would be so easy to surrender.

The thought rocked her. Abruptly, she pushed against his chest.

"Hey now, what's with that, sugar?"

"You're . . . you're getting me wet."

"I thought it'd take a little longer, but—"

"That's not what I meant!"

"Maybe not." His grin spoke volumes. "But I did."

Her earlier dilemma returned. Should she? Shouldn't she?

"Rain or no, Jack, I have work to do and . . . and no time for fooling around."

"Who's fooling?"

The man's incorrigible streak ran as long as Florida's contiguous coastline. Covering up a laugh, she shoved again, breaking his hold enough to step back. Jabbing a finger at him, she did her best to sound firm. "I have work to do."

"All work and no play . . ."

"Means progress. I am not going to let you distract me."

"Oh no?"

With one step, he closed the distance, backing her against the desk. Gently grasping her upper arms, he held her steady for his kiss. She willed her bones not to melt, not to give in to the urge to yield to the firm, warm press of his mouth. It took effort, but she forced herself to stand straight and not lean into his body.

Her steely resolve was outstanding. For all of five seconds. Then her traitorous lips softened, and her body's resistance ebbed. As soon as she weakened, he deepened the kiss, his tongue stealing in to tease a greater response. He groaned and, with one smooth move, lifted her atop the desk.

Her butt knocked over the mug of tea. Liquid splashed the seat of her jeans.

She yelped and he let go. "What's wrong?"

Saved by the spill. "My reports!" She shoved a stack of papers into his hands before grabbing the roll of paper towels and mopping up rivulets of tea running over the desk. Thankfully, the damage was minimal. She pitched the soaked mess into the trash.

"That could have ruined weeks of work." Taking back the papers, she arranged them in a neat stack on the now-dry desk. "No more funny stuff during business hours, mister," she declared. "Is that understood?"

Clearly holding back laughter, he snapped off a salute. "Aye, aye, boss!"

"Good. Now, stay or go, but find something to keep yourself busy." Positive he'd gotten the message, Victoria turned back to her desk and pulled out the most recent signature-whistle, spectrograph printouts.

His arms stole around her waist pulling her back against his solid body. Warm breath fanned her skin right before he placed a searing kiss on the exact tender spot where her neck joined her shoulder.

A wave of heat rippled through her, stalling her breath in her throat. "I said no funny stuff."

"I'm flat-out serious, sweetheart." Lifting her hair away from her neck, he ran a string of moist kisses up her throat. His thumb feathered the pulse point under her jaw.

His other hand, splayed against her stomach, began a slow, circular climb, sweeping over her abdomen, her ribcage.

"Jack, I—" The protest lodged in her throat when his big palm closed over her breast. The jolt shot down between her legs, and her entire body went pliant.

He smiled against her throat as he played with her breast. His other hand tangled in her hair, slowly tilting back her head. She caught a glimpse of heated turquoise eyes before he covered her mouth again, drawing her into a soul kiss that obliterated the rest of her misgivings.

No more wondering. No more questions. She shifted to slide her hand up around his neck while she returned the kiss, welcoming his tongue like a long-anticipated treat. Her heart leapt under his hand, while he continued to caress her, and the kiss spun them higher. Each breath she drew brought in the scent of heated male. The taste of rain mingled with a flavor that was uniquely him. She drew the tip of her tongue along the inner seam of his lips and craved more.

He pulled back and turned her the rest of the way. His broad chest rose and fell, showing that he was as affected as she was by the shared heat. His eyes were deadly serious, his voice rough.

"This is your last chance to say no, Victoria. Are you in or out?"

On weak legs, her insides churning but her head still clear enough to make a decision, she walked to the door and turned the lock. "I'm in."

It was all the answer he needed. Catching her to him, he lifted her in a hug, melding her to his body. She could feel his heart thudding in his chest and the hard arousal in his jeans when she wrapped her legs around his waist.

Her heart soared, knowing that she caused such a reaction. Thrilled, she laughed, grabbing handfuls of his coffee-dark hair and holding on tight while she scalded him with another kiss. Grasping her butt in both hands, he walked her toward the dilapidated couch against the wall. Each step brought that impressive erection into closer, stroking contact. Even through both of their jeans, the sensation set her nerve endings on high boil.

A bend of his knee lowered her to the couch. He broke the kiss to slide her tank top up and off her body. For an instant she wished she'd thrown on some sexy, satin, and lace creation when she'd dressed in the morning, instead of the plain white sports bra. The regret disappeared when he unsnapped the fastening and stripped the undergarment from her body.

"Have mercy," he rasped, staring with pure, male appreciation at her naked breasts.

Her nipples hardened instantly, although he did no more than look for a long moment. Then, he knelt over her and slowly, deliberately, thumbed the rigid peaks.

She nearly shot off the couch. Her reaction made him smile and he continued to play, teasing first one breast then the other. Within seconds she was squirming, torn between enjoying the pure pleasure washing over her and wanting to give him the same.

She rose, targeting the buttons on his denim shirt. He helped her make short work of removing the garment from his broad chest, but before she got one good stroke on his skin, he drew her hands behind her back. Holding them securely in a single grip, he pulled her onto his lap, then arched her over his arm.

"You don't play fair," she protested weakly.

"Sure I do, sugar," he drawled, bringing his head down to blaze more moist, open-mouth kisses down her throat. "I just always play by my rules."

His other hand shifted under her breast. "Rule number one . . ." He molded it with his palm, lifting it as his head slid lower. "Ladies first." His mouth closed over the nipple with a single hard suck.

She would have launched to the ceiling if he hadn't held her tight. While he suckled and laved the taut peak, she wriggled in his lap rubbing against his erection. He switched to the other breast, giving it the same sensual attention until she shuddered in his arms.

By the time his hand slipped inside the waistband of her jeans, she was nearly beyond rational thought. When he wrestled off both her pants and underwear and cupped his palm between her legs, she knew thinking was highly overrated. At that point, everything centered on the throbbing ache.

"Jack . . ." she moaned.

"What, sweetheart?" The question rumbled against the over-sensitized skin of her breast.

"Please . . ."

"This?" A single finger dipped inside her cleft and wiggled.

She gasped.

"Oh yeah, sweetheart. That's it. Show me you like what I'm doing." The hoarse whisper and lightning strokes of his finger drove her wild, and her hips pumped, inviting him deeper to do more, faster. Pulse points throbbed and her breathing took off in quick pants as he worked magic, all the time encouraging her with dark, sexy words.

Her flesh vibrated like a tuning fork, drawing a whimpering moan from her throat. Still he stroked and fondled, rubbing the taut pulsing knot of her clitoris while he penetrated her with slick fingers. Still he urged her on to her release until suddenly, with magnum force, she hit the swell and crested, crying out his name.

"That's it, sweetheart." He took her mouth in a wild kiss, and then laid her back on the couch. His hands yanked at the snap of his jeans.

Still trembling, she propped herself up on one hand and reached for him. "Let me."

Carefully, she worked the zipper down and pressed against the hard length still concealed behind snug navy briefs. A groan encouraged her to pull the undergarment free. She looked up as she encircled his smooth shaft and watched his eyes go dark. Delighted, she stroked up and down the full length and heard his breath quicken, while he grew impossibly harder in her hand.

"I'll give you an hour to stop doing that," he ground out as he shoved his jeans down his hips and kicked them off. "Next time."

Abruptly, he grabbed her hand away, bearing her back down on the couch. He ripped open a foil packet—he must have gotten it from his jeans—and covered himself. Then, he sat back on his haunches, slid his hands under her thighs and pulled her forward.

Never taking his heavy-lidded gaze from hers, he rubbed himself against her sensitive flesh. Quicksilver shimmered through her veins, and her head dropped back against the cushions.

"Victoria, look at me," he ordered softly. "I want to see your eyes when I take you."

She could only obey, the dark promise of his words sending curls of heat and desire through her. Her nerve cells quivered and she flexed her hips, pressing up against him. The crown of his penis breached her opening and her flesh stretched to receive him.

"Oh! Ohh, Jack!"

In a swift move, he surged forward on his knees. She jackknifed her legs around his waist, taking him deeper. He filled her so completely, she couldn't tell where his throbbing ended and hers began. She only knew that the slick friction of him stroking her from the inside out created the most exquisite pleasure.

He dipped down to kiss her, plunging his tongue into her mouth with carnal hunger as he thrust his hips forward and back, forward and back. His long hair brushed like damp silk against her naked skin, and the crisp curls on his chest teased her breasts until it felt like every inch of her was alive with sensation.

Lightning pulses jolted her where their bodies joined, and he quickened his thrusts. The world lost focus, except for the intense pleasure she saw written on his face, the heavy sound of their breathing and the desperate, skyrocketing pleasure building inside her veins. Suddenly, another powerful, molten wave hit and she shattered, crying out her release.

His powerful body rocked harder once, twice, and then once again before he hit his own release on a hoarse shout of her name.

Chapter Twelve

Swamped in sensation with tiny pulses of pleasure still throbbing inside, it was a long time before Victoria registered conscious thought. She lay still, too absorbed in the warm, solid weight of Jack's body to care that the tweed cushions of the ancient couch scratched her skin. They were a tight fit, the two of them, on that sofa, but she loved cradling him between her thighs and feeling his chest rise and fall. Stroking his back, she combed her fingers through his hair.

A satisfied moan rumbled in his chest. Smoothly, he rolled to his side, shifting her at the same time. Drifting a hand to her hip, he snuggled her close, entwining their legs. "There, you should be able to breath easier."

She could, until a slow, thorough kiss stole her air again. When he finished, he furrowed his brow in mock concern.

"You're mighty quiet, sweetheart."

Everything she felt could be expressed in a single word.

Wow!

Nothing else seemed quite right, and words wouldn't come anyway, not while she was losing herself in his eyes. Looking into their turquoise brilliance was like gazing into the endless depths of the ocean.

He traced her cheekbones, her jaw, the curve of her eyebrows, and the outline of her lips. "You sure you're okay?"

She nodded, fascinated by the gentle caress of his fingers on her skin.

Playing with her hair, he drew the ends across his mouth, and tickled her nose. "Then why aren't you talking?"

Because my body's still singing Hallelujah. Because her world had never been rocked like that, and she was overwhelmed.

She could never admit that to him, though. It said too much about her previous experiences or lack thereof. "Jeez, can't a woman bask in the afterglow?"

"That's more like it," he chuckled. "You had me worried."

"Excuse me, but I never figured you'd suffer performance anxiety." She couldn't keep from giggling, which earned her a friendly swat on her backside.

"My performance is the last thing I worry about, sugar. You were right there with me the whole time. That wasn't a scream of disappointment I heard a few minutes ago."

"I did not scream!"

"Did too, right when I . . ." He finished the sentence with a naughty description of exactly what he'd been doing to her at the time.

Laughter sputtered out, completely ruining her tone of fake outrage. "I have news for you, buddy, the last time I heard a sound like the one you made, it came from a blue whale a hundred miles away from the boat."

He laughed out loud, hugging her tightly. "I've been called a lot of things, sweetheart, but that's a first. Now about that afterglow."

Rolling to a sitting position, he pulled her onto his lap. "While I'm forever going to have fond memories of this couch, I think this place lacks the proper atmosphere." He nuzzled her neck and whispered in her ear. "What do you say we sneak on over to your place and play hooky for the day?"

"Respected research scientists do not play hooky, hot stuff."

"Oh no? Then what would you call spending an afternoon naked in bed, while I explore every inch of your body with my mouth?"

That got her pulse rate revving at top RPMs.

"A good plan."

* * *

Without any trouble at all, afternoon turned into night and rolled right over into the following morning. Victoria lost count of the number of times they'd reached for each other and the different ways he'd shown her how to play hooky.

An hour ago, he'd suddenly remembered that a shipment of fencing was due to be delivered. He'd jumped into the shower, pulled on his clothes, and then planted a hard, swift kiss on her mouth before running out the door.

Her body felt . . . incredible . . . inside and out. True to his promise, there wasn't an inch of her that hadn't been kissed, tasted, stroked, nuzzled. Minor muscle aches reminded her in particular of a few unfamiliar, but thoroughly interesting positions. From the look in his eyes before he dashed out, she'd get introduced to a few more tonight.

In the meantime, she couldn't lie around and waste the day. Yesterday's storm had blown by, leaving a trademark Keys' day of bright sunshine. Quickly, efficiently, she took her own shower and dressed, then turned on her laptop. While it booted up, she pitched out the empty cartons from the Chinese dinner they'd ordered and changed the sheets on the bed.

She caught herself humming as she sat down at the computer and logged online to access her trust fund account. The day before, she'd been doing just this very thing when Jack returned, and look what had happened since. For a minute, the downloading information blurred in front of her eyes. Jack-style seduction was enough to make anyone's mind go numb.

Ah, finally, there was the deposit information. She scrolled down to the income summary and froze.

The dividend deposit was listed, but the amount was less than half of what she'd expected.

Quickly, she grabbed her cell phone and punched in her broker's number. The number rang several times before connecting to an electronic recording. Of course! It was too early in the morning; the office wouldn't open for another hour.

No need to panic. She sucked in a couple of deep breaths. Although, she'd planned on a certain amount from the bank dividend, her account held plenty of other monies. She'd call again in a little while and talk to her broker. In the meantime, she needed to act as if nothing was the slightest bit amiss. That meant getting over to Dolphin Land at her usual time.

Everything's normal, she reminded herself. She grabbed a brush to pull her hair into its customary ponytail. Her reflection in the mirror made her pause. Well, maybe not exactly normal. Her eyes shone more brightly than usual, her lips were slightly swollen, and there was a trace of whisker burn on her jaw.

The signs were as obvious as if she'd donned a T-shirt that read, "I Got Lucky." Ruby would take one look at her and know what happened. That was pretty much a given. Good Lord, a stranger walking down the highway would guess, and the best part was she didn't care. Slinging her backpack over a shoulder, she left the room. No matter what happened between her and Jack in the future, yesterday was something she would never regret.

Nobody was in the office when she arrived. Jack must still be dealing with the delivery. Since Ruby's Jeep sat in its customary spot, she had returned from her evening spent not playing pinochle with Willie and was probably in the fish house prepping the morning buckets. Victoria filled some time at the computer running a program to produce random samplings for the day's tests. Without them, there was always a chance a human might make selections in a subconscious pattern that the dolphins could pick up on. The program kept the test data pure.

Nine o'clock rolled around, and she placed her call. After giving her name to the receptionist, she drummed her fingers on the desk and fiddled with some paper clips.

"Why, hello, Victoria. How nice to hear from you."

Since the days when he'd served as her grandparents' financial advisor, Mr. Kennedy always sounded delighted, no matter when or why she called. They exchanged pleasantries before she got down to business.

The news wasn't terrific. The bank's earnings had fallen below projections for the third quarter in a row. Investment analysts had lowered the institution's rating and stockholders were nervous. The share price had dropped significantly. In order to restore confidence, the bank's directors had announced a full program of cost-saving measures and had slashed the dividend to improve immediate cash flow.

"It's still a solid investment for the long term," Mr. Kennedy assured her. "The management team is strong, and their plan will help the bank recover from this rough patch."

Bully for them, she thought. Those cost-saving measures wouldn't fix her immediate problem. Plan B.

"Mr. Kennedy, I need to make up the shortfall with interest income right away," she explained. "Next month, I'll need a similar amount."

"Victoria, the monthly income from the trust account won't cover that amount, not at the rate you require."

"Then surely there's a short-term holding we can sell a little early."

"Of course, but if you do that, you're not only liquidating principal now, you're reducing the earnings' potential of the trust for the future. I really can't advise it. Overall economic indicators hint at the risk of recession, so the wise investor must act conservatively."

"I realize that, Mr. Kennedy, but this is a special case." She hated talking so tough, but she was desperate. "Please proceed with my instructions. I'll expect the check in a few days."

An audible sigh came over the line. "Victoria, I need to remind you that I am also a trustee of this fund. Therefore, I have a fiduciary responsibility to protect your holdings."

"What exactly do you mean?"

"Quite simply, most of the time, you've been perfectly able to live within the monthly income generated by the fund. Your needs have grown suddenly, for whatever reason, and now you want to sell off principal investments. I'm sorry, but I cannot permit you to do so. We cannot produce a check of this size. You will have to make do with the lesser amount."

It wouldn't be enough. "But it's *my* trust fund!" she exclaimed.

"And your grandparents appointed me to oversee it so that you would never have to worry about money. That, young lady, is what I intend to do."

From the tone of his voice, she could picture him donning armor and picking up weaponry to defend the treasure room of some ancient castle. She was sunk.

"I understand," she choked out from a throat tight with worry. Thanking him, she disconnected the call.

What in God's name was she going to do now? Suddenly, every question she'd asked herself about getting involved with Jack seemed ridiculous. What was the point of wondering what kind of relationship they'd have in the future? Forget protecting her research project for a minute. Without the "grant" money she'd pledged to Dolphin Land, how would she keep Ruby and Jack from hating her?

He would be furious! The most important thing, as he'd made a hundred percent clear, was that his aunt be financially secure and happy. He'd had his plans in place, she knew, and been forced to put them aside because of her arrival and the funds she'd promised.

After this week, she would no longer deliver adequate money, and who knew if the developers he'd lined up were still available? Guilt imps again marched in her head like soldiers. Her deception wasn't so harmless anymore.

She felt sick, as if she were rocking aboard a small boat in the middle of a hurricane. An image of a huge "For Sale" sign stuck in the middle of Dolphin Land's parking lot made her stomach churn even more. *Think, Victoria, think!* What was the use of an above average IQ if she couldn't come up with a solution? She would not let this setback destroy her dreams, or the people and place she cared for so deeply.

She needed time, and then surely an idea would present itself. An idea, an opportunity, a miracle. Instead, Jack arrived back at the office at the worst possible time.

He caught her up in a bear hug and delivered a bone-dissolving kiss.

It would be so easy to melt, to let the embrace obliterate her worries, but she couldn't. Here he was, the most amazing man she'd ever met behaving like her dream lover, and instead of being able to enjoy it, she felt like a slimy, giant squid-sized fraud.

She broke the kiss and wriggled in his arms. "Put me down." Her words came out more sharply than she'd intended, and his face changed. *Bad move.* Right now it was imperative he not suspect anything was wrong. If he did, he'd pester her without mercy until he uncovered the whole story.

"That's not the reaction I expected."

Damage control, Victoria. "I'm sorry. I didn't mean that the way it sounded. It's just, you know . . . Someone could come in at any moment."

"They'd see us kissing, so what?"

"There's a time and a place for kissing." Way to sound prissy and lame.

Thankfully, he laughed. "You know, sugar, your secret's out."

"What?" she gasped. Had he heard her on the phone?

"The rest of the world may believe your starched-spine scientist routine, but I know the real you."

Oh God, this couldn't get any worse. She had no idea how he'd discovered the truth. Then a sick realization struck. "Kel! Have you been talking to Kel?"

Jack snorted. "Like I'd waste my time. I don't call a lady's ex to brag or compare notes. Not when I can find out everything I need to know on my own."

Her deception hung around her neck like a thirty-pound anchor. Now, in addition to the money problem, somehow he knew she wasn't the accredited researcher she'd claimed. Misery curdled in her stomach. She stared at his shirt buttons, unable to look him in the eye.

"How did you figure it out?" she asked weakly, waiting for the sword to fall.

"Well, I started to suspect the first time I kissed you." A thumb beneath her jaw lifted her face. "I was pretty sure after our time on the couch over there." He pressed her lower lip gently. "Last night settled the question. Underneath that brainy, by-the-book attitude beats the heart of a red-hot babe."

Without his thumb bracing it, her jaw would have hit the floor. He didn't know after all!

And he thought she was a babe. A red-hot one at that. Instant delight rushed through her, but unfortunately, her worries returned almost as fast, deflating her spirits. Still, she kept her expression neutral and her tone light. "Well, this babe is still serious about her work, and I'm a day behind." She jerked her head away from the caress of his fingers and leaned back against the desk. "I thought you had a list of projects scheduled to complete today."

"You in a hurry to get rid of me?"

Yes! she thought. "Of course not, but . . ." But what? She needed a plausible excuse. "But, you know, there's something I need from my place." She turned away from his too-perceptive eyes and rummaged for her keys. "I'm running over to my room, and on the way back I'll pick us up some lunch." She'd make sure to take as much time as possible to clear her head and devise a way to repair the financial mess. "How's a Reuben sandwich from Downtown Deli sound?"

"Great, about three hours from now when it's actually lunchtime. Can't you wait?"

"No."

"What's so important that you have to go this minute?"

Her brain spun like a whirligig. "Well, I've reached the stage where I need to . . . to chart the current results in relation to the global overview of the entire project. Taking into account, of course, historical data perspectives."

Pure and total gibberish. No wonder his expression was blank.

"If not, there's the risk of . . . of incorrectly weighting the test scores in ratio to the desired subject responses."

At the moment, she was very, very glad he wasn't another research scientist.

"And that would be bad."

"Terrible. If I'm not completely precise, all the conclusions could be skewed."

"Wouldn't want you to screw your conclusions."

"I said skewed." Too late, she spotted the glint in his eyes. Why did he have to be so damned much fun when she was in crisis mode? Oh, how she'd miss his teasing when the truth came out. She would miss him, period.

The realization landed like a rock in the middle of the lagoon, sending ripples of sadness through her before settling at the bottom of her stomach.

It must have shown, because he instantly responded. "Hey, c'mon. You oughta know by now when I'm joking. About the results anyway. I still wish you weren't heading out right now." He rubbed his knuckles under her chin, lifting it so she looked into his eyes. "It's been almost two hours since we were alone together. If I promise to behave myself, won't you wait?"

Jack, the smart aleck, she could handle. Jack, the new lover, was a whole other thing. The combination of charm and cuteness weakened her resolve and he knew it, because he pulled her closer. Fighting herself as much as him, she brought her arms up and pushed, breaking contact. "No, I need the historical data now or the whole day will be a waste." Quickly, she turned toward the door.

A gentle tug on her ponytail stopped her progress. "Hold it, Victoria."

Turning her, he cupped her jaw. The intense focus was back in his gaze as he searched her face. "You're mighty jumpy. Something else going on that you want to tell me about?"

"No."

"No, there's nothing going on, or no, you don't want to tell me?"

"Why do you insist there's something going on?"

"Call it a hunch, sugar. You're on edge, and this time I'm not the reason."

"Maybe I don't like you interrupting my work."

"You're a rotten liar."

His estimation made her feel even worse.

"So, what happened? You brought up your ex-fiancé a while ago. Did he hassle you again this morning?"

She closed her eyes and stifled a sigh. Without realizing it, he'd provided the perfect excuse. "I can't help but be upset about Kel."

"I told you not to worry. Like you said, he doesn't know where you are, and if he figures it out, he'll have to deal with me. Put it out of your mind."

Now, when she deserved it least, she finally had someone ready to look out for her. His solid protectiveness made her feel lower than the deepest bottom feeder. In another minute, she would break down in tears.

"Jack, I appreciate your support, more than you know, but the best way for me to get Kel off my mind is to dig into my analysis and be by myself for a while." She looked up with a forced smile. "I'll be back in a few hours with lunch, okay? This will give you time to finish your projects, and then you can help me run tests this afternoon."

Searching her face again, he finally acquiesced.

"I'll hold you to it, sugar. Get your work done now, because later on, I'm going to want you all for myself."

So he could rip her apart without witnesses, unless she figured out something. There was no good way to answer him, so she stowed reports into her backpack. Before she left the office, she reached her hands to the sides of his face and kissed him thoroughly. Before the moment could turn into something sweeter, she hurried out the door.

She sensed his stare and knew she'd only succeeded in delaying his questions. Not that it would matter in the long run. If she didn't come up with a solution soon, this would be the last time he wanted anything to do with her.

Chapter Thirteen

Jack pushed the roller up the fish house wall, applying white paint with the same precision he used to rig explosives. Damned if a couple of coats of fresh paint didn't spruce up the place. Sure, it wasn't as important as blowing up that cocaine factory in the Colombian jungle, but he got a charge out of it anyway.

He whistled as he dipped the roller back in the paint pan. When he finished with the walls, maybe he'd paint the door and windowsills blue for contrast. Later on, he'd tighten the railing facing the front lagoon. The tiki roof that sheltered the benches there needed some holes plugged. It made a nice shady spot for his aunt and Victoria to sit while they discussed the research progress, but he knew nothing about weaving palm fronds tight enough to block out rain. Well, maybe he could figure it out. By the time he finished, it'd be close to quitting time and he had definite plans for the evening, all of which involved Victoria.

The weather report promised a warm evening with light winds, and she might enjoy a sail on his boat. Sunsets were beautiful in the Keys, and he'd get a kick out of watching her take in the sight. She had a way of experiencing things totally in the moment. That pretty face got all animated, her eyes shone and she talked with so much enthusiasm, he got caught up too.

Except when they were naked together; then she fell quiet, absorbing every single sensation. The pleasure on her face was so rapt, so incredible, he wanted to draw out his touches, multiply his strokes and kisses for the pure enjoyment of watching her come undone. Then he wanted to do it all again.

The weeks prior had taught him all about her mind, her sass, and her commitment to her work. Yesterday, he'd learned her inside and out. What turned her on, what made her blush, what drove her wild.

What upset her. That ex-fiancé hit her buttons, for sure, no matter how she'd tried to cover it up with that intricate load of bull about global overviews and historical perspectives. He'd give her the afternoon to stew and then cajole her onto his sailboat, where he could take her mind off everything.

Except him.

She better grow used to it. From the day she arrived at Dolphin Land, she'd come under his surveillance. Now that they were lovers, she'd come under his protection too.

Although most of his relationships lasted the average length of a holiday weekend, the few times he did get involved for longer periods, he'd followed hard and fast rules. He didn't cheat or make false promises. He didn't share his woman with other men, and Jack Benton always took care of his own.

Whoa. Thinking of Victoria as his woman went a lot farther than the mind-blowing sex he'd anticipated. When exactly had the mission objective changed? He couldn't pinpoint the exact minute, but it fell somewhere between their first kiss and last orgasm.

Oh, baby. The thought took getting used to. Like new intelligence received from an unexpected source, he needed to process the info.

He leaned on the long handle of the paint roller and took stock. He'd never really been sorry to part ways with former lady friends. There was always another mission waiting, a different battle to fight, and when completed, a new woman to enjoy during down time. That kind of life wasn't long on permanence, but it kept a man on the cutting edge.

Was he ready to give it up? Coating the roller with more paint, he attacked the wall. He was no more prepared to settle down with one woman than he was to swap field assignments for a desk job. So what if his injured leg throbbed like a son-of-a-bitch from the over-the-top activity of the previous twenty-four hours, and he still couldn't jog more than a mile or two at a time? After a few more weeks of recovery, he'd start a fitness regimen that would really kick his ass into shape and then reapply for active status. They'd force him to go through a battery of physical tests, but he'd pass. He had to.

Life in the DEA was tough, but it mattered. He was doing something important for his country down in the jungles, cutting off the Colombian drug supply before it got to the streets of America. The conditions sucked, with the native poverty and lousy hygiene in the small villages. Hard-eyed men and sad, worried women raised skinny kids on next to no money. No wonder the drug lords had a never-ending supply of cheap, willing labor to grow and harvest the coca and turn it into white crystals of cocaine.

There were times when it felt like they waged war on an enemy that had a limitless supply of soldiers. Some days they won, but mostly they kept even. The constant edge, living with his nerves wound as tightly as piano wires, could wear him down, but hot damn, he knew he was alive.

So why the hell was he smiling and whistling while he worked? Rebuilding sorry-ass buildings, fixing fences, and slapping gallons of paint around the place didn't compare to fieldwork. Sometime in the future, when he was good and ready to quit the agency, this wouldn't be a bad gig. But in the meantime, it was only a stopgap. Something to keep him from going crazy while he healed. It gave him the bonus of seeing to his aunt's welfare.

Even that was going better than expected. Sure, he'd thought the whole research idea was a cockamamie scheme, but Victoria had delivered as promised. For the first time since Gus's death, they were current on their fish account and had money left to tackle fix-up projects. The place hadn't looked this good since back when, as a kid, he'd come to live at Dolphin Land.

And they had Victoria to thank for it. Beautiful, brainy, sweet-to-tease, and even sweeter to make love with, the woman was accomplishing what she'd set out to do. He had to admire her dedication, and as soon as he got her alone again, he planned to do a hell of a lot of admiring.

Geezus, she got to him. Alone, with nobody but the dolphins near, he could admit the truth.

He was nuts about her. Crazy, loco, gone-overboard-without-a-life-vest nuts. If most of his life had existed in dark, dank jungles with the underbelly of humanity, then Victoria was sunsets, warm breezes, and bright, golden light.

Oh, Christ. Somebody stop him before he broke out in song.

The wall finished, he threw down the roller, grabbed his tool belt, and stalked to the front lagoon. He needed to hammer some nails into the railing to tighten it, and at the same time, bang on his head.

If he didn't reclaim his senses fast, in another minute he might say the "L" word.

No, effing way. I am not in lo— Lust, maybe. Probably. Okay, definitely with a capital L, but Jack Benton did not do love. Love led to commitment. To settling down. To sitting side-by-side at sunset, holding hands while the day's last light sank into the sea.

Hey, Bubba, that's exactly what you planned for the end of the day.

Two dolphins popped up nearby. The noises they made sounded like laughter.

"Knock it off, you two. You aren't funny and I'm not in love."

Arrrgh. He sounded like Aunt Ruby again, talking to the dolphins and attributing them with human reactions, when he knew very well the noises came from manipulating air sacs around their blowholes. They didn't even have vocal cords. Despite what his aunt said, he refused to believe they understood the concept of laughter, and even if they did, they couldn't know he was the punch line.

He walloped a nail so hard, the force vibrated up his arm.

I am not . . .

Bang!

In . . .

Bang, bang!

Love!

Three more hits drove the nail home. He grabbed another and repeated the process, then another still, hammering as if the key to his survival lay in securing the sturdiness of the wooden railing. Sweat dripped down his forehead. The salt stung his eyes by the time he'd finished, and his jaw ached from gritting his teeth. Finally, he dropped onto the bench and swabbed his face with the hem of his T-shirt.

"Whooeee, I'm sure glad you're through, Bubba. That wood can't take the punishment."

Aw, hell. How long had Aunt Ruby been standing there?

He stretched out his legs and stared at the water. "At least now

145

the rail won't come off in your hand when you go down to the dock."

Ruby plopped down next to him, handing over a glass of iced tea. "What's bugging you, darlin'?"

"Nothing." He gulped down the cold liquid and crunched the ice between his teeth.

His aunt threw him a *bull crap* look. "I heard you whistling outside the fish house not too long ago, Jack. Now you look as grumpy as a grouper with a hook in its mouth."

"It's hot. I'm tired. I'm taking a break." He shrugged. No big deal.

She snorted. "Victoria wear you out last night?"

Iced tea spewed from his mouth. "Aunt Ruby!"

"Oh don't give me that shocked look. You're as bad as her. I've been waiting for you to make a move since she got here."

"A few weeks ago you told me to stay away from her!"

"Hah. Aintcha ever heard of reverse psychology? Besides, I knew after I said that, you wouldn't press the issue unless you really wanted her for her and not just because she's beautiful and available. Finally you came to your senses and did something about it. The only thing I can't figure out is why you went from glad to mad so fast. So, I'll ask again. What's bothering you?"

How could he explain his dilemma to this beloved old woman? He'd only just realized it himself. "It's complicated."

"How come? You like her. She likes you. Something clicked, or you wouldn't have spent the whole night together."

He made a strangled sound. "How do you know?"

She *thwapped* his arm. "What? You think I wouldn't notice you drove in this morning instead of walking over from where you docked the dinghy? Gimme a break."

His skin heated, horrifying him. All of a sudden he felt like he had when he was fourteen years old and had tried to disguise that he'd been in a fight at school.

She studied him, eyes sharp in her wrinkled-parchment face. "So, if sex isn't the problem, what is?" All of a sudden, she clasped her hands over her chest and her blue eyes sparkled. "My stars! The problem is you like her too much!"

He caught sight of a toothy grin before she threw her skinny arms around him in a tight hug. "Well, I'll be damned. My boy's in love."

"Don't say that!" He tried to shake her off, but she clung like a barnacle.

"Why the heck not? Lordy, you didn't catch some dreadful disease. You're in love!"

He reined her in hard. "Aunt Ruby, this isn't what you think. It's not good. In fact, it's a catastrophe."

"It's damn near a miracle! I didn't think it would ever happen. Not with you slogging away in that godforsaken wilderness down in South America. Not that I'm not proud of you, and I sure as hell didn't ever want you to almost die. I swear, I near about aged twenty years when I got the call that you'd been hurt. But still, it got you out of the jungle and back home here with me.

"Now, not only are you safe, but you're in love with a wonderful woman who's going to make you happy. Heck, y'all even saved Dolphin Land for me, and now you'll be around to help me run it."

Something cold swept over him. "What do you mean? I'm going back to work as soon as I pass the physical."

Her expression dimmed. "But . . . you can't!"

"Aunt Ruby, I have to. It's my job."

Worry washed the glow from her eyes. He squeezed her shoulder. "By the time I leave, Dolphin Land will be back on its feet all the way. We're almost ready as it is, and you'll be able to hire people to help.

It might never be as popular as it was way back when, but you'll pull enough tourists to stay in the black."

She shifted, facing him, and grasped his hands in her own. Her lively face was as still and serious as he'd ever seen it.

"That's not what I meant, darlin'."

"Then what?" A nasty shard of suspicion stabbed him in the solar plexus.

Her voice quiet and achingly sad, she delivered the knockout punch. "Jack, surely you can tell your leg's healed as much as it's gonna. Yeah, it's better, but it isn't where it needs to be for you to go back to active duty. Your doctors and bosses knew it from the get-go."

"No." He jumped to his feet, ignoring the telltale twinge shooting through his knee. "You're wrong. They're wrong. That's all there is to it." He shoved the empty glass back in her hands and grabbed his tools.

"I'm sorry, but you gotta listen to the truth. I thought you'd accepted this by now."

"No," he repeated, barely keeping from roaring the word. Refusing to look at his aunt and the fretful expression on her face, he stared over her head. "I don't care what everyone else says. I'm not finished until I say I'm finished."

"But—"

"But nothing. I belong in the agency. This . . ." A sweeping gesture dismissed the facility. "Doesn't compare. Any idiot can fix buildings and pull weeds."

"Now just a damn minute. Don't you write off Dolphin Land like this is crap beneath your shoes. It's your home. And even more, it has purpose and . . . and meaning."

He snorted, and she smacked him in the chest.

"Don't give me that look! It isn't the same purpose you're used to, I'll grant you that, but you think back to when your uncle was alive and you were a young 'un. Remember the visitors we'd get? The families, especially the kids? Think back to what it was like when they'd all come here and see our dolphins strutting their stuff. We entertained people, Jack. We made them happy."

"Fine. While you're making them happy, I'm keeping them safer by cutting down the drug supply before it gets to those kids. Which is more important?"

"They're both important, but that's not the point."

"You've got a point?"

Thwap.

"Don't get smart with me." She grabbed him by the arm and yanked him around. "Take a look at what you've accomplished in the past few months. Really look."

He heaved a gigantic sigh. God knows she wouldn't quit pestering him until he obeyed. His gaze took in the buildings, fresh paint gleaming white in the sun. New roofs practically dared the rain to fall. Hibiscus flowers bobbed in the breeze on neatly thinned bushes. Wood fences that used to sag with big, splintered holes, now stood straight.

A reluctant smile quirked the corner of his mouth. Yeah, so the old place no longer looked like a minefield after the bombs had discharged. Still . . .

"Aunt Ruby, this is a day at the beach compared to the job I'm used to doing."

"It's good honest work, just the same. And it won't stop once we get back up and running. There's a place for you here, now that you can't—"

"Don't say it!" That time he did holler, suddenly desperate to make her understand. "The DEA needs me."

"You need the DEA. That's what you mean. Admit it."

He shut his mouth, so angry he believed he might just breathe fire. Stalking off, he stopped short when she ran around and planted her much smaller body directly in his path.

"I have work to finish," he spit out.

"I got more to say. I know what your problem is. You're no different than any man I've ever known. You've got it in your head that what you do is who you are."

"Yeah, so what's wrong with that?"

"You've got it backwards. It isn't what you do that makes you a man. Whether you're in the DEA or right here, it's the man you are that gets the job done."

"Are you finished yet?"

She glared at him, exasperation evident from the stance of her bandy legs to the topknot of hair quivering in the breeze. "You want to be pig-headed about it, that's up to you. Go off and wallow for a while." With a disgusted jerk of her head, she stepped out of his way, but delivered her parting shot. "Sooner or later you'll see that I'm right, and not just about this. I'm right about your feelings for Victoria too!"

Chapter Fourteen

Victoria's heart hung like ballast in her chest, as she approached the front lagoon. Hours of thinking and she was no closer to a way out of this disaster. It was time to come clean.

From the looks on their faces and their posture, they were arguing about something, but she didn't think much of it. A day that passed without Ruby and Jack disagreeing wasn't normal. In fact, she'd noticed they enjoyed the little spats, particularly Ruby when she came out the winner.

She shifted the bag of deli sandwiches. Lunch wasn't the best peace offering, but the least she could do was feed them when she delivered the bad news.

With a little luck, Jack would still be able to put together a development deal that didn't involve his aunt giving up her dolphins.

With a miracle, they wouldn't hate her by the end of the day.

* * *

"All this time you used your own money?" Ruby stabbed the air with a plastic fork. "You let us believe it was a grant, but all this time you were funding the research. Jesus, Mary, and all the saints, what were you thinking?"

"I didn't think it mattered where the money came from, as long as I produced it on a regular basis."

The older woman turned as red as a bougainvillea blossom, and her eyes blazed. It hurt to see her upset, but Victoria refused to look away. Besides, if she glanced at Jack again, she'd freeze in place from his sub-zero glare.

"I can't believe you did this."

The reproach drove another shaft of pain into her heart. "I know. It was inexcusable, really, and sorry doesn't begin to cover it."

"Then why?"

Bitter condemnation dripped from the words—the first he'd spoken since she had revealed the truth.

She faced him. "I needed a place for my research. When I checked into the facility's background, I discovered that you could use the money a project would bring."

"Why Dolphin Land? Why not a bigger, better established facility—and don't give me that crap about our dolphins not being overused."

"There's high demand for the other facilities and—."

"And your institute couldn't get in? Yeah, right. Your father's the top man in the field, isn't he? So there's got to be something more." He pushed himself off the wall and stalked toward her. "I want the whole story. Now."

She swallowed hard. "It's complicated."

"Try me." His drawl turned cornpone. "Y'all speak slow, no big words, I bet us backwards hicks can follow along."

"That's unfair. I don't consider either of you backward. I never did."

"Instead, you figured that we were desperate enough that we'd take the first handout that came along."

"No! I thought—"

He threw up a hand, cutting her off. "Save it. We jumped all right, like a tarpon after baitfish. You reeled us in, gaffed us tight, and hauled us on board."

His anger wrapped around her like a hand to her throat, choking the protests she wanted to make.

Mute, miserable, she shook her head.

"Now that you're through, you think you'll leave us flopping on deck, is that it?" He leaned in so close, she could see that rage had dilated his pupils, darkening his brilliant eyes.

"Think again, Vic. Nobody leaves my aunt twisting in the wind. Pack your gear and get out. I want you off Dolphin Land in two hours. Hydrophones, video cams, and all. Anything not stowed in your truck gets left. We'll sell it for the next fish delivery."

"Now hold on just a damn minute, Bubba. Give the girl a chance."

"We gave her all the chances she's getting, Aunt Ruby." He turned and walked off, his final words tossed over his shoulder. "Two hours, *Dr.* Sheffield. Clock's ticking."

Ruby sputtered and started after him, but Victoria stopped her, putting a hand on the woman's arm. "Don't. He's right. I need to leave."

"Now don't you go agreeing with him. I swear the two of you could give stubborn lessons to a brace of mules. I ain't saying what you did was right, but that don't mean you were all the way wrong."

Victoria stared in amazement. "I came here under false pretenses. I took advantage of you, and let you think I was someone I'm not."

"Did you ever actually say you were your father? No. Did you come here to do research? Yes. Did you pay us? Hell yes. So, what's false about those pretenses, girl?"

"I lied!"

The older woman narrowed her eyes and jutted out her chin. "You stretched things a bit, I'll give you that, but from where I'm standing everything you've done has helped, not hurt."

Victoria opened her mouth to argue, but Ruby waggled her bony finger and stopped her.

"Sometimes a woman's got to be creative to make her way in this world. The ends don't always justify the means, but if you hadn't come along when you did, Dolphin Land would probably be sold by now and my gang gone, God knows where, to other facilities. So, Miss Dr. Victoria Sheffield, if you need to feel guilty, buy yourself sackcloth and scoop some ashes out of the barbecue grill. Beat yourself up a little, and then get over it. You hear?"

Stunned, Victoria managed a shaky, speechless nod.

"Good. Now that we know the problem, we've got to figure out how to fix it," Ruby continued.

"I've tried," Victoria answered, miserably. "I thought about it all morning and still came up with nothing."

"Then we'll all just have to think some more because nobody here's a quitter. I ain't giving up and neither are you."

"What about Jack?"

"That nephew of mine has a powerful mad on right now, but he'll calm down. Then, like as not, he'll brood for a while. Nobody could match that boy for brooding when he was younger, but he'll get over that too. Especially when we work out a plan. Jack's big on planning."

"*If* we work one out, you mean."

"*When!* Now go on off by yourself again for a bit. You've got solving to do, and you're better off doing it where you won't run into him."

It wouldn't matter if she went off the grounds or off the end of the world. She'd never lose the memory of the cold anger in Jack's eyes that had teased her earlier, and then heated with desire time and again in the last twenty-four hours.

She blew out a breath, reaching deep inside for what remained of her guts. Her hope for the Delphinid Prize lay crushed at her feet, but that didn't hurt nearly as much as she expected. Far greater pain came in knowing that Ruby's dreams were again in jeopardy.

Her own future be damned! She owed it to Ruby, Jack, and the dolphins to make things right before she left. She picked up her backpack and headed toward the parking lot. For every problem, there was a sane and reasonable solution. Her heart might be breaking into as many pieces as her dreams, but somehow her mind would bail her out. Any other result was unacceptable. In the meantime, she'd give Jack a wide berth and do her thinking back at Pirate's Cove before returning with a new, workable strategy.

One that would restore the damage she'd done.

One that might melt the twin ice caps in his eyes.

* * *

After locking the gate behind her, she could barely drag her feet across the gravel driveway. Despite Ruby's reassurances, she deserved every bad thing Jack had thrown at her. She'd arrived at Dolphin Land with a head full of dreams, a healthy fund of cash, and the confidence that here she'd make her mark.

Oh yeah, I made a mark all right. I came, I saw, I ruined everything.

Even Kel's research thievery hadn't knocked her down this low. Her own father, on his most disapproving day, couldn't make her feel any worse. *Summa cum laude screwup.*

"Okay, fine. I didn't cover all the contingencies," she muttered, as she crossed the parking lot. "Now come up with an idea to fix the problem."

May as well wish for a shower of gold to rain from the sky. She looked upward into the endless blue. Barring that phenomenon, she'd settle for a lightning bolt of inspiration, a Divine messenger or—

"Excuse me, miss?"

The timing was too perfect, as if the universe had a cosmic funny bone and her wishful thinking tickled it.

She whipped around and saw a tall, skinny man marching across the weedy gravel, followed by a gaggle of high school-aged kids.

"I say, miss, we'd given up hope that someone would come to let us in."

"Let you in?"

Judging from the man's crisp British accent and everyone's whiter-than-pale skin, none of them were native Floridians. The man clutched a dog-eared, faded guidebook, and each younger person carried a small notebook.

"I don't understand. Who are you and why are you here?"

"Professor Jeremy Brumfield, miss, and these are my students. We're on holiday from Westminster Academy in Essex, Great Britain."

"I gathered you're on vacation, but why are you *here* specifically?" She waved her hand, indicating the facility.

"To see dolphins, lady," piped up one of the students.

"Quite right," added the professor. "This is Dolphin Land, is it not?"

"Well, yes, but we're not open."

"Oh, bother. We've come too late in the afternoon, then. I was afraid of that when we hit traffic after the turnpike."

A chorus of groans broke out among the students, but their teacher waved them silent.

"Not to worry, people, we'll go on to Key West as planned and return tomorrow." He turned back to Victoria. "Very well then, see you in the morning. Come along now, class, back to the van."

"Professor, wait. You don't understand. The facility isn't open to the public."

His patient look suggested she had the IQ of a dugong. "I can see you're closed for the evening. We'll simply rearrange our schedule and do our observations tomorrow."

The man was a steamroller in madras shorts and polo shirt.

"Observations?"

"Why yes. We're using our holiday as a field trip to observe marine mammals in various facilities. You're the last stop on our excursion."

"The orcas in Orlando were brilliant!" exclaimed a petite girl with long, cinnamon-colored curls.

"The manatees are my favorites," added a gangly boy, his Adam's apple bobbing excitedly.

The others chimed in until a dozen voices debated their preferences at the same time.

"Excuse me, Professor? Class?"

Victoria tried to get their attention, but they talked right over her. She'd need a traffic cop to direct this conversation. Too bad she didn't carry a training whistle like Ruby, but when in doubt, improvise.

Sticking two fingers in her mouth, she blew a piercing whistle. "All right. Everybody, hold it!"

As one, the visitors gaped at her as if she were a lunatic.

Professor Brumfield's wire-haired eyebrows met in the middle of his forehead when he frowned. "Is there a problem?"

"Yes! No! Well, I'm not sure."

Ahh, the polished response of a Phi Beta Kappa. Victoria forced in a steady breath. "What I'm trying to say is that Dolphin Land is not open to the public *anymore*. Not at this time anyway, although that will change. But for right now . . ."

The audience reaction ranged from surprise to annoyance to utter dismay. She could relate.

"Well, I must say, this news comes as a bit of a disappointment, eh?"

The professor thumbed through his guidebook, opening it wider at certain pages to show her a number of marine mammal care facilities and parks throughout Florida: Seven Seas Park in Orlando; Jacksonville Aquarium; and Manatee Refuge Park in Crystal River.

"We've been making a trip of it, as you can see, and expected Dolphin Land to put the proper cap on our tour."

"But, sir, this book must be at least five years old."

"Of course it is, my dear. I don't bring a class across the big pond every year, but I remember very well the excellent experience I had right here. The proprietors were such good folk, perfectly willing to spend extra time talking to us when we were last here." He looked around, obviously hoping to spot those good folk.

"Well, I'm terribly sorry, but the facility is closed to the public because of—"

Me. Victoria couldn't bring herself to finish the sentence. The man obviously had positive memories of his earlier visit, and to tell him that financial problems had forced Dolphin Land's demise seemed a disservice to Ruby and her late husband—the people this professor remembered so fondly.

"Yes, miss? The facility is closed because . . ."

She owed him some sort of explanation.

"Because they . . . were chosen for a private research project."

It wasn't a bald-faced lie. The truth twisted in there somewhere.

"Private research project, you say?"

Professor Brumfield didn't sound all that upset. She nodded, spreading her hands in a "there-you-have it" gesture.

"Well I say–that's brilliant!" Far from being disappointed, the man beamed. "Miss, my class would be quite keen to observe this research. It is right in keeping with our trip, you see. Now, to whom should I speak to arrange a meeting? Perhaps a short presentation of the project's objectives and a demonstration of data-collection methods?"

"Sir, I'm afraid you aren't listening." Victoria had to put her foot down, even if she tromped on his sandal-clad toes. "We can't welcome visitors at this time. So—"

"So what?" sneered one of the students. "How hard can it be? We pay our admission. You open the gates and show us your work with the animals."

Rude brat! Why couldn't they all just get it? "Look, I know you're disappointed, but we simply are not in the position to—"

The sentence stuck in her mouth. What had the kid said about an admission fee?

Victoria checked out the faces of the group. Some disappointed, some sullen, and yet some still regarded her with hopeful anticipation. Ideas started spinning in her head like a weather vane in high wind. As miracles went, this wasn't quite a shower of gold, but maybe, just maybe, it was something she could make work.

Despite the dryness in her throat, she plastered a bright smile on her face and addressed the professor. "What I meant to say, of course, is that we simply aren't prepared to make a presentation to your group as early as tomorrow. We do, after all, have our research protocols set for the day and shouldn't deviate."

Brumfield nodded earnestly, buying every word. Encouraged, she continued.

"We weren't expecting you, but if you can rearrange your itinerary a bit more, we can accommodate your group the day after tomorrow. Does this work for you, Professor?"

He thumbed through a small travel journal. "Well, I suppose we might be able to move our snorkel excursion up a day. So, yes, miss. That will suit us quite well. What time should we arrive?"

"Let's say 2:00 p.m., shall we? Plan on being here for several hours." That didn't leave much time to accomplish the plans whirling in her head, but she'd get it done even if she had to work straight through. If the idea paid off, she'd catch up on her sleep later.

"For whom should we ask when we arrive, miss?" the professor questioned, reminding Victoria that she hadn't introduced herself.

In for a penny, in for a pound, she decided. "It's Doctor, actually. Dr. Victoria Sheffield, the project's principal investigator." She extended her hand to be pumped enthusiastically.

"Sheffield, you say? Well then you must be related to Dr. Victor Sheffield. My classes and I review his papers on echolocation development in *Tursiops Truncatas* every term. Oh my, this certainly *is* brilliant."

Finally releasing her hand, he turned to the class. "All right now, people, we're off to Key West and will return here on Thursday. Good day to you, Doctor."

As he herded the group toward their van, she heard him explaining the details on her father's echolocation study and the excited chatter of his students. They'd certainly been an easy sell.

Visions of PowerPoint presentations and audio samplings danced in her head. A ton of work lay ahead if she was going to pull this off, and she knew that once she explained it to her, Ruby would help in any way possible.

Before they could start, however, she faced an even greater obstacle.

First, she had to convince Jack.

Chapter Fifteen

Victoria snugged the dinghy's bowline to an aft cleat on Jack's sailboat. Excitement and nerves congealed into a solid mass in her stomach. She didn't see him right off and took advantage of his absence, swinging her legs over the side and climbing on deck.

If he wanted her off his boat, he'd have to throw her overboard.

The man had ears like a cat, so why wasn't he waiting, ready to shred her with a double-blast of sarcasm? He wasn't anywhere on deck, that was sure.

A quick glance showed her a tidy ship. Weathered teak, rubbed smooth. Sails furled. Lines coiled in tight circles. Chrome rails polished mirror-bright. Not a crushed beer can or empty pizza box in sight.

No Jack either, although he must have heard her arrive. He must be down below. Ignoring her.

This didn't fit his behavior pattern. Invade the territory of a classic alpha male, and he'd erupt from the lair snarling, with claws swiping, not loll around in a passive-aggressive snit. Unless she'd pushed him so far over the edge of anger that he didn't trust his own reaction. "Powerful mad" might have been an optimistic assessment.

Her knees wobbled, but she blamed it on an unexpected sway of the boat. She refused to acknowledge the clench in her stomach as real fear.

Well, darned if she'd let him get away with ignoring her. If he wanted to yell, toss more accusations at her, fine. He could rant non-stop for the rest of the day and all the night if, at the end, he gave her new plan a chance. All in all, she'd rather row the dinghy into a waterspout than face a fully enraged Jack, but she had to try. She owed it to them.

No more stalling. The sooner they had this out, the sooner she could get to work.

Her stomach jostling like a buoy in high seas, she stepped down into the well and rapped on the cabin door. "Jack?"

No answer.

Knocking more loudly, she called again, her voice firm and calm. "I know you're angry, but we need to talk. Come out, okay?"

Please, she nearly added, but caught herself. Now was no time to beg. First she'd lay out her idea and explain the details, drawing on all the cool, practical logic she could muster.

If that didn't work, then she'd beg.

First he had to get over his stubbornness and open the door.

"You have to hear me out." Desperation surged through her system. She drew back her foot, ready to kick the bottom panel. "Open this door and talk to me or—"

"What?"

The single icy word came from above. Jack loomed over her from atop the cabin. Water ran down his body, and his dark hair was plastered against his head. One look at his face confirmed that, if he'd taken a swim to work off his anger, he'd wasted the effort.

Not a promising start, but she couldn't afford to back down. She stepped up on the bench and climbed back onto the deck.

"It's a good thing you finally answered me, or I might have gotten worried and done something drastic, like break down the door."

His snort indicated what he thought of her bravado.

"I was scrubbing the hull." He jumped down to the deck. "If you came to say goodbye, save your breath."

Victoria crossed her arms, as much to keep them from trembling as to indicate that she wasn't budging until she was darned good and ready. "We need to talk. I have an idea for—"

"For what? Saving my aunt and her dolphins? Oh yeah, I'm in a real hurry to hear this, seeing that the last plan worked out so well."

She resisted flinching. "Whether you want to or not, you still have to hear me out. For Ruby's sake."

Anger darkened his face. "You dare to bring up Ruby's sake? Since when did you consider what's best for her? If it hadn't been for you, I'd have her set up for life." He spit the words like venom. "I had the deal almost in place until you got in touch with your big-ass scheme and your non-existent research grant."

His big hands clenched into fists, as if fighting the urge to shake her head loose from her neck. "You drove in here with your fancy equipment and made her think you could save this place. Now, when we were this close . . ." He held up two fingers an inch apart. "This close to making it work, you trashed our best shot."

The bitterness stung, leaving welts of hurt on her heart. Her breath shook in her chest, but she spoke calmly.

"I can make it work again. I found a way and we can put it into action as soon as the day after tomorrow."

"No."

"But, Jack, I—"

"I said no."

"But . . ."

"I meant it. I had a chance to save Dolphin Land for Ruby. You blew it. It'll take a miracle to resurrect the deal, and my bargaining power is gone. We'll have to crawl to the developers, and their offer will be thousands lower. Now get off my boat and off the property."

The last bloom of hope shriveled. He wouldn't even listen. The guilt she'd felt before didn't come close to this choking, bitter weight in her chest. She'd failed.

Again.

Deflated, she turned to go. Hands on the rail, she swung a foot up to boost herself over and into the dinghy, but a loud splash and piercing whistle caught her attention.

She looked across the water to the lagoons of Dolphin Land. Three graceful dolphins leapt high out of the water in tight synchrony. The whistle blew again and she saw Ruby on the floating dock, cheering the dolphins' dives before handing out fish from their buckets.

Ruby threw her fist in the air, signaling a different behavior, and the dolphins executed a series of perfect back dives.

Even from a distance, she could picture the brilliant smile on Ruby's face. There, on the dock, an elderly woman experienced all the joy of living a dream, of owning a life she loved. In that moment, her resolve flooded back.

She whipped around. "This doesn't have to be the end. I can give Dolphin Land another shot. The plan is good."

His stern face would have deterred her if saving the facility didn't mean more than anything else that had ever mattered.

"You have to let me try."

"Like hell I do," he snarled. "I gave you an order, now I'm giving you a choice. Either climb on that dinghy and row away, or I'll dump your ass on it and cut the line myself. When I get back to Dolphin

Land, whatever equipment isn't loaded in your truck gets pitched into the Gulf. One way or another, you're leaving."

"That's not your call."

"What the fu—it sure as hell is!"

For the life of her, Victoria didn't know where she got the strength to stand up to the wave of male anger pouring off him, but she did.

"No it isn't. You're not the final word on this matter, or on Dolphin Land. Ruby is, and she's already given me the go ahead." She snorted. "I told her I wanted to talk to you first and get your agreement, too, so all of us could work on it as a team, just like before. My mistake."

Out from under the avalanche of pain and hurt climbed a new realization. She cared about Jack, but she didn't need his approval. Come to think of it, she didn't need any man in order to succeed. Not her ex-fiancé, not her father, not the man standing three feet in front of her, with a glare that struck like a lightning bolt.

On the heels of the epiphany came a whip crack of power. Ohh, it felt strong, a rush of pure flame spurring her on as she laid it on the line. "I wanted your help because I know how important it is for you to see Dolphin Land prosper for your aunt. I wanted your help, but you know what? I don't need it. You can throw me overboard, out of your bed, and out of your life, but you can't toss me off the property. If Ruby wants me to stick around, that's what I'll do."

Moving forward, she jabbed a finger onto his broad chest. "If you don't want to be a part of it, don't want to help, fine. I'm going to make this work with or without you. If you force the issue and make her choose, of course she'll choose you—you're her flesh and blood—but you better think hard about what you'll be making her give up. While you're thinking, do us both a favor and stay the hell out of my way."

Swaggering like a swashbuckler in a classic movie, she vaulted into the dinghy. A twist of her wrist freed the line. She shoved off from the sailboat, set the oars in the locks, and settled into a steady rowing rhythm.

She didn't bother checking to see if Jack continued to glare. She had far more important things to do.

* * *

"Looking good, Victoria. That whistle match game in the middle is a real nice touch."

"I don't know that I'd use it in an all-adult presentation, Ruby, but I think it will work with younger students."

Ignoring the gritty burn of tiredness in her eyes, she reviewed her notes. "I still need to tighten the section on cooperative feeding behaviors in wild dolphins, and I'm a little concerned that I get too technical in other areas. The quickest way to lose students' interest is to talk over their heads."

She gulped down her umpteenth cup of coffee, before picking up the clipboard. Her pen raced over her printout, marking sections, and scrawling notes in the margins. "It will take awhile, but I still have time to make those adjustments on the presentation and burn a new CD. You know, I think I should add the Raymond study to the handouts. The office supply store opens early enough for me to make copies tomorrow."

Ruby clamped her hand on the pen. "Darlin', stop a minute."

"What?"

"Gimme that." She wrestled pen, papers, and clipboard out of Victoria's grasp. "You've worked non-stop on this presentation. Take a break and breathe, will you?"

She started to protest, but clapped her mouth shut at the first, fierce, blue glare.

"You've got this thing as darned near perfect as it's gonna get. It's brilliant, that's what. If an old conch like me can understand the research, those Brit kids are for sure gonna get it. You made it interesting as all hell and, best of all, fun!"

"Oh, I hope so. That's the mood I want. Research is fascinating, but so many presentations are loaded with jargon and dry data that they don't appeal to a mass audience."

"You bring it alive. When that group shows up tomorrow, you'll blow them away and make 'em beg for more."

"I want them to learn, but I also want them to feel they got their money's worth."

"Heck, at thirty bucks a head, they're getting a bargain. I'm damn sure certain top scientists get bigger speaker fees than you're charging."

In the past, her father commanded fees in the thousands, not hundreds, when he addressed adoring masses at the world's most prestigious universities.

"Yes, that's usually true, but this group is only listening to me, not a top scientist."

"Says who?"

"I haven't published a single major study on my own, and in research if you don't publish, you don't count."

She twisted her fingers together. "I still can't believe the professor agreed to this price when he talked to you about the final arrangements. I don't know how you convinced him."

"That was easy. I told him the truth. He and his class are getting off light. We could have asked twice this amount and gotten it."

She shook her head at Ruby's assurances. "I'm not my father."

"Thank God for that." The fierce glare returned to Ruby's eyes.

"Huh?"

"Darlin', now that I've worked with and gotten to know you, I realize that we'd never have made it this far if anybody else but you had driven up to Dolphin Land." A crack of laughter broke out. "Hell, someone like your father never would have approached us, and if he had, he'd have taken one look, turned right around, and headed back home.

"But you. You gave us more credit than anyone else has in a real long time. So, don't you think it's time you gave yourself some credit too?"

Emotion ballooned in her chest as the older woman's words sank into her soul. "You don't understand the way it works, Ruby. Unless I publish a study on my own, I'll always be second-rate as a scientist."

"Don't you dare say that about yourself! Maybe that's what you grew up believing, and you haven't had the opportunity to prove yourself before, but you're doing it now."

"That was before the bottom dropped out of my trust fund."

"Did you let that stop you? Hell no. Instead, you went right out and came up with another solution. You are absolutely brilliant, girl. How come you can't see that for yourself?"

"You know what my father's accomplished in his life."

"I've seen what he hasn't accomplished too. You know, the big man might be a top scientist, but he sucks at being a dad."

"Oh my God!" The blunt words made Victoria laugh. "Nobody's ever said that before."

"Then it's long overdue."

Tears welled up, and she wrapped her arms around Ruby in a tight hug. "Thank you so much," she whispered. "You're the first person who has ever really believed in me."

Ruby harrumphed, but returned the hug.

"I mean it. You have every reason to hate me, but instead, you're here in my corner giving me another chance and telling me that it's going to be successful. Nobody I've loved has ever done that for me before. Not my father, not my ex, not . . . anybody else."

Realizing what she was about to reveal, she tried to cover, but it was too late.

"Not Jack? That's what you meant, right? Well hot damn and Hallelujah!" Ruby smacked her hands together and pumped her arms like a football fan.

Victoria gaped. "How is this a good thing? Not only did he refuse to help with the presentation, but he was out there disconnecting my hydrophones until you threatened to dump a bucket of capelin on his head."

"He'll come around about the project, just you wait and see," Ruby chortled. "But that's not the important thing."

"It isn't?"

"Hell no! The important thing is you love him."

Tears turned bitter in her throat. "For all the good it does me. I've ruined any chance I had with him. He hates me."

"Don't even think that for a second. He's still angry, but I know he'll get over it. Don't you worry."

"But, but . . ."

"Quit sounding like a motorboat. I know my nephew, and you're the best thing that could have happened to him in a hundred years."

Ruby gathered papers into a neat pile. "He's a stubborn one, I'll give you that. And as long as we're being honest, you blindsiding him stung his pride."

"Blindsiding him?"

"Yep, sure. Think about it. He had his plans all set, how he was going to be the big hero and save Dolphin Land for me, bless his heart. Then you came on the scene and knocked him flat." She chuckled. "He'll find his feet again, and when he does, oh darlin', you just better watch out."

"That's what I'm afraid of," Victoria muttered. Standing, she closed out her computer and pressed the buttons to shut it down. So far, Jack's avoidance was a plus if it kept him from interfering. Over the last day, when they crossed paths by accident, she'd felt his glare stab her like a stingray barb.

Sliding the laptop into her backpack, she hoisted the load onto her shoulder and shoved him out of her thoughts.

"Ruby, the best I can hope for is that the presentation will be a success and we spread the word to encourage more customers. Even starting on a smaller scale, we can attract enough visitors to keep the gang in fish. If we accomplish that much, maybe Jack will tolerate my presence long enough for me to finish the research."

Although working day after day with her heart broken by his disdain would be nearly unbearable. She shoved away the hurt and focused on the main goal.

"At least I'll know I didn't destroy your dreams."

Ruby placed wizened hands on her shoulders. "You listen to me. You didn't destroy anything. You've already helped us get in a whole lot better shape than we were before you came. Don't look so godawful beaten down, you hear?"

She turned her around and gave her a gentle push toward the door. "You're worn out from creating the seminar, that's why you're talking so blue. Go on home, get some dinner, and go to bed early. You've got to shine tomorrow, Dr. Victoria Sheffield. We're counting on you."

* * *

Damned if she didn't pull it off. Jack slouched against the fish house, watching the class absorb Victoria's every word. Somehow she'd boiled down complex data and extracted the info that made her study fascinating, and then turned it into something entertaining and educational. When she amplified the dolphins' whistles coming from the lagoon, the rapt faces looked like they were listening to the hottest pop star.

He glanced around. The women had worked like mad sprucing up the place until it looked as neat as a military barracks, but more welcoming. Spruced themselves up too. They'd found someone to embroider the name Dolphin Land over a leaping dolphin on blinding white polo shirts. Ruby and old Willy wore them with neat khaki shorts. The two stood as straight as their aging bones allowed, playing the role of official staff of the newly reopened facility, home to what he'd heard Ruby proclaim was,"the cuttingest-edge cetacean research around."

Someone dared to buy him a matching polo shirt, one that, at first, he flatly refused to wear. Then his aunt put her foot down, nearly on his toes, declaring it was now the required uniform of all Dolphin Land staff. He started to argue that he was family, not staff, but the look in her eyes threatened him with consequences at least as dire as a bucket of half-thawed herring dumped on his head.

He'd been tempted to stay away. This crackpot idea would flop soon enough, and he was too big a man to rub Victoria's nose in her failure just because she'd broken his trust.

No way you could trust a woman who barged into your life pretending she was one thing, only to have her turn out to be someone altogether different. No wonder he'd been fooled. She'd thrown him off with her quirky combo of beauty, brains, and insecurity.

So what if his Y chromosome straightened to attention when she came into range. Regardless of his aunt's greeting-card romantic streak, every other part of his body remained intact. Granted, trust was a big enough casualty, but it could've been a hell of a lot worse. The ache that sneaked up on him now and again, stemmed from suppressed anger.

Full of righteous indignation, he'd been ready to boycott the evening, but he owed it to his aunt to drop by for a few minutes, just in case she needed him. He didn't intend to stay long, but then Victoria began her computer presentation. He figured he might as well stick around, if for no other reason than to prop up Ruby when she realized this crazy idea of a research seminar series for money wouldn't fly.

Somewhere between the computer presentation and the dockside live demo, that crazy idea sprouted wings. Now he couldn't decide if he was happy or horrified. He could see the outrageous vision working in his head. The snowbird visitors, not to mention local residents, always looked for something new and interesting. For whatever reason, half the world seemed fascinated by dolphins. Why not learn from an expert?

Victoria provided the hook that compensated for their lack of size. They might not have the Mouse in their house, but they had their own resident scientist. One who, judging by the professor and students hanging on every word, made her topics come alive in full Technicolor.

Look at his aunt. Neat as a soldier in her "uni," she was fit to bursting with pride. Her weathered face glowed as if she'd won the lottery. That was the whole damned point, wasn't it? Nothing made

Ruby as happy as her dolphins; nothing else ever would. Certainly not a million-dollar deal for the land. If it meant keeping the gang, she'd rather live out her life in a tin can trailer than in the most exclusive beachfront condo.

With fleeting regret, Jack bid adios to his development dream. Almost on cue, the audience burst into applause, signaling the end of Victoria's presentation. She barely had time to draw a breath before the kids attacked her with still more questions.

She never turned a hair. Every question got an answer phrased simply enough that one didn't have to be in Mensa to understand. He stifled a snort. Hell, she even stirred his interest.

And this time he wasn't thinking with his little head.

Okay, not entirely true.

At some point he'd gotten over being angry. Now, he was back to wanting her with every breath, but he couldn't claim it was only lust. Without his anger buffer, other emotions ran wild.

One in particular burned like a jalapeno pepper, chased down by bad tequila. Raw, hot, and gut-sickening. He hated even acknowledging its existence. It had no place in his life. Not now, not ever, but he couldn't defeat it with denial or conquer it with lust. So, like he'd done with every other challenge in his life, he named it and claimed it.

Fear.

A chill skittered down his spine. He glared at the air conditioner, assigning blame where it belonged. The day hadn't come where fear froze him in his tracks. He'd fix that unit first thing in the morning, but for now, he needed a good wave of warm air. Quietly, he levered off the wall and slipped out the door. Gravel crunched under his feet as he walked away from the building. Veering away from the benches arranged like an outdoor classroom, he headed toward the lagoon.

The distance took him far enough for his peace of mind, but kept him handy in case Ruby needed him. Not that she would. She and Victoria had everything under control.

And tomorrow? There were still fences to repair, boardwalks to replace, and coats of paint to be slapped on buildings. With Dolphin Land's restoration back on track, he could name a dozen different projects that required his attention and muscle.

He looked out over the lagoon. Ashley glided on his side, chasing minnows. The tiny fish skipped out of the water, evading his snapping jaws. Melanie hovered in the corner, dozing. The other four circled the lagoon, swimming in perfect synchrony. If he were given to projecting human emotions on a non-human species, he'd say the dolphins looked content.

What about him?

Geezus! Jack hadn't asked himself that question since his parents died when he was an eleven-year-old boy, wondering where he would live and with whom. From the day Aunt Ruby and Uncle Gus arrived to bring him to Dolphin Land, he hadn't needed to ask. He'd known.

Sure, he didn't decide as a child to enter the DEA, but at least he'd known that, whatever he chose, he had a future. With his head and his body, he'd built a career that made him proud.

That career, as he knew it, was gone. Even he could accept the truth when it whopped him upside the head. No more fieldwork, no midnight deals in dark jungles where you survived by your wits, your quickness, and your willingness to use whatever weapons you had at hand. At best, he could expect a desk job with the agency. Give him a month of nothing but phone contact, paperwork, and department meetings, and he'd strangle someone with the necktie they'd force him to wear. He was no more cut out to work cases from inside a government building than old Willy was to work security for the President.

So, here he stood. Twenty-five years later, asking the same question he had as a child. Talk about something sucking big time. He'd better come up with an answer fast. Damn it all, he was too old and too tough for a crisis of confidence. The only way to meet the situation was a hundred percent head-on.

Behind him, the door swung open, spilling a gaggle of chattering students into the twilight. He heard the excited chorus of good byes and Willy offering to show them off the property to their van. Knowing Ruby, she'd hurry out before all light faded to "tell" the gang that the plan had worked and they were safe. A bigger man would stay to apologize to Victoria for the way he'd treated her and the things he'd said. A really big man would congratulate her on her success. He added both those things to his "to-do" list, scheduling them for tomorrow.

Tonight, there was only room for one at his pity party. He needed time to figure out his future. A future in which, as long as he was being honest, he hoped she would play a major part. First thing tomorrow, he'd grovel. If he did it right, he'd only have a short bridge to cross to heal the rift he'd stubbornly created.

Defeat was not an option. He would find a new, meaningful career. He would make things right with the woman who held his heart in her very capable hands, even if she didn't know it yet.

His acute hearing judged that the British guests were gone and someone was heading toward the lagoon. With the quiet step that had saved him in a number of tight spots, he melted away into the growing darkness.

Chapter Sixteen

The sun had hardly risen high enough to provide light for a meter reading on the video camera, when Victoria pressed the record button and slipped on her headphones. Pumped from the successful presentation the night before, she'd slept fitfully, waking up every hour or so with new ideas. Dawn had just poked a pink finger over the horizon, when she'd bounded out of bed, eager to resume data collection for her project. After an hour of video and sound recording, followed by a couple of hours of analysis, she and Ruby had a strategy session scheduled.

Now that they knew the idea worked, they needed to keep things rolling. Before the day was out, she planned to call home and ask her father's caregiver to package and send her copies of previous papers and the support materials. There were a number of her father's lectures from which she could glean great information. Since she'd worked on those projects and helped design his presentations, she was qualified to explain their methods and findings. She jotted a quick note in the margin of her data journal. Her doctoral thesis was also neatly boxed and stored in the attic. Rosa could unearth and send that mega-document too.

Ruby was, in her words, "Hauling butt into town to the office supply store as soon as it opens to make up some brochures and flyers ASA humanly P!" After that, she and Willy planned to take the flyers to every merchant in town and leave a stack at the Visitors Center.

"Victoria, darlin', by the time I'm through, everybody in town's gonna know that Dolphin Land is back. Maybe not like they're used to, but in its own way even better!"

A quick glance confirmed that all her equipment was functioning. Victoria sat cross-legged on the dock and jotted down more notes. While her older compatriots plastered the town with flyers, she would access the power of the Internet. Give her a couple of hours, and an announcement promoting the new experiential education programs would be in the computers of every school system, community college, and university in a three-hundred-mile radius.

A few hours more and that same announcement would spread across the country. By the following day, she'd have it buzzing around the world. The Sheffield name meant something in the halls of academia. It was her name, too, and she'd make the most of it. Finally.

Once they'd hosted more groups and worked out a few kinks in the overall program, they could call in the media and see what sort of groundswell that would build. As soon as she could squeeze in the time, she would use a template-ready design shell and build the skeleton of a workable web site.

The sheer number of plans swirling in her head almost made her dizzy, but she welcomed the sensation. Anything to keep her brain occupied. Anything to keep from thinking about Jack.

She'd seen him last night, of course. Although he'd kept out of sight ever since their war of words on his boat, she should have guessed he'd show up for the presentation—to gloat if it failed. When he slipped in the door and took up wall space at the back of the room, she nearly lost her place. Sheer determination kept her on point. No way would she give him the satisfaction of seeing the extent of the hurt ripping her apart.

He'd left early, skulking away in defeat, she told herself. Fine. Let him hide on his boat and sulk. She and Ruby still had a lot to accomplish, and if he wasn't willing to do his share, then staying out of their way was the next best thing. It wouldn't do her heart any good to have him in her face all the time.

Indifference she could handle. She'd learned from a master and had the lesson driven home by his apprentice. If she needed to, she could shove the hurt into a box and lock it away, but it would certainly be easier if she didn't have to look at its main source all day long. The longer Jack stayed away, the better, even though each day broke off another piece of her heart.

The dock behind her dipped unexpectedly, and she wobbled like a kid's toy. Reaching back to steady her balance, she grabbed Jack's leg instead. She jerked back her hand like his skin was draped in fire coral. Surprised, she spit out angry words. "What the hell are you doing? Trying to sink me?"

His lips moved, but she heard nothing.

"Damn it." Ripping off the headset, she glared. "What did you say?"

"I'm sorry I startled you. I was trying not to attract or disturb the dolphins. That's the protocol when you record at this time of day, isn't it?"

She nodded without answering. Prepared for cold-shoulder silence, she hated that he'd caught her off guard. Why had he chosen this hour to appear? Just once, couldn't he behave according to expectations?

Her stomach muscles tensed, and a horrifying bubble of unvoiced feelings swelled in her throat. Suddenly furious, she struggled to conceal her emotions. There were a hundred things she wanted to say to him, but that didn't mean he got to pick the time and place.

Figuratively speaking, there was only room for one of them on this dock. She switched off the video camera and began disconnecting the audio cables.

He moved quickly, stopping her with a hand on her arm before she could collapse the tripod. "You don't have to pack up because I'm here."

"I won't try to work and fight with you at the same time. If you want to argue again, you should have waited." She yanked her arm from his grip. "Pistols at dawn are passé."

She stowed the audio equipment in its carrying bag, hoisted the camera tripod over her shoulder, and swung around, but the low tide foiled her grand exit. There was a three-and-a-half foot distance between the boardwalk and the floating dock—too far for her to step up, especially loaded down with the gear.

Biting back a snarl, she laid the tripod on the boardwalk and prepared to boost herself up, but Jack beat her to it. He vaulted to the boardwalk and reached down a hand. "Here."

Behemoth show-off. Delivering a look that could topple a statue, she clambered off the dock under her own power. "I don't need your assistance."

He beat her to the tripod. Hoisting it up one-handed, he turned and strode off the boardwalk.

She kept on his heels. "I said I can handle it. Give me back my equipment."

The annoying man continued down the causeway as if what she said, what she wanted, didn't matter. To his way of thinking, it probably didn't. What nerve!

Cold realization rimed her heart. The last words they'd exchanged on his boat included a blunt threat to jettison her equipment like useless ballast. Having seen the presentation, he couldn't possibly carry out that threat. Could he? She sped up, but even taking two steps to his one, she lagged behind.

"Jack, you can't do this to m—to my—equipment. Be reasonable."

He kept walking, damn him. Still nursing his "powerful mad," huh? Well, if he thought she'd cave and let him intimidate her into leaving, he was about to learn differently. She'd had enough male intimidation and disapproval in her life to sink a ship. No more.

The snarl curling her lip felt good, as she growled a threat through clenched teeth. "Return my camera to me this minute. I swear to heaven if you throw it into the bay, I'll . . ."

He tossed a look over his shoulder. "You'll what?"

"Shoot you with a spear gun!"

A raised eyebrow mocked her warning.

"I'll gaff you like a bloated whale carcass."

A bark of hoarse laughter answered her, but at least he slowed down a little.

Pressing the minute advantage, she pulled out the big ammunition. "If you so much as put a micro-scratch on the waterproof housing of that equipment, I will tell Ruby."

It worked. He stopped walking and set the tripod upright, leaning on it with crossed arms. To her dismay, he chuckled from deep in his chest.

"That threat held more teeth when I was a kid."

"How fitting," she sneered, "since you're a classic case of arrested development."

"You're the one who decided to pack up your gear early. I just gave you a hand. Don't blame me because you're in a snit."

A snit? "How dare you! First you breathe fire and rain brimstone on me for messing up your precious plans. Then, you follow up that routine with a deep freeze. Now, you miraculously regain a scrap of civility and expect me to act like everything's fine?"

If she'd had a speargun handy, she might have been sorely tempted to nail him to the fence. "You've got a lot of nerve, Jack Benton."

"No argument here."

"Well that would certainly be a first. God knows the only thing you like better than fighting is—"

That blasted eyebrow rose again, challenging her to finish the sentence.

Her chest rose and fell several times while she struggled for control.

He had the gall to give her an encouraging look. "The only thing I like better than fighting is . . ."

Thinking fast, she substituted, "having things your way."

When he hesitated for the barest second, she pounced.

"That's really the crux of the matter. You didn't get your way, and it makes you mad." Warming to her theme, she advanced a step. "You had control of everything before I got here, and from the beginning you were against me doing my research. You only agreed to help me because you were suspicious and wanted to keep an eye on me. Oh, and because your aunt insisted. Am I right?"

Not giving him time to answer, she continued. "Of course I'm right. I'm a scientist. I know how to interpret behavior, particularly when it takes place right in front of me." She moved closer.

"That's what it comes down to. For once in your life, you didn't get your own way. I admit that I deserved your anger before, but now

I have things back on track. We can make good things happen here and everyone's happy. Except you, of course. So now, I have only one thing to say. Get. Over. It." She emphasized the point with a not-so-gentle smack to his rock-hard chest.

Not the wisest move, she realized when he grabbed her hand, but she didn't back down. She refused to pull away, opting to stand still, returning his narrowed-eye glare with the coolest look she could muster.

He growled. "I am happy."

"Ha!"

"I am!" The grip on her hand nearly fused her bones. He must have realized it because he let go and planted his hands on his hips. "No matter what you think, I didn't come down here this early in the morning to fight with you."

Posture stiff, stance belligerent, breathing hoarse. Any second now he'd paw the ground like a bull ready to charge. Classic signs of a male temper about to erupt. Instead of running for safety, she got in touch with her inner nerve and smiled coolly. "Could have fooled me."

"You're the one who got pissy and packed up."

"Excuse me if I couldn't get a clear recording over the sound of you breathing fire."

"I was being quiet."

"Like a chuffing whale!"

His darkly tanned face flushed to an interesting shade of maroon. If he clenched his jaw any more tightly, he'd crack teeth.

"For the last time, I did *not* show up here to give you a hard time."

"Yeah right," she snorted. "Then why?"

"Damn it, woman, I came to apologize!"

The roar could have lifted roofs all the way down in Key West.

Oh God, he was a sight. Eyes burning like blue flames. Voice thundering. Long hair hanging like coarse brown silk to his powerful shoulders.

A sane woman, faced with this potent show of anger, would have dissolved at his feet in a puddle of liquid fear. Anybody else would have run as the flight instinct for self-preservation kicked in. Apparently, she fit neither category, because she froze, fairly sure her jaw would drop open from amazement.

Shock inhibited an intelligent response. "Huh?"

"Don't make me repe . . ." His yard-wide chest heaved, but with obvious effort he forced his voice into a calmer tone. "I said that I came here . . . to . . . apol-o-gize."

If he'd rattled off a treatise on inter-species territorial conflict, she couldn't have been more surprised. A man making amends, yet alone going out of his way to do so, was a brand new experience. Could he blame her for being suspicious?

Then she thought—really thought—about it, and instinctively she knew that she could trust his words. In fact, she'd stake her chance at the Delphinid Prize on the fact that he meant them. After all, she had insight into his psyche that no other woman besides his aunt could claim—because no other woman loved him like she did.

Oh yes! With a joyful shout, Victoria leaped, clasping her hands around his neck and wrapping her legs around his waist.

"Well, why didn't you say so?"

"What the—"

She cut him off with her kiss, a thirsty press of her mouth to the sculpted lips that haunted her dreams. She sensed his initial shock, but he recovered quickly, shifting his hands to cup her butt and steady her in his arms.

She didn't need to hear "I'm sorry" in so many words, not when the apology was ripe in his kiss. Whatever had happened before, he was over it. They both were.

Everything he felt for her, everything he should have said, came through loud and clear. She savored the taste of him, the feel of his muscles bunching beneath her grip, and gloried in the mad rush of her blood heating her skin.

When she ran out of breath, she broke the kiss and smiled.

"Apology accepted."

He grinned. "You sure, sugar? I could apologize again, another two or three times, if you promise to kiss me like that again each time. Four or five times if you need to be convinced enough to take it back to your room."

"You are such a jerk," she laughed.

"Nice talk from a PhD."

"I could say a lot worse, but since you're so remorseful, I'll let you off the hook." She tilted her head back and laughed again, hanging onto his shoulders when he spun her around and carried her over to the bench.

"I'll count myself lucky. You had me a little worried with that speargun threat." He sat, cradling her on his lap. "Seriously, I have been a jerk lately, but, believe it or not, I'm glad you proved me wrong."

A tender kiss confirmed his words.

He looked into her eyes. "If it isn't too late, I'd like to start helping again."

She sat up. "Terrific! There's so much still to do. You told me before that you have computer experience. Can you man a scanner? I have presentations to convert from slides." At his nod, she continued. "With an extra body, we can speed up distribution of our flyers and brochures to schools. I could use your electronics experience to rig up a listening station. I thought it would be cool if students could hear some actual underwater whistles and echolocation live instead of on tape."

He appeared to be listening, but he was staring at her mouth, so just in case . . .

"Jack, how long will it take to build a fully functional outdoor theater?"

"What?" He nearly dropped her, but quickly grabbed her thigh, securing her on his lap.

"Just checking that you were paying attention." She smiled. "You know this will thrill Ruby to no end."

"Yeah, I know, but that's not why I'm doing it." His eyes searched hers again.

"I treated you like crap," he admitted bluntly. "Are you really happy that I'm jumping back in again?"

Touched by the question and the strange uncertainty dimming his brilliant eyes, she rested a palm against his cheek. "Of course I am." Should she tell him now that, no matter what, she loved him? Her inner defense system kicked in, blocking the words. The realization was too new to be revealed, especially when she had no evidence that he reciprocated.

Besides, they'd just taken a giant step forward on the road to healing their rift. For the time being, she couldn't handle another emotional upheaval. So, until the time was right, she'd cradle the knowledge in her heart and tend to it all on her own. For now, she just wanted to enjoy the moment.

Pursing her lips, she bussed him affectionately on the chin.

"I'm delighted you're back on the team. After all, we already bought you a shirt."

"Hey now. Don't press your luck." The chuckle rumbling in his chest belied the words.

"Who's pressing whose luck?" She gave him a look of mock sternness. "You're apologizing, remember? You're happy that the idea works and you want to help. We're in this together, Bubba, for the good of Dolphin Land."

"All right, all right," he groaned. "I'll risk looking like a preppy idiot and wear the darn polo shirt, if it'll make you happy."

Another victory. "Oh, I'll be ecstatic seeing you in your official Dolphin Land uniform." Pausing, she ran a finger up the center of his chest, enjoying the tensing of his muscles. "Almost as happy as it will make me to peel you out of it."

Chapter Seventeen

Jack closed his eyes, controlling through will alone his body's reaction to her touch. *Oh yes! He hadn't lost all ground.* She still wanted him, as a lover at least, but that was no longer enough. For the first time in his life, he wanted a hell of a lot more. Closing his hand around hers, he reluctantly moved it away from his chest and prepared to do some big time convincing.

"Darlin', hold that thought. I need you to hear me out first."

"You've already apologized and I accepted. What more is there to say? Unless . . . Oh, well, I never considered, I mean, I guess I shouldn't have assumed that this meant you'd also want to resume our . . ."

Even in the early light, he saw her eyes lose some of their sparkle, and he tightened his arms instinctively when she tried to squirm off his lap. "Just a minute. Don't get the wrong idea." Bending his head, he whispered an explicit list of the many things he wanted to resume, all of which necessitated both of them being naked. Her face turned a full flamingo pink.

"Okayyy. Point taken." She coughed and swallowed hard. "So, what's the problem?"

He settled her comfortably again in his lap, or as comfortable as he could be when the sweet butt of the woman he loved was pressing against already aroused flesh.

Where to begin? He cleared his throat.

"Victoria, when you showed up here, I admit I was pis—er, surprised, and I didn't like it one bit that Aunt Ruby picked your offer over the deal I was setting up. You were right that I wanted my own way, but that's only half of it."

She was listening with the keen intent she used in her research observations. It would have made him uncomfortable, but it mirrored the focus that showed on her face when he introduced her to something new in bed. *Don't go there, now, Bubba, or you won't get through the rest of what you need to say.*

"Anyway, it isn't that I wanted to have my way, it's that I wanted, no, if I'm going to be truthful, I *needed* to be the one who saved the day."

It wasn't hot yet, but droplets of sweat popped out on his forehead. He was walking perilously close to that other dreaded "F" word—*feelings.* Like, he was feeling vulnerable, as open to attack as if he'd left the protective cover of the jungle to run across an exposed clearing in the middle of a firefight. No wonder he wanted to crawl into a foxhole.

"Jesus. How do you women do this? Talk about your feelings all the time."

She laughed, but it was a good, encouraging laugh, not one that mocked his discomfort.

"Keep going, big guy. I know it's tough, but you can handle it."

Stalling wouldn't accomplish the mission. She cared for him, he knew that much, even if he didn't know to what extent. So like a paratrooper, he jumped, trusting that her feelings for him would be the

189

parachute that kept him from splatting on the ground.

"Okay. Here's the whole deal. Victoria, from the beginning, I let you keep thinking that I was no more than a fix-it guy, content to do a little work, some fooling around, and a whole lot of relaxing."

"So? What's wrong with that? Not everybody's meant for the corporate world. In fact, according to Ruby, not too many folks in the Keys are interested in that kind of routine. What's more, in case you've forgotten, without you this whole place would have caved around Ruby's ears. Over the last few weeks alone, you put in the most sweat and labor to have it looking this good. On top of all that, you almost had that deal in place when I showed up."

How quickly she jumped to defend him, even against himself. A Phi Beta Kappa genius applauding him for being a top-notch handyman.

"There's more. You're right. I'm not meant for big business, but carpentry and painting aren't my chosen careers either."

He paused, drawing in a deep breath and catching her gaze.

"I never told you, but until a couple months ago, I was an undercover field agent for the Drug Enforcement Agency."

"You're a federal agent?" Her eyes grew as big as helium balloons. "Oh my God, what did you do, save up all your vacation time to help out your aunt? That explains a lot. No wonder you were so annoyed when you'd gone to all the time and trouble for her sake!"

She so totally didn't get the whole picture that she hugged him instead of smacking him in the face for being a jackass.

"Roll back, sugar. I didn't sacrifice my vacation plans. I got injured when an operation went sour, and I came home to recuperate. I've been on medical leave trying to rehab myself back to the physical condition I need to be in to return to field assignment."

Half afraid to look at her when comprehension finally sank in, he rushed to finish.

"Truth is, I'm kidding myself. My leg won't return to that level. My DEA career is over unless I want to spend the rest of it sitting behind a desk, which I don't. I got all caught up in planning for Aunt Ruby's future because I don't have a clue what to do for mine.

"Then you arrived with your research project and gave her what she wanted most of all. A way to keep her dolphins and make Dolphin Land like it used to be, only better."

Regret swelled in his throat, flavored with the bitter sting of uselessness. He closed his eyes and fought against the sharpness. Any minute now, she'd make the connection that the whole time he was blasting her for false pretenses, he was hiding his true story.

"Jack?"

He steeled himself for the first hit.

"Yeah?"

"I am so sorry." She tentatively squeezed his shoulder.

"You got nothing to be sorry for, Victoria. Thanks to you, Aunt Ruby won't lose her dolphins or Dolphin Land."

The squeeze turned to a nudge.

"You're right. I'm not sorry that all this was successful, but I *am* sorry that you've been hurt and that, in the course of doing your duty, you're forced to give up work that obviously matters to you."

Instead of scorn, she offered him compassion. The sweetness of it dissolved the sting in his throat. He opened his eyes and started to thank her, but she placed a finger against his mouth.

"Let me finish. Given everything you're going through, I understand why you wanted to rescue things for Ruby. I'm sorry that my dream superseded your plan to save the day."

"Ah, hell, it was a pretty pathetic need to prove myself."

Her hair tumbled around her face when she shook her head. "No it wasn't. You love your aunt and wanted to be her hero."

"Yeah." He snorted. "Pretty sappy of me."

"No! Not sappy. It's sweet and loving and wonderful."

Terrific. Here he confessed why he'd acted like such an S.O.B. to her in the beginning, and she complimented him instead of knocking him flat with righteous anger. *Sweet and wonderful*, she said. He ought to be mortified, but knowing she thought of him that way felt too damn good. He hugged her tightly, soaking up her warmth and scent.

"You're letting me off the hook way too easy, you know," he whispered.

"Not completely." She laughed. "Now that I know how strongly motivated you are to make things right, I plan to take full advantage later."

"Oh really?"

"Really! I'm only half-kidding about that outdoor theater."

He raised an eyebrow, knowing now that she'd laugh at the mock intimidation.

"Okay, okay, actually, all we want is some sort of covered pavilion where we can at least put in a television, a VCR, and some benches. That way, if it rains, we can still conduct presentations outside and accommodate more people."

"I oughta be able to handle that much. I think I'm getting the knack of this tiki-hut technique."

"I'm not the least bit surprised." She paused, looking up at him, her eyes serious. "You know when you said you don't know what to do in the future?"

"Yeah."

"You left out something."

"Trust me, Victoria. I've been thinking about it for days and haven't left out a thing. I honestly don't have a plan."

"Yet. You don't have a plan yet."

She shifted in his lap, straddling him and putting her hands on his shoulders. Despite the fact that her position increased the ache in his shorts, he concentrated on her face and words, picking up the vibe that indicated she was a hundred percent serious.

"You don't have a plan yet, but that won't last forever. Give yourself a break. For weeks you've focused on the idea that you would return to the DEA. I don't know when you accepted that you weren't, but it couldn't have been very long ago. You haven't had time to turn your thought process to a new direction. When you do, you'll come up with something." She emphasized her point with a lip-smacking kiss.

Her absolute confidence in the face of his self-doubt rocked him.

"I wish I were as positive."

"I know you. There probably isn't one thing in your life that you've set your mind on and not accomplished."

"But this—"

"But nothing." She waggled a finger. "Do I need to remind you that I am a trained behavioral scientist?"

He couldn't hold back a chuckle. "No, ma'am."

"Exactly. So let me tell you what I've observed." She sat back on his knees, the motion almost making him moan.

"You're smart—oh, and nice move making me think you were dumb. I guess in retrospect, that's just more evidence that you're resourceful. Given your previous profession, you've had to be. You're strong, capable, and . . ."

He'd ask her later why she blushed mid-sentence, but for the time being he just listened.

". . . inventive. You're no stranger to hard work, and you're obviously willing to do whatever must be done."

"Should I apply for sainthood now instead of waiting until I'm dead?" He scrubbed a hand over his own heating face.

She grinned. "Don't tell me it's possible to embarrass an ego like yours?"

"Hey!"

"Oh puh-leeze. A healthy ego is a good thing, and I've noticed that when yours gets too healthy, Ruby adjusts it."

"That's putting it mildly. You don't do too badly in that area yourself."

"I'm a quick study and you made it necessary. Now, let me continue. Strength of character, natural intelligence, inventive thinking, strong will, and an ego that won't permit you to fail. Given the data with which I'm presented, I can only conclude that you will succeed at this task."

He shook his head. Un-freakin' believable.

"Don't disagree with me, Jack. I'm right."

"I'm not disagreeing." He snorted. "I wouldn't dare when you're so adamant. But, sweetheart, you amaze me. I've gone out of my way to show you every bad quality in the book. That ego you mentioned, my temper, stubbornness."

"I'm not forgetting any of those traits, either, but remember what you've given me." Her smile glowed more brightly than the sun that had now risen to its full morning glory.

"You probably don't realize it, but going one on one with you has taught me a lot about myself. You challenged me to believe in myself and prove it to you, even when you didn't want to be convinced. I've even learned that I can't please everybody all the time and, in spite of it, we'll all survive."

She moved again, leaning forward this time to nestle against his shoulder, her arms around his neck.

"You've also shared with me the magic of swimming with dolphins, the thrill of kissing underwater, and the wonder of making love until my bones dissolve and my heart turns inside out." Her sigh caressed his skin like a warm summer breeze.

"It's all part of the total package. All the things that make you *you*." Her lips pressed warmly to his throat, and then she sat back and again looked deep into his eyes.

"All the things that make you the man I love."

The breath lodged in his lungs. "You what?"

"You heard me."

"Say it again."

"I love you."

"Damn!"

She froze in his embrace, and then began struggling. "That's your response? I tell you a dozen reasons why you're wonderful. Then I go all the way to the end of the limb and open up my heart, and all you can say is 'Damn'?"

Shoving and prodding, she did her best to break his hold.

"I don't expect you to reciprocate with some big declaration, but if nothing else, the bulge in your shorts tells me you feel something. Of course that might be all you feel and all you want. Now let go of me!"

In answer, he shifted his grip and tightened his arms around her until he regained his breath. Did finding out that the woman he adored also loved him in return rob him of his speech? He was the worst at talking about emotions on a normal day, and this was huge. Enormous! Geezus, he wanted to pound his chest and roar in triumph.

Instead, he'd uttered one wildly inadequate word and had given

195

her the totally opposite idea. The hurt on her face hit him like the speargun she'd threatened him with earlier, and he launched into immediate damage control.

"Victoria, stop fighting me a minute and listen. Please."

"Thank you," he breathed when she finally settled. He wanted to erase the frown and chase the insecurity from her eyes forever.

"I don't have a lot of fancy words, so I'll say it straight. All I feel for you is everything."

Gently, he cupped her cheek. "Everything, Victoria. Heart and soul." He kissed her forehead, her cheeks, the tip of her nose, and then brought his mouth an inch from hers. "I love you," he said, sealing the pledge with a kiss.

Her lips were stiff at first, but he didn't give up, coaxing, warming her until the wariness softened and gradually melted away. He let the caress of his mouth prove the truth of his words. When she relaxed, he released the grip on her arms and splayed his hands around her back to draw her closer.

When she finally responded, pure happiness zipped through him and he poured it into the kiss, deepening the contact with the play of tongue and teeth. His heart lurched inside his ribcage and his breath tightened.

He broke the kiss to whisper, "Don't ever doubt it, sweetheart. I love you."

She sighed, and nestled against his chest. "I love you too. Every stubborn, infuriating male pound of you."

Laughter rumbled in his chest. "When it comes to stubbornness, you could win a few titles yourself, you know." He held her easily anchored with one arm, stroking her hair with his other hand. "Next to Ruby, you're the only person I've never been able to intimidate."

"What, are you crazy? You intimidated me to death in the beginning."

"But you never backed down, did you? Even when things were at their worst, you brought the fight into my territory. That tells me something."

"I was desperate."

"You were determined," he corrected. "You were also right." He chuckled. "So, with everything out in the open, do you still believe me when I tell you I'm honestly happy that you hit on a way to make Dolphin Land succeed?"

She nodded. "We still need your help, though, so don't think you're getting out of your fair share of the work."

"I wouldn't dream of it."

"Excellent." She traced a lazy pattern on his shirt. "It'll be good for you, too, Jack. "You aren't a man to sit around idle for long when there's work you could be doing. This at least keeps you active while you work on picking your next career."

"Good point." Still holding her in his arms, he stood and walked toward the office.

"What are you doing?"

"Getting down to business."

"What kind of business?" She laughed, then squealed when he loosened his hold, pretending to drop her, before pulling her tight to him again. "Funny business, probably."

"There's work to be done, and like you said, I'm not one to sit around idle."

"I have a list of projects in my bag."

"We'll get to that soon enough, but right now it's first things first." He kissed her while he walked, teasing her sweet lips open and deviling her mouth with his tongue. A smile curved on his face when her lips grew pliant, then clung, moving against his with tantalizing softness.

Her voice was breathless when they broke the kiss. "Is the first thing what I'm hoping?"

"Well, you mentioned wanting to see me in my uniform shirt. I assume it's in the office."

"Your uniform shirt. That's where all this is leading?"

"Sure thing, sugar." He dipped, unlatched the door, and then opened it with his foot. "I gotta put it on first if you still want the chance to watch me peel it off."

Chapter Eighteen

A long time later, they left the office to search for Ruby. After all the determined effort she'd put into showing each of them separately how good they'd be together, they figured she deserved to know her hopes had come true.

Victoria felt like she was gliding over the gravel between the office and the lagoon where Ruby sat tossing tokens, little fish snacks, to the dolphins. The old woman turned her head when she heard them approach, and a wide grin spread across her parchment face.

"Good thing you surfaced. I figured I'd hold off for another hour before I checked to see if you were both still breathing."

"You knew?" Victoria gasped, and whipped around to Jack. "She knew!"

He only shrugged acceptance when his aunt hooted.

"I got a lot of years on you, girl. You think I can't tell what's going on when Jack's runabout is tied up at the dock, your stuff's out here . . ." She gestured to the audio bag and tripod. "And the office door is shut and locked?"

She chuckled again. "Hot damn. Ain't make-up sex the ever loving best?"

Jack roared with laughter, and Ruby swatted him playfully on the arm. Even the dolphins seemed to get the joke, blasting giggle-like sounds from their blowholes. Victoria waffled between joining in and jumping in the lagoon to cool off what she was sure was a full-body blush. Joy won out over embarrassment, and she merged her laughter with theirs.

Oh, how she loved these two people. In a relatively short time, they'd become more than friends. More like . . . family. Although, to be honest, her father never joked about sex, at least not in her hearing. Nor had he given her a tenth of the praise and encouragement she'd already received from these people. Hoot with laughter? Please. Talk about unreasonable expectations. Someone would solve the ancient mystery of Stonehenge before that happened.

Don't go there. Today was made for joy, laughter, and if so inclined, spinning around until she was dizzy with glee. She refused to let old baggage bring her down. Her father had chosen to put his work ahead of all else and celebrate only his own success and acclaim. He'd left next to no room in his life for anything else, and now with his ability to work gone, he was left with next to nothing.

God knows how he'd ever convinced her mother to spend a minute in his cold company, yet alone devote several years to being his wife, supporting his career, and raising their daughter. He'd never experienced the kind of bond shared between Ruby and Jack—and now her. Victor Sheffield's inability to show support, affection, even true love, was his loss. Now that she had all that and then some in her life, she couldn't drum up any of her usual resentment. Left in its place was a real sense of sadness. Her brilliant father, who had measured his life only by his accomplishments, had bankrupted himself emotionally.

Another round of laughter erupted. She'd lost track of the fun, but it was obvious the two of them were deviling each other to their mutual delight. Jack was as different a man from her father as lava was from an ice floe. Volatile? Sure. Perfect? Heck, no, but neither was she, and that was just fine with both of them.

Comparing him to Kel, it amazed her that they were males of the same species. She and her former fiancé had known each other for years, worked side-by-side, and, yes, been to bed together. But in all that time, they'd never achieved the connection she had with Jack.

The scientist in her could study pheromones and the chemistry of attraction. The sociologist would consider backgrounds, upbringing, and life experiences. The woman knew only that he filled the open spaces in her heart.

One quick glance and his smile shot heat down to her toes. Okay, there was also something to be said for pheromones. Whatever the case, she and Jack clicked in ways that Kel left her cold. In a flash of insight, she locked on another elemental difference. Kel based her value on what benefits he could gain from her hard work. Jack valued her for herself.

"What's wrong, sweetheart?"

She looked up and smiled at the concern in his amazing eyes. "Nothing, why?"

"You're frowning." He stroked the corner of her mouth.

He would always notice, she realized, and even more wonderful, he would always care.

"I'm fine." She slipped her arms around him, knowing instinctively that he would gather her close. "Better than fine, actually. I'm happy."

"Happy doesn't make you frown." He tipped up her chin. "So . . ."

She kissed him, thrilled that she could without reservation. "Old memories, nothing more, and as of right now, I'm banishing them to where they belong."

"Okay."

They stood quietly, enjoying each other while Ruby finished feeding the dolphins.

"I guess we better get working on that list of projects instead of wasting the whole day."

"Oh, heck yes! There's so much to do! I want to review my notes from last night and develop more program options."

"I'll start measuring and sketching out that pavilion. But, Victoria?"

"Yes?"

He reached behind her, plucked a red hibiscus flower off a nearby tree, and tucked it into her hair.

"Don't wear yourself out, love. We've got a date for tonight."

***

The students' questions last night had truly been excellent, she thought as she watched the video. Not only did they make for a lively, more interactive discussion, but they also targeted a few areas where she could refine the presentation. If she was going to present herself in the academic world as an expert, she darned well would need to deliver the best possible program.

Programs, actually. They'd never achieve long-term success without additional presentations. Ideas poured out of her like bees from a busy hive. With minor tweaks in approach and handouts, she could tailor versions of the current presentation for different age groups, but she needed fresh material too. By offering more choices in curriculum, they would appeal to a wider range of classes.

Her thesis on alloparenting was a good place to start. During those two years in Hawaii, she'd learned so much from assisting the second-best-known marine mammal researcher in the world. With his mentoring, she'd done top-notch work and earned her doctorate. She had a ton of slides from the study, too, for visual impact.

The sooner she got hold of Rosa and asked her to ship the stuff, the sooner she'd have another seminar ready to go.

She punched in the telephone number on her cell and swiveled her chair around to prop her feet on the desk. As long as Rosa was packaging up the data and paper from one study, it wouldn't be much trouble for her to do a second. Several years before, while she was still an undergraduate, she'd documented her father's Inter-Modal Matching Study with videotapes and copious notes.

Strange. The caregiver usually picked up on the second ring.

Hunching her shoulder to hold the phone receiver close to her ear, she scribbled a reminder. *Talk to Ruby about training a simple match-to-sample behavior.* A live demonstration of the dolphins looking at an object, and then finding a similar one, was a great visual aid and would help students grasp the more advanced study.

"Good afternoon. De Sheffield House."

"Hi, Rosa. I was starting to think you weren't home."

"Ah, Victoria. Hello. We were out in de backyard. It's a fine, sunny day and your fahder, he wanted to be outside."

"I saw online that Massachusetts was having a warm sp—"

Her feet fell off the desk when she straightened.

"My father wanted to go outside?"

"Yes! It's a wonderful ding. Now dat he sees some progress wid his derapy, he has more interest in oder dings too."

Victoria digested that for a second. Since his stroke, he was more likely to react with displeasure, rather than indicate a preference. Amazing.

"His speech, too, keeps improving. We work on it every day at home, even when he doesn't go to derapy."

Perhaps she wasn't the only Sheffield whose life recently had improved.

"That's good news, Rosa. Thanks for telling me."

"You're welcome, girl-child."

"Listen, would you please do me a favor? There are some old papers and things in the attic that I need. Do you mind gathering them up and sending them to me?"

"Of course not. Wait just a moment while I get a pen."

One thing she shared with her father was a dedication to organization. All materials related to a particular study were packed in appropriately labeled boxes. It was an easy matter to give the project names to the caregiver and tell her where in the attic they were located.

"Dis sounds like you're busy all right, girl-child. Are dese all to help wid your study?"

"Indirectly. In addition to my project, we've decided now to offer a series of research lectures."

"You're teaching seminars? Wonderful!"

Bless her heart, the woman was always excited at whatever news Victoria shared. She grinned and prepared herself for the questions sure to follow, but Rosa surprised her.

"Doctor Sheffield, did you hear what your daughter is doing?"

After asking Victoria to hold on, she repeated the news to her father. Give her credit, the caregiver didn't know the meaning of "wasted effort," but Victoria appreciated the attempt to interest her father in her activities.

"Girl-child, you still dere? De doctor, he wants to talk wid you."

Shocked, she wasn't sure she could respond, even if she knew what to say. Thank God, it took a moment for the woman to transfer the phone to her father. She waited, listening to soft rustling while they got the receiver situated, and heard Rosa gently remind her father to take his time "wid de words." Then . . .

"Vic-dor-a?"

"Ye-yes, Father. I'm here."

"How . . . arr . . . you?"

I'm stunned. "I'm good. And I'm happy to hear you're doing better."

Clearly, speaking was a struggle, almost as if he had to remember how to move his mouth to shape each syllable. That he even tried to talk to her, when it was obviously difficult, touched her in a way she never expected.

"Vic . . ." He managed an upward inflection.

"What, Father?"

"W-will you . . . tell me . . . p-p-pro-ject?"

"Tell you about project. My project?"

If she'd been stunned before, it was nothing compared to this new bolt. She had no way to know why the request came now, when it never had before. It would have been so easy for him to show interest at any time during her years in school or on any of their travels since. Now, every word took immense effort, but he made it.

No, she might not know why he asked now, but taken in perspective, she didn't care. He could be bored out of his mind, and it didn't matter. He had asked. She shook off the last of her daze and got ready to present her study to the man who knew more about marine mammal research than most people could ever hope to learn.

"Well, Father, my premise is that cetaceans don't just learn by imitation, but that dolphins actively and deliberately communicate knowledge to each other. To prove this theory, I developed a protocol and . . ."

The conversation was almost entirely one-sided, but she continued for at least half an hour, encouraged by the occasional question, laboriously phrased, and a series of grunts.

Whether he accepted her methods as sound and her study as significant, she couldn't tell, but again, at that moment, it didn't matter. He was actively listening. Despite all the years of strife and coldness behind them, even though she no longer needed his approval for validation, this meant the world to her.

Finally, worried that she might be tiring him out, she paused. "Father, there's so much more, but I don't want to overdo. What if . . . would you like me to call again tomorrow?"

"Umm-hmm. Y-yes."

She beamed. "Okay. We'll talk more then."

"W-wait, Vic-dor-a."

"Yes, Father? What is it?"

"G-good j-job."

* * *

"We really focus on experiential education," Victoria explained a couple weeks later over the phone to a professor in North Carolina. "I guarantee that your students will come away with a greater understanding of marine mammal research in a way they simply can't get when limited to the classroom."

It was the third such pitch she'd made this afternoon, and if her record held, she'd have a commitment from the professor before she hung up the phone. "Absolutely we incorporate hands-on, or rather, an eyes-on portion where the students can practice observations." They didn't, but it was a terrific idea, so she jotted a note to include it in their next presentation.

"Two weeks from today? Let me check the schedule." She paused for effect. "Yes, Doctor, we can arrange a field trip on that day. Oh, you'd like to study with us for two days? I'd be happy to design a two-day experience. Yes, there are several good campgrounds and RV parks in the area." She rattled off the web site for the local Chamber of Commerce. "Now forgive me for veering from the scientific to the financial, but in order to reserve that date for your class, the proprietors require a signed application and deposit."

After another few minutes of taking credit card information and promising to fax some preliminary reading material, Victoria disconnected the call. Score! Another customer hooked and landed. She marked the school name on the big master calendar tacked to the wall and allowed herself a very satisfied smile.

They weren't just on a roll; they were flying at warp speed. The month ahead was filling fast. She could probably book more presentations than they had available dates, but Ruby refused to let her.

"You've got to leave yourself time to continue your research, darlin'," she'd said in a firm voice that defied disagreement. "There's a Delphinid Prize out there with your name on it. Damned if there isn't."

Maybe, maybe not. She wouldn't pretend that she was so devoid of ego that winning the prestigious prize didn't mean anything. It just didn't serve as the ultimate, all important goal anymore. Even if she didn't know in both her head and her gut that her theories were sound, her father's reactions would have confirmed it.

With each subsequent phone call, his speech improved. Last night, he'd even managed to remind her of a terrific journal article.

"The one . . . on co-op-pera-tive fishing per-actices. B-Brazil. You helped."

She was still smiling over the memory when the telephone rang again. The way word had spread, it could be another prospective field trip waiting to be booked.

She snatched up the receiver. "Dolphin Land Research Department. Dr. Sheffield speaking."

"Victoria. How good to hear your voice."

Kel.

Her smile shriveled. He hadn't called on her wireless phone since she'd hung up on him weeks ago. That he was calling now on the office number, could only mean one thing.

Word had spread even further and faster than anticipated.

"Hello, Kel." She returned the greeting smoothly, pleased that her voice sounded calm and gave away no hint of her instantaneous apprehension.

"How are you, love?"

The endearment grated. When it came to her ex-fiancé, love equaled deceit. "I'm fine. Busy. So, whatever the point of this call is, please get to it quickly."

"Victoria, Victoria. From the buzz in the field, I would say you're more than busy, but surely you have a few moments for an old . . ."

He paused, and she could imagine his smirk.

"Friend."

"I'd give the entire afternoon and then some to an old friend, Kel. You don't qualify. So, since I don't have time to spare for former cheating colleagues, move it along."

Take that. His observation skills fell far below her level, but even he had to realize that she was now a wiser woman than the one he'd so easily duped.

Still, he dared laugh like one would when amused at the bravado of a puppy.

"All right, if you choose to focus on practical matters over pleasantries, I'll comply."

He paused again, the tactic intended, no doubt, to wear on her nerves. She out-waited him, not letting even an impatient breath escape. Finally, he continued.

"Everyone's talking about Dr. Sheffield's daughter and her new research education program. When I first heard the news, I was shocked, and then very concerned."

With effort, she held back a snort.

"I suspected that with your father incapacitated, you hadn't yet convinced another top level scientist to sign you on as an assistant. Still, I'd never imagined that things had gotten so bad that you'd give up for a teaching position. Then I remembered that you've always been a clever girl, and I knew that there had to be something more."

Had he always been this pompous? Good Lord, he was only thirty-one and talked thirty years older. In fact, he sounded a lot like her father. *Whoa, Electra! Don't go there now. You still need to concentrate.*

"So, how does it feel to work on your first solo project? Is the research going well?"

Talk about a shot in the dark. Well, simply because he'd asked didn't mean he was entitled to an answer. Thinking fast, she phrased a non-committal response.

"I enjoy what I'm doing, Kel. I've always liked talking to people about marine mammals and what we've learned."

"I'm not interested in boring lectures delivered to uninteresting minds. Tell me about your fieldwork, and don't try to make me believe you aren't deeply involved in a fully developed project. I know better and I know you."

He fished with as little finesse as a drunken rube on a party boat. Fed up with the game, she let it all out. "You're the last person with whom I would discuss any study until after I've published the paper, and even then only if you purchased a ticket to a lecture."

"Ah, you're still smarting because I beat you to the punch on our last collaboration."

"Is that Kel-speak for stealing the data and pretending you were the sole investigator on the research I designed?"

"You designed? Now who's stealing sole credit? We worked on that study together."

"C'mon, Kel. Just between us. Without me, there wouldn't have been anything to work on. Left on your own, you wouldn't have generated any data. No solid theories or conclusions. And there certainly wouldn't have been a paper to publish with only your name on the credit."

"That's one paper more than you've published. What does that tell you?"

"That you're a deceitful jerk who made his name using someone else's work."

"Emphasis on the phrase 'made his name.' I had as much right to that material as you, and if I didn't give you equal credit, oh well. How many times did your father remind us that research doesn't count until it's published? I beat you into the journals. So, as far as the rest of the field is concerned, that was my study, my findings. Ergo, I'm the one who's known in the field. Right now, you're just a sick old man's unpublished daughter who can't get a job."

Bastard! "I come to work every morning. By anyone's definition, that's a job."

"You're trading on your father's name, hawking research lectures at some rundown, worthless roadside attraction in the middle of the

Florida Keys. Now why do you suppose that could be? Possibly because no self-respecting facility would make their animals available to you for whatever study proposal you submitted."

Oh how she longed to plant a fist in his smug face. Lucky for him, he was calling from miles away instead of standing within reach in the office.

It took effort and acting skill, but her laugh sounded natural. "You got me on that point, Kel. You're published, and I'm not. So, here I am at this little unheard of place scraping together the means to perform a study and hopefully publish the findings in my own name."

Now it was her turn to pause, let him think he'd gained an advantage.

"It may not be much, but it's more than you're currently doing. In fact, you haven't accomplished a thing since that study, and from what I hear, you don't have any prospects lined up either. Let's look at that information. Could it be because without my father or me you don't have a source for creative ideas? Even if you could finesse your way into a research facility, you wouldn't have a study to conduct once you arrived."

Oh, it felt glorious to finally vent everything she'd been too hurt, too shocked to hurl at him before. She fed on the power and knew exactly how a predator felt when it had its target trapped. "Face it, Kel. You don't have what it takes on your own. Once you alienated me, you lost any remaining edge."

He was pathetic, really, but saying so would be overkill. Instead, she sat back, immensely pleased with her attack, and waited for his response.

Did he realize his agitated breathing came through loud and clear over the phone? Every hitch and stifled growl signaled a struggle for control. He must have nearly strangled on the words, but he kept his tone moderate.

"You couldn't be more wrong. I have the perfect project waiting for me. Yours."

This time nothing kept back the snort. "In your dreams. Fool me once, shame on you. Fool me twice? Not in this lifetime."

"So strong, so positive. I'm almost impressed. Had you shown this much determination years ago, your father wouldn't have continued to keep you from the credit you deserved. Your basic mistake was that you always underestimated your own abilities. There was no reason for anyone to respect you. It's too late now, so we can leave that in the past. However, the one mistake you are determined to repeat is that you continue to underestimate *me*."

"I know exactly who and what you are."

"But, you don't know how far I'll go."

"I saw exactly how far when we were still engaged."

"No. I only did what I needed to achieve that particular goal. Right now, my goal is to be included as an investigator on your current project."

Something cold and scaly slithered down her spine. She shrugged it off and sneered into the phone.

"Get over yourself. The time is long past when you could intimidate or outwit me. The closest you'll get to my work is when you read the published paper."

He had the unmitigated nerve to laugh. "I'll give you a little time to think about it, but don't try to cross me on this, Victoria. You'll discover you don't like the results. Remember, love, the absolute truth is that I will always go as far as necessary to get what I want."

"No way in—"

The miserable sea slug disconnected.

Damn him! He was *not* going to upset her. She stomped around the small office, wishing she wore heavy-heeled boots, not leather sandals, while she imagined kicking him where it hurt the most. A paper cup from the water cooler crumpled satisfactorily in her hand, but fluttered to the ground when she tried to hurl it across the room. Grabbing a pencil, she launched it like a dart, but then snarled when it rolled weakly down the wall.

"That pompous, arrogant, lying, cheating . . ."

The office door opened and reflex spun her around.

". . . son of a bitch!"

"Whoa, sweetheart." Jack threw up his hands, the picture of instant surrender. "Whatever it is, I swear I didn't do it."

"Not you. Him!" She flung her hand toward the phone. "He's conceited, oily, intellectually inferior, which actually makes me happy, but ohhhh, the rest of it."

A half-spin brought her around so she and Jack were face-to-face. "He had the colossal nerve to tell me, not ask mind you, tell me that he was joining my research project."

"Kel called you."

"Yes, Kel called. Who else? Why else would I get this ridiculously upset? That . . . that . . . bastard!" Anger burned in her veins. She hugged her arms to her waist.

Jack spun her into his embrace. "It doesn't matter what he said. I won't let him put one miserable foot on Dolphin Land property. Don't worry. He's spitting into the wind."

His hug wrapped around, drawing her closer to his heart while he stroked her from the nape of her neck to the small of her back. The deep rumble of his voice and sure, steady caress soothed her more than his words. Tight muscles loosened, and she slipped her hands around his waist letting her head rest against his chest.

"That's it, sweetheart. Let it go."

"He won't be successful, will he, Jack? We won't let him

anywhere near our work."

"Damn straight."

"Without access, he won't even know our intent, yet alone our observational process or testing protocols."

"Right."

His chin rubbed companionably on the top of her head.

"So, there's no way he can steal my study again?"

"Nope." He held her away from him, smiling down into her eyes. "Based on a quick evaluation of the evidence at hand, your conclusion, Doctor?"

"Kel's screwed."

"I love how you science brains think."

She giggled, beaming at him like she'd just solved the most impossible physics equation.

"God, you're good, Jack. Problem solved." A sloppy, friendly kiss served as his reward. "Thank you. I feel a whole lot better."

"Oh yeah? How much better?" He waggled his eyebrows at her. "Enough to let me lure you to my boat for a sunset sail?"

"Hmmm. Tempting, but I need to make a few more calls." She glanced at her watch. "It's that late already? Wow."

"Aunt Ruby left half an hour ago. Plans with Willy, and she said she wants to look hot." He winced on the last word, making her giggle again.

"You know, Jack, you can never tell where a game of pinochle will lead."

"Please don't put any more images into my head."

"Ohhhh, so only fantasies involving you and me are okay?"

"Well, except for the ones involving you, me, and the babe from the new fictional forensic show on Thursday nights."

"You pig!" Laughter spoiled the disgusted tone she'd tried to inject.

"Hey, I'm a guy. I can dream." His eyes softened, as he slipped a warm hand to cup the back of her neck. "I can dream, or I can find some private time with my woman and put those dreams into action."

The sudden kiss speared lightning to her toes.

Consigning Kel to the mental dungeon where he belonged, she answered the kiss with her own, promising heat and more.

"You don't have to lure me anywhere. You've already landed me—hook, line, and sinker."

"Kiss me like that again, and we won't make it to the boat."

His theatrical groan made her laugh in spite of the passion burning through her limbs. Confident that he'd catch her, she jumped, wrapping her legs around his waist. "Get a move on, sailor. That sun won't wait for us before it sets."

"You know, I didn't think it was possible, but you're even bossier when you're in love," he complained good-naturedly, even as he swung around and kicked open the door. "Is this what I have to look forward to from now on?"

"That and all the fantasies come true that you can handle." She nipped the side of his throat. "Except for ones that include third parties."

In a move that would have been complicated for most men, he smoothly maneuvered her so she was clinging to him piggyback style. His back was strong, as solidly muscled as the rest of him. His dark hair hung to his shoulders like a pirate's, and she itched to thread her fingers in its raw silk texture.

Long strides ate up the ground between the office and the dock where he'd moored the dinghy. He lowered her carefully into the small craft as if she were priceless treasure.

"Not a problem, sweetheart. I got plenty more where that one came from."

* * *

Seventeen hundred miles away, Kel slammed his empty coffee mug against his desk hard enough to chip the ceramic. *How dare the little witch deny him?* She should be grateful he had any interest in her work and be on her knees begging him to help. Among the people who mattered, she was practically nobody. Without her father's weighty influence to help her, she'd be lucky to get a credible journal to even look at her work. Whereas, with his own past publishing credit, his name would add authority to the project.

She'd never been capable of exploiting a situation to her own advantage. Nor did she understand that the worst he could do was far greater than she imagined. Did she honestly think he'd give up simply because she told him to? She'd learned nothing from their earlier involvement if she thought he listened to anyone or anything other than his own desires. His needs took priority over everything, and everyone, else.

Victoria was very sadly mistaken when she accused him of not having what it takes. He'd not yet failed at a goal. What Kel Griffin wanted, he got, and never wasted time worrying about the means. To date he'd never needed to, so why change? His methods had served him well before, and certainly would again.

She was right on one point, he conceded. She was a terrific source of creative ideas. During those years of assisting her father, when he realized she was privately conducting a smaller, but fresh, study on her own, he'd begun formulating his own plan.

Desperate for support for her abilities and theories, she never noticed his skillful manipulation. In showing her enthusiasm, he encouraged her to share more of her ideas—a response he then rewarded with praise. By treating her as a respected colleague, instead of the boss's lowly assistant, it wasn't long before she trusted him enough to discuss her observations on family recognition in migrating dolphin pods.

Pity, her father had never acknowledged her exceptional gift. Then again, had she not been so starved for approval and recognition, it might have taken him slightly longer to seduce her. He'd played her emotions with the skill of a sport-fishing master. First, she gave him her trust, then soon after, her body, and finally, full access to her data.

Appropriating her study proved even more satisfying than taking her virginity. Women's bodies, after all, were more readily available and a lot less challenging than good research studies. A conquest in bed didn't bring him the professional distinction he craved.

Oh, but the paper he authored certainly had, and he still maintained a fine appreciation for her brilliant source work. In retrospect, perhaps he'd cut her loose too soon. Given her love-struck adoration of him at the time, he most likely could have found a way to get credit for that first study while keeping her on the line for the future. That would certainly have been more expedient. Over the last few weeks, she'd proven surprisingly difficult to locate. He'd succeeded, of course, but he had wasted his valuable time.

Now, she'd wasted even more of his time by stonewalling him and refusing him access to her project. She'd thrown brave words at him when she declared he could no longer intimidate or outwit her. She'd acted much more self-assured than he remembered—a definite change in her personality and not one that suited his purposes.

This was the wrong time for her to experiment with a backbone. Given that her determination placed a direct obstacle in his path, he had no choice but to teach her a lesson. There must always be consequences for negative behavior, in his opinion.

Kel swept the broken chips of his mug onto a sheet of paper.

Clearly, she needed to realize that there was only one master in this game, and it wasn't she. What could he do that would upset her project and rattle her confidence? He needed to provide indisputable proof that refusing him was a very, very dangerous move.

Rising from the desk, he walked over to the trash receptacle and dumped in the ceramic pieces, while he contemplated his options. Whatever project she had underway, she obviously needed this inconsequential roadside attraction. So that's what he'd use to deliver his message.

He'd promised her a little time to reconsider her initial refusal, he thought as he returned to his desk and accessed the Internet, the perfect lesson already coming together in his mind. Amazing how the contact information he needed appeared almost immediately with a few keystrokes. Picking up the telephone receiver, he glanced at the clock.

Time's up.

Chapter Nineteen

Jack would never again see anything as beautiful as Victoria illuminated by the melting blaze of the setting sun. Purple, red, and orangey gold slashed across the sky. The vibrant colors staged a dramatic backdrop to her golden tan and her thick brown hair with its sun-streaked highlights. The play of light did something to her eyes, brightening the deep color to amber.

They sailed a mile from shore. While he guided the rudder and set the sails to capture the breeze, she tucked her feet up on the bench seat and entertained him by reporting all she'd accomplished during the day. The woman knew how to get things done, that's for sure. When she set her mind on a task, there was no stopping her.

From the start, he'd recognized it as a trait he'd always prized in his colleagues, but there was a major difference. No DEA partner brought out his romantic streak of protectiveness.

Jack meant every word of his promise. Victoria's ex-fiancé wasn't getting a foot in the gate of the facility. If he tried . . . Given the depth of his previous betrayal, Jack almost hoped the SOB *would* try. He'd enjoy rolling the weasel's carcass across the gravel parking lot all the way back to the Overseas Highway.

Knowing the man had badly hurt her in the past was reason enough. Hearing the lingering worry in her voice, catching the hint of fear in her eyes, cemented Jack's determination.

If he dared approach her, Kel Griffin was fish bait.

"Honey?"

He looked over and saw her studying him, that familiar frown between her brows and her eyes sharp with concern. "Yeah, sweetheart?"

"What's wrong? You look very . . . fierce all of a sudden."

He leaned over and brushed his lips across her forehead. "Nothing's wrong." The tender press of his mouth to hers quieted the contradiction before she could voice it. "Honest. I'm only thinking about how much you mean to me."

Suddenly he felt fierce, just as she'd described, and the need to make sure she understood the depth of his feelings beat at him. He cupped her cheek, tilting her face up to stare into the rich depths of her eyes.

"You are everything to me, Victoria. There isn't anything that I won't do for you." He took her mouth again, swift and urgent, sealing the promise.

When they broke for air, her breath shuddered and her voice trembled. "Wow. You sure can convince a woman."

"I'm serious."

"I get that. But I don't understand what brought this on right now."

"Just believe I won't let you down, even though I don't have a clue as to what's ahead." He swallowed hard and continued. "Or what I'll do when I leave the DEA."

"I'm not worried that you'll disappoint me. Ever." Unexpectedly, she laughed. "You know, that's the first time I have ever been able to say that to a man without reservation?" She slipped her hands around his neck and kissed him, sweetly, in a way that wrapped around his heart. "Thank you."

This woman could humble him with the simplest phrase. With her easy acceptance, his mood lifted. He brushed another light kiss against her cheek and, with a squeeze, turned her in his arms, drawing her back against his chest. They settled together, her head resting in the curve of his shoulder, his cheek against her hair. In silent appreciation they watched the sun's last flare as it lowered in the sky.

In the span of a heartbeat it melted into the horizon, and immediately a distant green light speared up in its place.

"Oh my gosh! What was that?"

"It's the green flash, darlin'. A little special Keys' magic that doesn't happen every night. Quick. Make a wish."

"A wish?" She laughed and closed her eyes. "Okay. Here goes."

He took advantage of her closed eyes to sneak in another kiss— one that promised her he'd do everything in his power to make this and every future wish come true. In the meantime, there wasn't anything wrong with working on a wish or two of his own.

He deepened the kiss, tracing the seam of her lush lips with his tongue. Her mouth opened and the slow burn flared hotter. She smelled of jasmine-scented shampoo, tasted like feminine sin, and the impact hit him in a rush. His hand swept down to her hip, then cradled her butt to pull her close.

The delicate skin under her jaw warmed with his moist, open-mouthed kisses, and the unforgettable fragrance that was hers alone rose to fill his senses. His mouth rushed down her throat. *Too fast,* he thought, but not nearly fast enough.

He barely kept from shredding the thin strap of her tank top when he tugged it down her shoulder, and then cupped her perfect breast, shaping it for the swirl of his tongue and hot mouth. Her moan was sweet music that he rewarded by drawing the taut peak of her nipple into his mouth and sucking hard.

She arched like a drawn bow and wrapped her arms around his neck. Breathy cries of pleasure spurred him on, and he continued to lave and suck. His hands roamed freely, possessively over her body, sliding inside the back of her shorts, pulling them, and her skimpy panties, down her legs. She kicked them free and simultaneously tore at his shirt while he ripped hers up her body and over her head.

Standing, he laid her gently on the boat cushions. He stared at her naked body, almost stunned that she belonged, willingly and totally, to him.

"You are so beautiful," he breathed as he knelt and kissed the unbelievably soft skin between her breasts. Inch by smooth inch, he paid homage in a pilgrimage down to her abdomen, the dip of her navel, and her belly with reverent kisses, teasing nibbles and slow, tormenting licks.

"Jack!" She wriggled, and he captured her hips, holding her in place.

"Easy, sweetheart. Let me."

Warm breath ruffled silky curls, and he smiled at the mingling of frustration and anticipation in her gasp. Making a vee of two fingers, he spread her for his intimate inspection, and grew impossibly harder at the slick proof of her desire. Even with urgent need pounding within him, he took his time stroking her with his finger and blowing warm breath over the tender knot while she writhed in his grasp.

"Please!"

He grinned and tickled the soft folds, feeling her grasp him as pleasure rippled up her body.

"I am so going to pay you back for teasing me like this!"

"I'm counting on it, sweetheart," he chuckled, then closed his lips over the sensitive nub and sucked.

"Oh, Jack!"

Pinning her with his hands, he got down to the business of driving her wild. Licking, sucking, the slick penetration and withdrawal of fingers inside quivering flesh that urged him to sample more. Her body shuddered and twisted on the cushions, and her cries carried on the wind as he urged her higher, hotter. Inhaling her scent, tasting her passion drove him to want more, to give her more. When her gasps mixed with pleas and he felt her muscles coil and tighten, he sealed his mouth on her, ruthlessly pleasuring her with tongue and lips until her body stiffened, then rocked in a huge spasm.

With the taste of her release still on his tongue, he shucked his shorts and briefs and stretched over her, parting her legs with his knees. Throbbing and huge with his own need, he nonetheless framed her face with gentle hands. "Look at me, Victoria," he demanded.

In eyes darkened by passion, he saw love, and his own answering emotion welled up, almost undoing him. He nudged the blunt, smooth head of his penis against her soft opening.

She cried out again and arched, opening for him. He surged into her and felt her muscles clench around him, drawing him in deep. In the twilight, their eyes met and their bodies found an escalating rhythm. Hearts merged, and the resulting passion launched them on a spiraling path for the stars.

✳ ✳ ✳

"You needn't look so smug, Bubba," she informed him the next morning. "Arrogance is not a virtue."

"I'm not arrogant. I'm confident. There's a difference."

The dinghy chugged across the water toward Dolphin Land, leaving the sailboat bobbing behind them in the harbor, right where he'd anchored it a few hours after sunset.

A very exciting, satisfying, and passionate few hours were followed by a meal of cheese, potato chips, and chocolate chip cookies that they'd scavenged in the tiny galley and then fed to each other, naked, on the surprisingly comfortable bed.

A bed they hadn't left until the last possible minute.

A bed she counted on returning to at the end of the day.

"Now who looks smug? That's a self-satisfied look if I've ever seen one, sugar."

"Sunset sails must agree with me."

"Oh yeah?"

Shading her eyes against the sun with her hand, she made a show of surveying his face and body. "Judging by that smirk, they agree with you too."

"Oh yeah."

Laughter lit his eyes, turning them to aquamarine. Then, suddenly, they darkened with real concern.

"What is it?" Instinctively, she reached out to him.

"Look on shore."

She turned around. In the distance, Ruby was waving her arms madly, clearly gesturing for them to hurry.

"Hang on." He opened up the throttle, kicking up the speed of the little boat. As soon as they were close, he killed the engine and latched onto the dock, bringing them alongside. A few quick twists of the bowline secured the vessel, and they scrambled out.

Ruby was almost breathless when they reached her side.

"Thank God you're here!"

"What is it? What's wrong?"

"The feds, Jack. APHIS is crawling all over the place."

"An inspection? They were just here for the annual visit a few months ago, and the few things they questioned, we fixed."

"I know, I know, but this is different. I tried to raise you on the radio. Someone called 'em with a complaint. They've got some sort of paperwork saying that we, that our gang . . ." Her breath hitched, and her lips trembled so hard she could barely form the words.

Stunned, Victoria realized the older woman was near tears. APHIS, or Animal and Plant Health Inspection Service, oversaw the welfare of all marine mammals in facilities. Inspections, performed annually at the very least, should be a familiar event.

Jack squeezed his aunt's shaking shoulders, his voice strong and gentle. "Easy, darlin'. Tell me what they said."

"Someone called APHIS and said we mistreat the dolphins, that we're in such bad shape that their living conditions are unhealthy."

"What?" Victoria couldn't hold back a shocked gasp. No wonder she was so upset. Those dolphins were part of her family. Suggesting she'd mistreat them was as bad as accusing her of child abuse. "That's absurd!"

"Tell *them* that!" Ruby flung her arm in the general direction of the front lagoon. A man in a yellow uniform shirt and khaki shorts was huddled over a clipboard, while another poured water from a small pail into a funnel to a vial. He sealed the sample, and then labeled the tube.

"There's another one in the fish house. I left Willy to watch him while I came out here. I was going to row over when I saw your dinghy."

The woman was so upset that watching her broke Victoria's heart.

"Don't worry," she assured Ruby. "Anybody with a working brain can see that the gang receives the finest possible care."

"Victoria's right. If anything, we're in much better shape than we were on the last inspection. This is bull, plain and simple. I'm about to make sure these inspectors know it."

He hugged his aunt and then turned toward the front lagoon. "Wait here."

"Jack, hold it!" Victoria and Ruby burst out in unison, stopping him before he got more than a couple of steps.

"Bubba, you can't run them off. It'll make things worse."

Victoria added her weight to the plea. "We need to approach this calmly and rationally. If we don't, they may think we have something to hide."

"I'm calm. And I can rationally see that this is harassment. Damned if we'll stand for them treating us like this."

"If the inspectors are responding to a complaint, it makes sense to let them do their jobs. It's the only way they can report back that the complaint is invalid." She looked from nephew to aunt and back again. "I know it's difficult, particularly when the allegations are so ridiculous, but instead of fighting with them, shouldn't we cooperate?"

For a full twenty seconds he gaped at her as if she'd lost her mind. Gradually his expression shifted from outrage to acceptance and on to a wallop of craftiness.

"You're right. We can turn this to our advantage."

Victoria got a glimpse of why he'd been an effective agent. Like a team leader launching a mission, he assigned them their duties.

"Aunt Ruby, you pull out a half-foot high stack of daily reports on every session with each individual animal from the last few months. Insist that they review every page. I'll ride herd on the guy in the fish house."

Wicked pleasure filled his expression. "Victoria, slip into your most official Dr. Sheffield persona and dazzle the hell out of those two with the clipboard and water sample test kit. Show them your research permit application and a few dozen days' worth of whistle graphs." He rubbed his hands together. "I wonder if they brought wetsuits. It's a might cold in those lagoons unless you're wearing one, but I don't see how they can check out our fences from dry land. Get ready, ladies, because we are about to cooperate the hell out of this inspection. Let's go."

They killed the men with kindness and ran them ragged. An inspection that might normally last three hours was stretched to seven, while the Dolphin Land team determinedly showed the inspectors every nook, cranny, frozen herring, and fence post on the place.

Jack gave them a blow by blow account of each maintenance project accomplished in the previous weeks. When it was time to inspect the fish supplies, he kept them in the sub-zero freezer for ten minutes, pulling out box after box and expounding on the virtues of their rotation system for air thawing. "We wouldn't hear of a water thaw with the greater chance of introducing bacteria," he emphasized, while they struggled not to shiver in the icy cold.

Even when the officials assured her that they'd read enough, Ruby pulled out another sheaf of documents, all detailed in her neat, small handwriting.

For her part, Victoria filled their ears with data, hypotheses, and observation methodology, purposely picking out the most minute, tedious details, but sharing them as if they were diamonds.

The dolphins did their part too. One by one, when Ruby signaled, they beached themselves on the floating dock, presenting their bodies for visual inspection. The animals were obviously fit and healthy, a fact confirmed by the medical records, which were also scrupulously noted every night.

Finally, the inspectors all but ordered them to stop and insisted that they'd seen more than enough evidence to refute the complaint. Still, for good measure, Jack continued to fill their ears on the exciting plans for Dolphin Land's future the entire time he walked them to the gate.

The women collapsed on the closest bench. Ruby was downright giddy with relief and could barely speak through her laughter. "In all my years, I have never seen APHIS agents so happy to finish their jobs and make tracks."

Jack returned and plopped down next to them. "I don't think we have to worry about that crew for a while. Good job, ladies."

"The two of you are a pair and a half," Ruby hooted. "The idea wasn't half out of Victoria's mouth, and you knew how to put it into action."

She looked at her beloved dolphins, swimming calmly around the lagoon. "I'm glad it's over, but I'd sure like to know what brought 'em here in the first place."

"Me, too, Aunt Ruby, but they aren't obligated to share the source of the complaint."

Victoria stared at the lagoon, fighting down the sick feeling roiling in her stomach.

Jack nudged her arm. "You've got your 'thinking' face on. What gives?"

An official complaint wouldn't reveal anything she didn't already know in her gut.

"It had to be Kel," she said, her voice choked and thready.

He swore under his breath while his aunt goggled.

"Now what the hell makes you think your ex-fiancé would give us a hard time right clear out of the blue?" Ruby asked.

"It isn't out of the blue. He called me yesterday. We didn't have a chance to tell you."

"He warned you he was filing a complaint?"

"No. Kel wants me to let him join the project, but I refused." But he'd warned her that there was no limit to how far he would go to get what he wanted. "This is his way of flexing his muscles, showing me he means business."

Victoria jumped up from the bench. "Damn him! Just when I have us back on track, he makes his move."

Jack followed her, but when he tried to wrap her in his arms, she avoided the hug and stepped away from the comfort.

"Don't. I need to think. I should have anticipated this and been better prepared."

She should have guessed that Jack wouldn't let her evade him for long. The next time she tried to dodge, he caught her snugly, making her face him.

"It wasn't, isn't, your fault. This is on him."

"Yeah, Bubba's right. Don't you go blaming yourself," Ruby said.

"I have to! If not for me, Kel wouldn't even know Dolphin Land existed. He wouldn't be a threat."

"I wouldn't give a hunk of chum for his threats, sweetheart. Look, he tried and we countered."

"That's right. He started it. We ended it."

They were both so sweet, she could cry on the spot.

"I wish I could believe that this was over, but he'll keep coming after me until I agree. Unless I give him his way, Dolphin Land is in jeopardy."

"You're not taking that slime into your project!" Ruby exclaimed.

"Don't even think about it," Jack whispered in her ear. He

squeezed her more tightly before releasing his hold. "Now, listen up, ladies."

That easily, he shifted back into leadership mode. The aura of power and command fit him like his custom wetsuit. How had she never spotted it before? A simple deduction. He'd concealed it, naturally, until he needed it again. The chameleon ability must have served him well undercover.

"Here's what we're going to do. Victoria, you and I will gather up every chart, journal, audio disk, and video, along with the backup disks from your computer, and stow them on my boat. Don't worry, I've got a watertight lock box."

"Hell, Bubba, do you really think this rat is ballsy enough to break into the facility?"

"First rule of strategy. Plan for what you think the enemy can do, not what you think he might try."

"Gotcha."

"Aunt Ruby, feed the gang their last meal of the day. I know it's a little early, but when you're done, clean up. We rendezvous at the front gate at 1800 hours. Got it?"

"Yes, sir!" She snapped off a spiffy salute, the effect totally ruined by a toothy grin.

Victoria wanted to take both of them by their shoulders and shake them until they took her fear seriously. How could they treat this so lightly? "This isn't going to accomplish anything."

"Maybe, maybe not, but let's look at the facts. The false complaint was for show, like you said. After all, he doesn't want the facility shut down. He needs us fully operational so you, and he, can continue doing research."

"You're right, so what good will it do us to call a strategy meeting?"

"Strategy meeting nothing. I'm taking us all out to dinner."

"Dinner? Why?"

"I'm hungry. Even us he-men have to eat once in a while, particularly if I'm going to keep up my strength."

"Why didn't I think of that myself? You're so obviously wasting away."

"And that's after only a couple of nights with you. I rest my case. Come on, sweetheart, we've got work to do." He grabbed her hand and walked with her toward the office. "See you in a few, Aunt Ruby."

"Right-o."

Forget sweet. They were nuts, both of them, spewing out all this matter-of-fact cheer in the face of disaster. Somebody had to be sensible. Apparently she was that someone.

"Hold it, hold it, *hold it!*" She dug in her heels, furrowing tunnels in the pea rock. "I cannot let you do this."

"Do what, sugar?"

"Yeah, do what?"

"Pretend that something as simple as locking up my research materials will be enough to protect this place against Kel. Don't you get it? We can't afford to joke around. Today's stunt is proof. He's ruthless!"

"Nobody's pretending anything. We're taking reasonable precautions until he makes another move. Then, we'll counter that one too. Pretty soon he'll get the hint and give up."

She pulled her hand free of his grasp and folded her arms across her chest.

"No he won't. I figured out that he can't get signed on to anyone else's project, and he hasn't come up with an experiment big enough to do on his own. I'm sure he's that desperate."

"Even better. Desperate people make mistakes. We'll be able to nail him."

"Jack, you weren't on the phone with him. He's out of control. I don't know how I never saw it years ago, but it is crystalline clear now. Failure isn't an acceptable option. When he finds out we thwarted him today, his next move will be bigger and, in all likelihood, nastier."

"Let him bring it on."

"Yeah. Let him!"

"Will the two of you stop?" She didn't know whether to demand that they listen to reason, or beg. "Whether you admit it or not, I'm the reason he sent the inspectors. I have what he wants. So, I'm the only one who can stop him." She pulled out her best Victor Sheffield stare. "There's only one way to do it."

Twin pairs of blue eyes projected expressions of unyielding determination.

Jack spoke for them both. "Don't insult us with the suggestion."

"You don't know what I'm thinking."

A raised brow disagreed.

"You *don't!*"

"Sure he does, Victoria. My Gus always knew what I was thinking, as much as I liked to pretend I could keep him guessing. Heck, even I can tell. You're thinking that rat-bastard ex of yours will leave us alone if you agree to a partnership."

The action she'd settled on would be easier to activate if they believed that was her plan.

"It makes perfect sense," she told them.

"Only to someone out of her mind."

"The only insane thing would be repeating the same behavior and expecting different results. I already said 'no' to Kel and look what happened. I won't make that mistake again."

"So instead you'll let him come in and grab half your glory, when you've done all the work? That's crazy if you ask me."

"It's the only way, Ruby."

"But what about the Delphinid Prize? What about your dream? That means everything to you!"

"Not anymore it doesn't."

Damn it, she couldn't afford tears. If she broke, they'd see right through her tough charade. But it was the truth. Making it to the top of the research echelon wasn't the only thing that mattered. Not even close.

"Bottom line, Ruby. I won't be so selfish that I sacrifice your security, your happiness, or the welfare of the dolphins to salvage my dream."

She had to look away or she *would* cry. Instead, she stared at the lagoon, breathing in deeply and watching the animals swim around, chasing each other and doing dolphin things.

"Victoria, listen to me."

Keeping her back to him, she shook her head. "No. My mind's made up."

Forget Jack's earlier tenderness. All of sudden he picked her up by the shoulders and turned her around.

Any hint of easy joking had left his voice.

"Don't do it."

"Jack, I–"

"Forty-eight hours."

"What?"

"Give me forty-eight hours before you do anything."

"But—"

"That's not much time, Victoria, but it's all I need to find a way to block your ex from causing further trouble. Two days. Come on, darling, I'm asking you to trust me."

Gone from his eyes was the stubbornness, replaced instead by love and an almost pleading kind of need. She'd never seen it before, but she recognized it anyway. He wanted to save the day. He needed to be her hero.

Even with her fears at their worst, how could she refuse?

"Okay," she croaked, her throat tight with worry. She cleared it firmly and repeated her answer. "Okay."

Chapter Twenty

Twenty-four hours felt like a lifetime. She'd be insane in another day. Only her trust and her love kept her from putting her plan into action. Her real plan.

Ruby and Jack both thought she was ready to give in to Kel's demands in order to save Dolphin Land. They had no inkling she was prepared to take even more drastic action.

She'd rip all the hydrophones out of the water, melt each disk and shred every last piece of printed data before letting Kel Griffin share her work. That would satisfy her pride.

Without her project as motivation, he had no reason to continue his extortion tactics. He'd leave Dolphin Land alone.

In the meantime, she'd feel a whole heck of a lot better if Jack shared the smallest detail of what he had in mind to thwart her ex. She'd asked, cajoled, and pleaded. She'd gone so far as to promise unlimited sexual pleasure.

"I'm getting that anyway, sweetheart," he'd said, before suggesting she fool with her sound triangulation analyses and let him get back to work.

All in all, he'd been as secretive as, well, as an undercover agent.

Big leap there.

Even Ruby didn't know, but it wasn't driving her crazy. The older woman wasn't the least bit concerned.

"That nephew of mine's a smart one. There ain't never been a time when he promised to do something and didn't deliver. Don't you worry."

Finally, when she couldn't badger, beg, or seduce the answer out of him, her only other option was to bury herself in work and try not to worry. Much.

She loaded up the equipment and wheeled it out to the lagoon for a session, but her heart wasn't in it. So, she leaned against a post, staring glumly at the water. How could she act like a scientist, when she felt more like the cursed seer Cassandra who couldn't get anyone to believe her visions?

Cassandra was too grandiose a comparison. They thought she was Chicken Little.

"Oh hell," she said to Melly when the dolphin popped up, gazing at her with what appeared to be real interest. "The sky may as well fall. Things can't get much worse."

The dolphin sank below the surface and swam off. That figured. Even the animals wouldn't listen.

"If your experiment focuses on inter-species verbal communication, then perhaps I am wasting my time."

So much for things not getting any worse. She'd know that oil-on-arrogance voice in the middle of a Harvard Square crowd.

"What are you doing here, Kel?" She spun around to face him, snarling. Civility and calm were forgotten, now that he'd actually invaded her territory.

"The answer's patently obvious. I'm here to reunite with you, the finest research partner I ever had."

"What part of 'no way in hell' don't you understand?"

"I understand more than you want to accept, love." He smiled, friendly as a shark.

He studied the equipment on the cart and scanned the lagoons. His smile grew even broader while she continued to seethe.

"Perfect set-up, Victoria. You planned well and the design is excellent. So, are your findings bearing out your hypothesis on social communication?"

"I scrapped that study in the first week. Too small a sample for reliable results."

"I would almost believe you if you'd been less quick to respond." He patted her shoulder, as condescending as a tenured professor to a first year C student. "I'm not as poor at behavioral observation as you'd like to think. I've done my share of studies."

"Been concentrating on Mustelids?" She made her smile syrupy sweet. "You and weasels have so much in common."

"It isn't wise to insult me. We're going to be working closely for quite some time."

"That's what you think."

"Wasn't yesterday's demonstration enough to make my point? Do you really want to push me any farther?"

"Is that why you're here? Did you want to see for yourself what havoc you created with your petty power play?"

She cast her hand around in a large arc, encompassing the freshly thatched tikis, the buildings gleaming with paint. "Does it look like you hurt us? It was an inconvenience, nothing more. So if that's why you came today, you may as well head back to wherever you aren't working. This trip was a waste of time. Mostly mine."

Displeasure flared in his eyes. "You're pushing dangerous buttons. If you weren't ready to cede the project, why did you invite me?"

"I didn't!" Scorn curled her lip. "That's a lame gambit, even for you."

Irritation steamed to narrow-eyed anger as he advanced.

"The email telling me to come to the Keys arrived yesterday morning. I caught the first plane out of Boston."

"Then catch the first plane back." Determined, she stood her ground. The days when she let any man intimidate her were long gone and far, far away. Power flowed through her like a potent elixir. The angrier he became, the more she wanted to laugh in his face. Arms akimbo, she settled for a cocky grin.

He grabbed her arm and shook her like a misbehaving puppy, tightening his grip when she tried to pull free. "Don't play games with me. If you didn't invite me, who did?"

"That would be me."

Jack's drawl had never been so welcome. He ambled toward them like a man with plenty of time on his hands. The casual pace and lazy tone fooled Kel, but she was wise to the act.

When he reached them, she watched his eyes turn icy sharp. Suddenly, he looked dangerous, tough, and willing to break Kel into teeny, tiny pieces. "Let go of her."

Even the dumbest species knew when not to challenge a larger, stronger male. Kel released her hand like her fingers had turned into jellyfish tentacles. She could almost see him regroup and decide how to neutralize Jack's brawn with what he considered his superior brains.

This was going to be good.

"So this is the guy, huh, sweetheart?" With a subtle shift of weight, he backed Kel away.

She nodded, smiling her love. Let Kel add that unexpected info into the new equation.

Jack grinned, Mr. Amiable, now that he controlled the situation.

Kel bristled. "Who is this person?"

She looped her arm around Jack's waist, smiling again when he pulled her to his side. The look he gave her in return would leave no doubt as to the exact nature of their relationship. "Meet Jack Benton, the owner's nephew. And the unequivocal, irrevocable love of my life."

Kel made his next mistake. "Clever of you to sleep with the boss's relative and cement your position. You learned something from me after all."

Jack didn't growl, didn't stiffen, he just sort of moved, and suddenly Kel lay sprawled on the gravel. He sputtered and writhed, but Jack pinned him with one foot on his chest.

"Sweetheart, what's the genus for jackass?" he inquired with mock seriousness.

"Given the evidence here, we might have to claim a new subspecies. How about *Kelus Griffinus*?"

"That works." Hauling her ex up by a handful of shirt, he jammed him against a post. "Now I know you science brains have a ton of methodology for determining levels of intelligence, but I've got tests of my own."

"Let go of me or I'll press charges for assault."

Jack's sigh typified utter disappointment. "You've blown the first test before I even had a chance to set it up. Never threaten someone who has the means and motivation to rip you apart." He shook his head. "Let's see if you can make it up on the next one. A smart man knows to apologize when he insults a lady."

Kel glared, but the look lacked punch considering he was single-handedly pinned like a bug specimen to a corkboard. He toned down the sneer. "I'm sorry for my comment."

"Not bad. There's hope. Now, tell me you realize your game is over. Stop trying to manipulate Victoria with stupid, useless power plays like filing false complaints."

"Manipulate? I wouldn't—" He sputtered when Jack tightened the grip on his shirt collar and twisted. "All right." He sucked in air when the grip loosened. "It was a misguided move, perhaps, but I was protecting the integrity of her work."

"What?" The man had more brass than a temple gong. "Give me a break!"

"We can't have the scientific community doubting the veracity of your findings because the facility and test subjects are sub-par. The inspection worked in your favor."

"You contacted APHIS for the sole reason of making me sweat and to scare me into giving in to your demands," she stormed. "Jack, let go of him so I can tear him to pieces myself."

"Easy, sweetheart. We're almost through, and then you won't have to deal with this scum ever again."

He turned back to Kel, and Victoria was sure that even if he didn't have him pushed up against the post, the force of his gaze would have locked the other man in place.

"A smart man knows when he's beaten, but it looks like you're a sub-par test subject yourself. Let's see if you can figure it out with a hint. Two words. Belinda Johnson."

Kel's winter-pale skin blanched.

Jack grinned. "Since you clearly remember her, it won't come as a surprise that she doesn't send her regards. In fact, it's a lucky break that she's far away. I'd steer clear of Hawaii, Griffin, unless you want her to braid your intestines."

"Who's Belinda Jackson? Why do I know that name?" Rifling through her memories, she finally hit on it. "I read a paper by her last year on cooperative fishing behavior in spinner dolphins. What does she have to do with all this?"

"You aren't the first woman he kissed before screwing, sweetheart. The two of them were an item in grad school, but somehow that collaboration ended and he finished his master's degree a whole year earlier. Seems somehow she was delayed in presenting her thesis."

"Let me guess. Perhaps she was delayed because her original work was stolen?"

"You're so smart."

She gaped and stared at Kel with complete disdain. "He's a serial lowlife."

"You got it."

"You have nothing, Benton." Kel jerked himself free, but remained plastered to the pillar, blocked by Jack's larger, stronger body. "Belinda and I were involved, true, and she may have assisted on my graduate project."

"It was *her* graduate project, I bet."

He shrugged. "I completed the paper and successfully defended the hypothesis to the jury of professors."

"You despicable ass! Has there ever been an original thought in your head? Have you completed a single thing on your own? No. Instead, you earned your degree because of someone else's creative thinking and hard work," Victoria said.

"Prove it." His sneer returned. "Prove any of it. You uncovered an old flame, a jilted lover out for revenge, and all you have is hearsay. Your threats and demands mean nothing."

"Think again," Jack disputed. "I did more than find Dr. Johnson. I spoke with her. When I explained why I was calling, she told me the entire story, including one very interesting piece of info. You couldn't possibly have conducted the study that earned you your master's degree."

"If that's the case, we can completely discredit him. Nice going, Jack."

"Dr. Johnson told me she performed her graduate study somewhere in Belize. The two of them reconnected when she returned to the States, so this joker was never present for any of the observations and data collection."

"That's a lie!" Kel's face had gone from bleach to boiled-lobster. "Even after all these years, Belinda is obviously playing the woman scorned because I ended our relationship."

"Give it up. This is exactly your method. I'm sure once she discovered your deceit, she didn't want any more to do with you. Don't forget, I've been in her position. When it comes to you, good riddance to a bad research scientist."

"Passport records confirm her statements," Jack added. "You've never been to Belize."

Leave it to a DEA agent to know how to access this kind of information. She beamed her approval. "Wow, that's impressive."

"Ridiculous! You're bluffing. A Florida Keys bum has no way to discover where I did or didn't travel."

"Wanna bet? Never underestimate a man with motivation." Jack's grin sharpened to a cutting edge. "I have connections."

* * *

After that, it was all over but the blustering. As a struggling grad student, Belinda Johnson may not have had the resources to prove Kel's perfidy, but her reputation had since grown considerably. With the passport records backing up her story and Victoria's additional information, the man didn't have a chance. Even he was smart enough to know that his brief career as a research scientist was over.

What's more, Dr. Johnson had told them that she planned to take the evidence that Jack had collected and present it to Washington State University. It was all but guaranteed that the university would revoke Kel's master's degree.

Just in case he harbored any thoughts of retaliating against Dolphin Land, they made it clear in succinct words that, not only would they consider bringing criminal charges against him, but there were also a dozen ways Jack could use his own government contacts to legally make him very, very sorry. When the truth of that hit home, Kel wilted like seaweed in the sun. He turned, and let Jack escort him off the property.

Victoria took a seat on the bench and stared out over the ocean. As daylight dwindled, it looked like someone had dipped handfuls of fluffy clouds in deep rose, violet, and pink paint and *swooshed* them across the sky. In less than ten minutes, Jack rejoined her on the bench, automatically hugging her to him. Her head rested on his shoulder. Content, more relaxed than she'd been in weeks, and thoroughly in love, she nonetheless needed more information to fill in the rest of the pieces.

"Honey, why did you bring him all the way down here when we could have handled this on the phone?"

He combed his fingers through her hair. "I did that for you, sweetheart."

"For me? I don't get it."

He grinned, obviously pleased with himself. "Griffin's a sneak. He stabbed you in the back. Sure, I could have warned him off long distance, but that would have let him off too lightly. I wanted him to see you succeeding with your research."

His lips brushed against her brow. "When you were engaged, he never would have beaten you using only his brain, so instead he took advantage of your heart. I wanted him to see you involved with a man who loves you completely."

If any cracks remained in her heart from Kel's treachery, the love she felt for and from Jack welled up and sealed them shut. For once, she needed no scientific correlation, no logical explanation of stimulus and response. For something so huge, the explanation was really quite simple. He loved her. She loved him.

They sat quietly for a long time, savoring the closeness. Eventually, he spoke.

"Victoria, how long will it take for you to complete your research?"

Half-drowsy, she had to think for a minute. "I need at least a year's worth of data for the first phase. It will take awhile to write up the paper, and Lord knows how long after I submit before it's accepted, maybe, for publication." She tilted her head. "Why?"

He cleared his throat and shifted. "Are you going to be happy here?"

"I already am."

"What about long term, when your research is over?"

"I'll still be happy and I'll still be here. I have so many ideas for the future, I could easily keep busy for the next twenty years."

She slipped out from under his arm to look him directly in the face. "If you're thinking of giving me the boot, forget about it."

He laughed. "Not a chance."

It was exactly what she wanted to hear, but he'd gotten her thinking. "What about you? Are you going to be happy once you leave the DEA?"

"There's still a lot to do around here."

"Will it be enough?"

"Maybe." He shrugged. "If the time comes when it isn't, I'll figure out something else. I think I've finally realized that I don't need to be in the DEA, working undercover in some jungle."

He cupped the back of her neck and tilted her face while he looked at her, his eyes glowing like fiery gems.

"It's good, honest work right here, and damned if I'm not proud of what we've done so far, and where we're going. But there's more."

His fingers were soft on her skin, stroking her cheek. "It doesn't matter what I do, or where. As long as I have you, I'm happier than I've ever been."

She raised her face to his, inviting his kiss, and he immediately responded. Before her head started to spin, she broke the kiss and looked at him seriously.

"You know, there are sociologists who claim that human beings are not meant to mate for life. That doing so goes against their psychological and sociological makeup."

"Oh yeah? Dr. Sheffield, what is your expert opinion of that hypothesis?"

"I think it's total hooey."

He burst out laughing.

"That's your scientific opinion?"

She giggled and nodded. "Yep."

"If you're positive it's 'hooey,' I think we owe it to the world to disprove the theory."

"That could take a while."

"Hey, I'm willing to work on it for the next twenty or thirty years."

He captured her mouth in another searing kiss, and with her securely snuggled on his lap, they began collecting their data.

The End

To Tame a Viking

Leslie Burbank

Two beautiful stories telling of the strength of love...

Lord Steele - Ambros Steele is a man desperate to strike a truce between the dreaded Norse and the Scots. So desperate in fact, that he agrees to marry a Viking Queen. Silke Thorganson wants no part of an arranged marriage. She would rather kill the man the Runes have foretold. Fierce wills clash while the flames of passion burn high.

Lady Thunder - Thora O'Donnahue must marry her enemy in order to save her people. Despising the Vikings, she prays for a way out. Her savior comes in the form of a Berserker, Aragon, who hides a dark secret. Can Thora love the man completely and break an ancient curse?

ISBN# 0-9743639-2-8

www.medallionpress.com

Charmed
Beth Ciotta

The Princess is in danger . . .

Beloved storyteller to hundreds of children, Lulu Ross champions non-violence. Just her luck, she's tiara over glass slippers for a man who carries a gun. Professional bodyguard Colin Murphy is s-e-x-y. Too bad he's delusional. Who would want to hurt Princess Charming—a low-profile, goody-two-shoes who performs as a storybook character at children's birthday parties? Surely the sexy gifts from a secret admirer are meant for her sister, a bombshell wannabe action-star. Or are they?

Murphy is determined to protect Lulu . . . whether she likes it or not. Perpetually cheerful and absurdly trusting, the locally famous kiddy-heroine refuses to believe she's in danger. Tipped off by the FBI, Murphy knows otherwise, but convincing Lulu that she's the fantasy target of a mobster's fixation is like trying to hang shades on the sun. Contending with a woman who favors bubblegum lip gloss and a pink poodle purse becomes an exercise in fascination and frustration for the world-weary protection specialist—almost as frustrating as resisting her whimsical charm.

ISBN# 1-932815-04-X

www.medallionpress.com

Jinxed

Beth Ciotta

Since the day beautiful socialite Afia St. John was born, her life has been plagued with bad luck. After losing her father and two older husbands in "freak" accidents, Afia now discovers her business manager has absconded with her fortune. Vowing not to rely on another man to guide her life, Afia refuses her godfather's help, and jumps at an unexpected job with Leeds Investigations.

With a pregnant, broke, sister, and an investigation agency in the red, control-freak Jake Leeds can't turn down the hefty but secret retainer offered by Afia's godfather for hiring her. Quickly seeing beyond her poor business skills, wacky superstitions, and sensationalized personal history, he realizes Afia is as generous in the heart as she is misunderstood.

But life is never easy for the woman born on Friday the 13th. Will the sexy PI be the good luck charm that puts her on a winning streak, or like everything else in her life, will their relationship wind up *Jinxed*?

ISBN# 0-9743639-4-4

www.medallionpress.com